I KNEW YOU WERE TROUBLE

SANDY BARKER

Boldwood

First published in Great Britain in 2025 by Boldwood Books Ltd.

Copyright © Sandy Barker, 2025

Cover Design by Alexandra Allden

Cover Images: Shutterstock

A CIP catalogue record for this book is available from the British Library.

Paperback ISBN 978-1-80549-889-6

Large Print ISBN 978-1-80549-888-9

Hardback ISBN 978-1-80549-887-2

Ebook ISBN 978-1-80549-890-2

Kindle ISBN 978-1-80549-891-9

Audio CD ISBN 978-1-80549-882-7

MP3 CD ISBN 978-1-80549-883-4

Digital audio download ISBN 978-1-80549-885-8

This book is printed on certified sustainable paper. Boldwood Books is dedicated to putting sustainability at the heart of our business. For more information please visit https://www.boldwoodbooks.com/about-us/sustainability/

Boldwood Books Ltd, 23 Bowerdean Street, London, SW6 3TN

www.boldwoodbooks.com

To my author friends,
Thank you for inspiring me with your incredible work and for your
unwavering support.
I couldn't do this without you.
Big hugs and love,
Sandy xxx

1

KATE

I've just pulled on my oversized *Gilmore Girls* T-shirt – a relic from my teens and my go-to for maximum comfort – when the buzzer to my flat bleats.

It's either a delivery driver who's got the wrong flat or Mrs Winterbottom, who lives below me, has locked herself out again. If it's the latter, that makes twice this week. I've told her I'm happy to take her rubbish out, but she insists that ninety is the new eighty and she's entirely capable of doing it herself. Only, she needs to remember her keys.

I cross the lounge and press the intercom button. 'Hello?'

'*Hallo*, is this Kate Whitaker?' asks a deep, husky, slightly accented voice.

'Yes,' I reply instinctually. Maybe I did order something and I've forgotten.

'My name is Willem de Vries,' he says, and I pinpoint the accent – Dutch. Though it's unclear why a delivery driver is introducing himself.

'Okay. Do you have a parcel for me? You can leave it by the door and I'll come down to collect it later,' I reply.

'Er... No, it's not a par— I have something to tell you – something important. Can I please come inside?'

Intriguing. But no matter how much he's piqued my curiosity, I'm a single woman who lives alone. I'm also trouser-less. I am not inviting a stranger into my flat, no matter how sexy his voice is.

'What's this concerning?' I ask, but there's no reply. 'Bug-ger,' I mutter – the intercom must have timed out. I wait, poised to answer if Willem de Vries buzzes again. He does.

'*Hallo?*'

'Hi,' I reply. 'Can you tell me what this is about? Please,' I add, remembering my manners.

But rather than answering, he sighs so loudly I can hear him over the intercom. 'It's *important*, Kate. Please, I need to speak to you. I understand if you don't want me to come inside, but— Look, I passed a pub on the corner. How about meeting me there?'

'When?'

'Now.'

'Oh, uh...'

I hadn't expected to be going anywhere. It's been an intense week at work, and I'd planned on a lazy Friday night on the sofa, watching something mindless and eating the rest of the curry I ordered in last night but didn't finish.

I *could* just tell Willem de Vries to sod off. If it's that impor-tant, why won't he tell me over the intercom?

Then again, he has me intrigued and I suppose that a crowded pub, one where I'm known by the staff and some of the local patrons, will offer some security.

'Fine, I'll be there in five minutes,' I say. 'Actually, make it ten,' I add, giving me an extra few minutes to make myself presentable – *and* to conduct a swift internet search on Mr de Vries.

Before he can respond, I release the button on the intercom and start googling 'Willem de Vries con man'.

* * *

As expected for 6 p.m. on a Friday, the pub is teeming – mostly with locals, and I say hello to the ones I know. There are also a handful of tourists, who stand out with their daypacks and weary, slightly sunburnt faces.

I scan the dark interior, sending a wave to Dave behind the bar, who smiles back, but don't see anyone who might be Willem de Vries. All the men are here with at least one other person.

'*Hallo*, Kate.'

I turn towards the voice, coming face to (formidable) chest with Willem, even though I'm five-eight. I take half a step back, craning my neck to meet his eyes.

Thor – the man looks like Thor. Well, the Hemsworth's version – and from the third film, after those signature golden locks had been shorn off. Strong jaw, high cheekbones, intense blue eyes under sexily arched dark brows, lips the colour of the last lip stain I bought (grossly unfair when men's lips are naturally that colour), and a five o'clock shadow. *And he's built like a god*, I note as my eyes drift to his biceps.

It's ridiculous how handsome he is – Willem, that is, not Hemsworth – although he is too, I suppose.

He extends his enormous hand for me to shake, and I do, mine instantly swallowed by his.

'Hi,' I say, so distracted by his eyes, all my other words have dried up. I don't think I've ever seen that exact shade of blue before.

I will myself to break eye contact and scout for a table. There aren't any free inside, so I signal towards the door. 'Shall we look for a table outside?' I ask and, not waiting for an answer, I head out.

I snag the end of a picnic table where we can sit opposite each other and Willem slides onto the bench, then rests his muscular forearms on the table.

'Sorry,' he says, 'I should have asked if you wanted something to drink.'

'That's okay. As soon as you tell me whatever it is, I'm going back to my flat.'

A frown mars his perfect features, and his lips disappear between his teeth. A few moments pass with him studying me intensely, which is beyond disconcerting.

Whatever he has to tell me – and I've been wracking my brain since he buzzed my flat – I can tell it's not good. It's obvious I haven't inherited a cupcake shop by the sea from a long-lost aunt. Or a bookshop.

'Just tell me,' I say, impatient for him to spit it out.

He nods, releasing his lips from between his teeth. 'You're engaged to Jon Dunn, yes?'

Oh god, I've been so thrown by a strange man showing up out of nowhere, I never imagined this might be about Jon. What a rubbish fiancée I am!

'Is he all right?' I ask, suddenly panicked. 'And how do you know Jon?'

Willem takes a deep breath as if he's steeling himself, which is even more unsettling – if that's possible. Unease lands heavily in my chest and my breath catches.

'*Willem*, is Jon okay?'

'As far as I'm aware, yes.'

I breathe out a sigh of relief, but I'm still confused. 'So, how are you connected to Jon? Do you work together?' It's plausible. There must be commercial pilots who look like Hollywood actors. Right?

'No. We don't work together. I know of Dunn through my sister.'

'Oh-kay.'

God, I wish he'd get to the point – he's really dragging this out. And why is he referring to Jon by his last name?

'Dunn is her fiancé.'

The words seem to float in the air between us.

But they don't make any sense. They can't make sense, because Jon is engaged to me. He has been for three months. He proposed to me on the observation deck of The Shard, and after I said yes, he took me to dinner at Oblix.

Dunn is her fiancé.

I stare down at the enormous solitaire affixed to the platinum band encircling my ring finger. Jon chose it – I would have chosen something smaller, less ostentatious, but he said he wanted everyone in the world to know that I was engaged.

Engaged to *him*.

'I don't understand,' I say eventually, my voice strangled. I look up from the ring, meeting Willem's eyes. Then something occurs to me. 'Wait, do you mean he *was* engaged to your sister – as in, past tense?'

'No. Dunn is engaged to both of you. *Present* tense,' he adds to drive the point home.

'But he can't be...' I say with a dry laugh. 'You're having me on, right? Wait, did Margot put you up to this? Because if she did, I will throttle h—'

He places one of his enormous hands on my forearm, silencing me instantly. When I'm quiet, he takes it away.

'I don't know anyone named Margot,' he says steadily. I fix my eyes on his, drawing strength from his calm demeanour. Because despite wishful thinking that this is a sick prank perpetrated by Margot, my cousin and closest friend, deep down, I believe he's telling the truth.

'What I *do* know,' he continues, 'is that my sister – her name's Adriana – recently got engaged to a man she barely knows, a man I've never met. So, I looked into him.'

I latch on to the detail with the least power to derail my entire life. 'You looked into him? You mean, you investigated him?'

'Yes.'

'How?' I ask, imagining Willem engaging a private investigator, an old-school one with a cluttered office, a sassy receptionist, and nicotine-stained fingers.

'I'm a cyber security consultant. I have access to information, and I know what I'm looking for – mostly.' It sounds simple when he puts it like that; though plainly it isn't.

'Which is how you found me?' I ask quietly.

'Yes.'

I drag my eyes from his tractor-beam gaze, dropping them to the table where someone has roughly carved 'S + B' into one of the slats. My mind starts vomiting up vignettes of me and Jon, which appear then vanish in quick succession.

Michelin-star dinners at Le Gavroche... Watching the world's greats play at Wimbledon... Champagne brunches at Duck & Waffle on a Sunday morning... Wandering through Hyde Park with takeaway coffees, and stopping to pet other people's dogs...

'I'm really sorry, Kate,' says Willem gently. 'It must be a shock. That's why I wanted to tell you in person.'

I jostle my head to dislodge the romantic snapshots. Because there are other memories lurking, more sinister ones, and they skulk into view, mocking me.

Jon excusing himself to take a hushed phone call in the other room... Jon suddenly leaving at 11 p.m. because the airline needed him to fly to Cairo at late notice... Jon not introducing me to his only family member, an aged mother who's in a care facility in Harrow, despite me asking numerous times... Jon dismissing my questions about his life before me with, 'Oh, you don't want me to bore you with all that.'

Were these instances of Jon's double life intruding on ours?

Something else occurs to me. Jon rarely wanted to stay in, always insisting that I 'put on something nice' and we go out. A sickening feeling washes over me. *Is everything I feel for Jon one-sided? Am I simply someone to wear on his arm?*

'Wait,' I say, my head snapping up, 'are you *positive* they're the same person? There must be dozens of Jon Dunns. What proof do you have that my Jon is the same man who's engaged to your sister?'

These are the desperate questions of a woman who knows better, but grasping at straws is far more palatable than admitting I've been deceived, that Jon is cheating on me. It's also easier than questioning the very nature of our relationship.

Willem presses his lips together, his jaw pulsing, then he reaches into the messenger bag by his side and takes out a document-sized envelope. He sets it on the table between us, his fingertips resting on it lightly. 'This is a summary of the evidence I've collected to date, but I suspect there is more to uncover.'

'More to...?' I look at the envelope, my heart pounding and

my stomach lurching. I lift my gaze. 'I think I'm going to need that drink after all.'

* * *

'Kate, seriously, what the actual eff?'

Margot is sitting cross-legged on the floor of my lounge, surrounded by the evidence Willem gave me at the pub. It's obvious she's shocked – and it takes a lot to shock someone like Margot. She's usually the one doing the shocking.

'I mean, this...' she continues, holding up the page she's been reading. 'This is irrefutable.'

'I know,' I squeak from the sofa where I'm curled up in the corner, legs tucked beneath me.

Her eyes soften, bathing me in her unique brand of love, as dozens of thoughts play behind her intelligent brown eyes.

Margot is my only cousin on my dad's side. She's eighteen months older than me and because her mum died suddenly when she was a baby and her dad worked away a lot, picking up odd jobs wherever he could, she mostly lived with me and my parents. Essentially, we grew up as sisters – even though we look nothing alike. She's petite and wiry with olive skin, a round face, and large brown eyes – almost pixie-esque, especially now that she's dyed her close-cropped hair bright pink. Then there's me: tall and willowy with wavy, dark-blonde hair, a pale complexion, green eyes, and attractive but otherwise non-descript features. Total opposites.

Regardless, Margot is my closest friend and fiercest ally. And as soon as I called with my news, she abandoned her Friday-night plans – a feminist poetry reading at a bookshop in Soho – and came straight here.

She picks up another page and continues reading, intermittently murmuring and tutting, her face set in a scowl.

As she reads, I eye the slew of papers littering the rug. Ostensibly, I've read every page – *twice* – but only some of the details have stuck. After a while, the revelations were so extreme, the words began swimming on the page, and an odd sort of numbness came over me.

Regardless, it didn't take long to get the gist. Jon lied – about pretty much everything – and he's currently engaged to both me and Adriana de Vries.

Memories of us start popping up again, only now they have the word 'LIES' stamped over them in fat red letters.

Was *anything* he told me true? Was any aspect of our relationship real?

'Bastard,' Margot hisses, snapping me back to the present. She haphazardly gathers up the pages and shoves them into the envelope. 'So, what do we do now?' she asks.

'What do you mean?'

She gets up and joins me on the sofa, sitting sideways and giving me a pointed look. 'I *mean,* how are we going to get back at the prick?'

'Wait, *we*?' I ask, struggling to form a coherent thought.

'Yes, *we*. I'm hardly letting you handle this alone. *Bastard,*' she says again. 'I never liked him.'

'Wait, really?' I ask, sitting up straighter.

'Really. Too cagey. He would never answer a direct question – it was always a convoluted response. Major red flag.'

'Hmm,' I mutter, more pieces of the puzzle slotting into place. 'I suppose you're right.'

'I am. *Anyway*, setting aside that he was never right for you—'

'I'm not really in the mood for "I told you so" right now,' I interject.

'Exactly, so setting that aside…' she says, missing my point entirely, 'we need a way to get back at him.'

'I don't know, Margot. This is all so fresh. I've barely got my mind around things. I'm not ready to start plotting revenge.'

I don't mention that I'm not really a revenge sort of person – that's more Margot's domain. And if I don't immediately quash her enthusiasm, she'll have me logged on to the dark web looking for mercenaries before bedtime.

'Besides,' I say, 'there's something else that takes precedence over dealing with Jon.'

She blinks at me, confused. 'What could *possibly* take precedence over chopping Jon's bollocks off?'

Margot has always had a rather graphic turn of phrase – more so since her divorce, a nasty, drawn-out affair that consolidated her hatred of (almost) all men. My dad is one of the few exceptions.

'I've been asked to go to Amsterdam,' I reply.

'Amsterdam? For what?'

'To help Willem. His sister – the other fiancée – she doesn't believe I exist. She thinks Willem made me up to prise her away from Jon.'

'You're not serious,' she says with a scoffing laugh.

'I am serious. He's asked me if I can go next weekend.'

'*If* you can go? Of course you *can*, Kate, but you need to consider if you *should*.' She slowly shakes her head disbelievingly. 'God, this is like something out of one of those books you're always reading – the ones with the black covers.'

She means the domestic noirs I like to escape into – and she's not entirely wrong. This *is* like the plot of a novel.

'*My Fiancé's Fiancée* coming soon to a bookshop near you,' she says in a deep voice. She chuckles at her own joke.

'If you're going to make fun, you can leave.'

Her laughter dies. 'Sorry. But you have to admit, it's...' I glare at her and she abandons her point, reaching over and patting my arm instead. 'I really am sorry, Kate. It's a shitty, shitty thing he's done, and I'm here for you no matter what, all right?'

It's rare Margot shows her serious side, but of everyone in my life, she's the person I can count on the most.

'Thanks.'

'Now, tell me more about the fit brother. Does he *really* look like Thor?'

My cheeks instantly flame and I try my best to stifle the smile, but it appears anyway.

'Ah-hah!' she says, wagging a finger at me. 'You fancy him.'

'I... Well, yes, he's a very handsome man, but a little perspective, please? I've just found out my fiancé is a fake. It's hardly the time to indulge in sexy thoughts about another man.'

'Au contraire, dear cousin, this is *exactly* the time for that – and not only *thinking* about him...' She shimmies her shoulders and raises her brows suggestively.

Laughter erupts out of me, a much-needed release after the evening's revelations. My love life may be in tatters, but at least my sense of humour is intact.

For now, anyway.

2

KATE

I jolt awake from a fitful sleep, feeling disgusting. My mouth's dry, my stomach is roiling, and my head might explode any second now.

I'm completely wrung out. Like if a used tissue were a person.

I roll onto my side and shut my eyes, deliberately slowing my breathing to quell the queasiness and ease the headache. It helps – a little.

Last night was... what? *Devastating* comes to mind.

My engagement is a lie.

I conjure Jon's face in my mind, tightness creeping into my chest. I was delighted when I met him through the match-making agency. He was everything I was looking for – or thought I was.

He's attentive when we're together, yet he also loves how independent I am, that we're not one of those couples who needs to spend every waking moment at each other's side – perfect for someone as career-oriented as I am. And he appreciates that I'm my own person, that my identity isn't dependent on his.

His identity – hah! Whatever that is.

Admittedly, sex with Jon has always been... well, less than mind-blowing, but I've never really minded. I fell in love a dozen times in my twenties and early-thirties – passionately, longingly, achingly in love – and each relationship ended in heartbreak. Heartbreak that knocked me sideways and took (what felt like) an eternity to recover from. At thirty-seven, I'm now far more pragmatic. I will happily forgo passion for contentedness, stability, and shared values, for a love built on mutual respect.

Only, all of that was bogus. Everything I thought I had with Jon was a forgery constructed by a crafty, scheming pretender.

For the fiftieth time since Willem buzzed my flat and blew my world apart, I ask myself, *Was any of it real?*

From my end, it was. I care for Jon – *cared*, I remind myself. All that's in the past now. I've drawn a proverbial line in the sand, never to be crossed again. Jon can sod off.

Of course, I'll have to confront him eventually – someday, as far into the future as possible – but the mere thought of it sends another wave of nausea ripping through me. It's all too fresh to be thinking that far ahead – there's a gaping wound in my heart. *And* my ego. How could I have been so stupid?

'Ugh,' I groan, throwing an arm over my face.

'That good, huh?' asks Margot, startling me.

I flip over and prop myself up, squinting at her. 'I forgot you were here.'

'I'll try not to take that personally,' she retorts dryly, surrendering to a loud yawn.

'Sorry. And thanks for staying.'

'I could hardly leave you alone – not once the crying started.'

'Right.' I plop back onto my pillow face-down.

If she were anyone else, I'd feel foolish for the loud and lengthy sobbing session that capped off our evening. Until then, I thought I was handling the situation well – *very* well.

After we put away the 'envelope of secrets' (as I dubbed it), we ordered takeaway. Then Margot insisted we open the bottle of Champagne I'd been saving for a special occasion. In her mind, my 'emancipation from Jon's evil clutches' – her exact words – *was* a special occasion. I relented, raising my glass to toast the 'lying bastard' then downing a third of it in one go.

We drank the rest of the bottle while we waited for our food to arrive, Margot entertaining us by listing all the things she disliked about Jon. Apparently, his caginess was the tip of the iceberg.

But when she said, 'And he's so *dull*,' I burst into tears. Because in many ways Jon *is* dull, but I've always looked past it because he's so thoughtful, always sending me sweet messages and bringing me trinkets from his travels.

Was so thoughtful, I remind myself again – past tense.

Though how thoughtful is it to deliberately deceive your fiancée? Make that *fiancées*.

By the time our takeaway arrived, I was too distraught to eat and Margot put me to bed. That may explain the queasy stomach – half a bottle of champers and no food.

'I'll put the kettle on,' says Margot, springing out of bed. She pauses at the door. 'And then we're making a plan.'

'Ugh,' I groan again. 'Can't I at least take the day to get my mind around things?' I ask, my voice muffled by my pillow.

'No, you can't.' I turn my head and peek at her through my

lashes. She has her arms folded over her chest. 'Do you think Jon's out there "taking the day"?'

'That makes no sense,' I reply. 'Why would he—'

'Of course he isn't!' she continues, talking over me. 'He's probably somewhere wooing fiancée number three by now! I'm telling you, Kate, we need a plan. We need to take Jon down.'

'Fine,' I say, more to shut her up than anything.

It does the trick – for now, anyway – and she leaves. Moments later, she's banging about in my kitchen. She must open every cupboard before she finds the one with the mugs. Anyone would think she'd never been here before.

We need a plan.

What we need – what *I* need – is to contact the matchmaking agency and ask them how in the hell someone like Jon got on their books. Though, maybe they did everything they could to screen him. If he successfully lied to me – *and* Adriana – then he probably lied to them as well.

God, I hope there aren't more of us out there. And it's not only Margot who's suggested there might be. Willem said the same thing before we parted ways at the pub.

Something comes to me – or rather, *someone*. A possible ally to help me untangle this godawful mess.

I kick off the duvet and, ignoring the protestations from my body, get up and go into the kitchen.

'Hey, Margot, I have an idea...'

* * *

'You *seriously* met Jon through a matchmaking agency? You told me you met through friends.'

'That was a lie – a little white lie,' I add hurriedly when

Margot's expression sours. 'Jon was embarrassed about using a matchmaker, so...' I shrug apologetically as her eyes bore into mine, her mouth taut and downturned. Another black mark against Jon's name – and possibly mine.

'Well, it's moot now anyway.' She waves her hand and I'm instantly forgiven. 'So, who's this *other* matchmaker then?'

'She's called Poppy – Poppy Dean – and she's with the Ever After Agency.'

Margot snorts. 'Is it really called that?'

'Yes, but it doesn't matter what it's called. What matters is that I really connected with Poppy. She's a lovely person – whip-smart and an all-round good egg.'

'Only not a good matchmaker.'

'Why do you say that?' I ask, taking offence on Poppy's behalf.

'Because you signed on with two agencies at the same time and she was pipped at the post.'

'Yes, but Poppy didn't match me with a two-timing liar, did she? *No,*' I say, answering my own rhetorical question. 'That was Arabella.'

'So why not go see Arabella then? She caused this mess – she should clean it up.'

'Because...' I say feebly.

How can I make Margot understand when, of the two of us, she's making the most sense? I *should* go back to Arabella at Perfect Pairings. But I don't want to. I never warmed to her, and I'm not convinced she'd be a sympathetic ear. She'll be one of those 'we did everything we could' people, fobbing me off with a non-apology and a shrug.

Oh god. Did I convince myself that Jon was a good match so I'd no longer have to deal with Arabella? Gah, there are so many layers to this. It might be years before I untangle it all.

'Because...?' Margot probes, bringing me back to the conversation.

I hedge, picking tiny bobbles off my pilled pyjama bottoms.

'Look, you'll need to inform them at some point,' she continues. 'They need to know who they're dealing with. *And* they should report him.'

'To whom? It's not like there's some sort of policing body for tossers who lie to their fiancées.'

She tilts her head, partly in sympathy and partly to make her point.

'I know, I know, I need to tell them – and I will – but I still want to talk to Poppy.'

Margot sips her coffee, wearing a far-off look.

'Hang about...' she says, her eyes lighting up. She leans forward, her coffee mug now at a precarious angle, and I grimace at the thought of her tipping coffee over my cream-coloured sofa. But she doesn't seem to notice that she's about to spill, *nor* my reaction.

'Do you think this Poppy gal would help you get revenge on Jon?' she asks.

I recoil. 'No! That's not why I— I'm not asking her to do that.'

She stares at me for a moment, then sits back against the sofa, letting me off the hook – *and* saving me half a can of upholstery cleaner. 'Well, in that case,' she says, her brows raised matter-of-factly, 'after I finish my coffee, I'm off to the nearest garden centre for a pair of gardening shears.'

'Gardening sh—' Her meaning lands and I can't help but chuckle. Then I remember who I'm talking to – a proud, man-hating divorcée. 'Margot, *no*,' I say firmly, which makes *her* laugh.

Clearly, Jon had better watch out. Facing the Wrath of Margot makes lifting the lid on Pandora's box look like tearing open a bag of crisps. I'm positive her ex-husband would agree.

She continues sipping her coffee, still chuckling to herself, and I'm about to go and put the kettle on again when Bruno Mars' 'Just the Way You Are' blares from my phone. I stare at it in horror. That's Jon's ringtone.

'Is that...?' asks Margot.

Unable to speak, I meet her eyes and numbly nod. I must look like I've seen a ghost, as I suddenly feel faint and clammy.

We wait out several bars of the chipper song, one I will immediately change to Taylor Swift's 'I Knew You Were Trouble', and when the call finally goes to voicemail, I expel a loud sigh.

'What do you suppose Jon the Con has to say?' asks Margot.

'Jon the Con?' I ask, scrunching my nose in distaste.

'Do you prefer "Arseface"?'

'Actually, yes.'

'All right, what do you suppose *Arseface* has to say?'

My phone chimes with a message notification and even though I was expecting it, I yelp.

'On edge much?' asks Margot.

'Wouldn't you be?'

She snatches the phone from the table and inputs the passcode. She's the only person besides me who knows it – a testament to how much I trust her and something I now regret.

'He didn't leave a voice message,' she tells me, 'but he's sent a text. Want me to read it to you?'

'I suppose.' I flop back onto the sofa and stare out the window at my neighbour's conker tree.

Margot reads aloud, adopting the unflattering, plum-in-the-mouth voice she uses when mimicking Jon. '"Hello darling. Missing you *so* much. Looks like I'm needed for another week on the Marrakesh/Madrid route. Back in London as soon as poss. Kisses." Bloody hell – he's laying it on a bit thick, isn't he? And he's added *far* too many emojis for a grown-arse man.'

'I feel ill.'

Margot sets down the phone and looks at me, her sarcastic expression falling away. 'I would too, hun. He's not even a fucking pilot.'

'I know. From what I can tell, the *only* truth he's told me is that he's British.'

I inhale slowly, bravely examining Jon's mounting number of lies. I'm positive that 'I love you' should be added to the tally.

Then that depressing question raises its hideous head again: *Was any of it real?*

'You know what?' says Margot, leaping up. 'We are *not* sitting around here all day moping.'

'We're not?' I ask. 'Because I could easily make a day of it – moping, wallowing... Maybe I'll throw in some wailing and intermittent cries of "Why me?" – give my neighbours something to talk about.'

'The only neighbour who *could* hear you if she weren't a hundred and three is Mrs Winterbottom. And you don't want to scare the poor love. She'd probably drop dead of a heart attack from sheer fright.'

'First off, she's ninety, not a hundred and three. Second, don't say things like that. It's—'

'Bad luck, I *know*. Only I don't know because I don't believe in all that rubbish.'

'Margot, can you please...?' I draw both hands across my neck, signalling that I need her to dial it down on the Margot-isms.

'Sorry,' she says sincerely. 'But one more thing and then I'll be quiet.'

'Fine. What is it?'

'Just a little reminder, dear cuz, that you have access to Mayberry's – for you *and* a guest. And the best part? The bill goes straight to Jon.'

I sit bolt upright as a tiny bubble of joy rises within me, elbows out and shoving its way through the muck and mire of shock and hurt.

'Oh my god, you're right. I'd completely forgotten. I've been so busy with work, I've only been there that one time – with Jon.'

'Exactly – that one time when he gave you access to London's most exclusive private club.' She waggles her brows conspiratorially.

'Yes, when he added me to his membership!' I exclaim excitedly.

'So, we're going?' she asks.

My smile falls away as reality intrudes on the too-brief reprieve. 'Oh, Margot... This really is proper shit, isn't it?'

'Yes, hun, it is. But for today, it can be proper shit with expensive champers and a fit bloke running his hands all over you.'

I cough out a laugh. 'A fit bloke— Oh, right... But how can you be sure the masseuse will be fit? Or a bloke for that matter?'

'Because the universe *owes* you.'

'I thought you didn't believe in all that rubbish?'

'Luck – no. But the universe is a powerful force, Kate, and today it owes you a magnum of Bollinger and a fit masseuse.'

Margot's logic may be flawed, but a day of indulgence – at Jon's considerable expense – could give me the boost I'll need to handle what's to come.

'You're right, we're going,' I say decisively, and Margot perks up. 'Spa treatments, lunch… the whole shebang.'

'And every bit of it on Jon's bill. It's the *least* he can do,' she says, breaking into an evil laugh. 'Right,' she says, 'I'm going to shower, then raid your wardrobe. You call Mayberry's and tell them to roll out the red carpet.'

As she closes the bathroom door, she starts singing 'Good as Hell' at top volume. I'm pretty sure that's for my benefit but regardless, cats in heat have better pitch than Margot, and her horrible singing makes me chuckle.

I really am glad she's here. If it weren't for Margot, I'd be curled up in bed right now, sobbing over a man who doesn't deserve even *one* of my tears.

3

KATE

Tuesday morning, my eyelids flutter open and I peek at the time. Fifteen minutes till my alarm but there's no sense in trying to get back to sleep – if I'd been asleep to begin with. Thank god I don't have a waterbed. I was tossing and turning so much last night, I would have made myself seasick.

Though, it would have been worse if I hadn't talked Margot out of setting up camp at mine while I 'process what's happened'. The woman snores like a grizzly bear.

In the pre-dawn light, I stare up at the lampshade above my bed, thinking for the fiftieth time that I should replace it with something less... well, seventies. Then my mind wanders to darker waters, to Friday night before my world came crashing down.

I'd had a massive week at work – hitting three competing deadlines and putting out several fires, something I excel at – and I was shattered, but happy.

Well, if not happy, then content. I have a good life – *very* good. If I were an influencer, I'd be hash-tagging 'gratitude' and 'blessed' all over the damned place.

I'm on track professionally as a senior project manager, the variety of my work keeps me motivated, and I get to stretch myself with each new project. I love my flat (seventies light fittings aside), which I purchased two years ago with my life savings, a little help from my great-aunt, and a mortgage that would scare some people, but which I plan to pay off by the time I'm fifty (if not before). I have a decent social life – a handful of colleagues who have become friends and a few of Margot's mates who've 'adopted' me. And most Sundays, I head to the pub for a roast lunch and chitchat with the locals.

Rounding out this audit of my (until four days ago) contented life, I'm engaged.

'To a scam artist,' I mutter out loud. 'Ugh,' I groan, scrubbing my hands over my face. 'And it's *was*, Kate. *Was* engaged.'

I lift my left hand – much lighter now I'm not wearing that (let's face it) monstrosity – and run my thumb over the pale, ring-shaped indentation where the ring used to be. I took it off on Friday night and shoved it in a drawer under the tatty knickers I only wear when I've got my period.

I stupidly forgot to put it on for work yesterday – a bare ring finger raises suspicions and I'm not ready yet for pitying looks from my colleagues – and eagle-eyed Sue asked where it was. I told her it was being cleaned, but I won't be able to use that excuse forever. At some point, I will have to end this 'engagement' and then I'll have to tell everyone it's off, enduring whatever well-meaning words pop out of their mouths. I suspect, based on something Margot let slip while we were at Mayberry's getting facials, that my parents won't be disappointed.

And what's the etiquette for keeping a ring given to you by a cheating liar? Maybe I can sell it back to the jeweller. No doubt it would be a significant sum, making a nice dent in my mortgage. Although, I can imagine Margot's reaction if I don't spend the money on something less practical – like one of those ridiculous designer handbags she's had her eye on since I can remember. Who spends thousands of pounds on a *handbag*?

I reach for my phone – habit – and check my messages – also habit. My loins (and the rest of me) are heavily girded for a message from Jon telling me how much he misses me all the way from Madrid. I have no idea where he really is. He could be right down the road for all I know, laughing his arse off at how gullible I am and congratulating himself for duping me.

I navigate to my messaging app. Nothing from Jon – thank god – but there is one from Willem, and my telltale heart flutters. I ignore it. No matter what Margot says, crushing on Willem is a *terrible* idea.

Besides, I'm sure it's only happening because my subconscious is in chaos and it's trying to distract me. *Look, Kate, look at the handsome man who could scoop you up in his arms and carry you upstairs without breaking a sweat, then do wicked, wicked things to you with those enormous hands of his.*

'Other parts of him are probably enormous too,' I mutter, making myself snigger. I read the message:

Adriana plans to introduce Dunn to our parents next week. I could really use your help.

Oh right. I haven't agreed to go to Amsterdam yet. The smile falls from my face as unease ripples through me. It may be the right thing to do, but am I ready to entangle myself further in Jon's web of lies?

Lies, such as Jon saying he was going to be in Sweden next week (not Amsterdam), flying the Stockholm/Bangkok route for two weeks. He probably googles flight routes and picks the ones he likes the sound of. I can't imagine where he gets the trinkets he brings me – a tiny, carved Buddha from Thailand, lingonberry jam from Sweden, a silk scarf from Istanbul. Does he simply order them online? He must have a great laugh at my expense when I 'ooh' and 'ahh' over them.

I read Willem's message again. If it weren't for him, I wouldn't even know I was one of two women engaged to the same man. Does that make me indebted to him?

My alarm chimes while I'm holding my phone, catching me off-guard, and I turn it off, shelving that question for another time. I fling back the duvet and climb out of bed, heading straight to the shower. Big day today – and I'm of two minds about it.

One of those minds is dreading going into work.

This is a first for me since I landed my dream job at Elev8te, a coaching organisation for C-level executives. I love my job – not only the work itself, but also my colleagues. And I am fully 'drinking the Kool-Aid' with Elev8te. We help organisations build a positive workplace culture, making people's working lives better. My boss, who founded the company, should be knighted. Or, as she is a woman, *damed*.

But yesterday, I was so consumed by this situation with Jon, I was completely useless – couldn't concentrate to save myself. My colleagues started looking at me oddly and exchanging loaded glances. I ended up faking a migraine and going home early – also a first. This puts me half a day behind, which I aim to make up by lunchtime, *and* I'll have to lie about 'feeling better', which makes me uncomfortable. It's one thing telling a small fib about a missing engagement ring, another to fake a malady.

The other of my two minds is eager for what's happening

before work. I'm returning to the Ever After Agency to meet
with Poppy Dean, something I teed up while 'convalescing' on
my sofa yesterday afternoon.

I was lying there, mindlessly scrolling through I can't even
remember which streaming app, when I thought about something Margot said on Friday night, about getting back at Jon.
And in that moment of perfect clarity, I realised that if Jon's
deception has impacted me *so* severely, completely upending
my world, including my ability to do my job, then I *do* want
him to pay.

I'm not sure how Poppy can help with that, but it's got to be
worth asking.

* * *

Poppy

'You're ready early this morning, darling.'

Tristan, who's usually up first, strides into the kitchen
dressed in a suit and tie – standard work attire for an invest-
ment banker, even these days. As always, he looks like he's
stepped right off the runway in Milan. Though, my handsome
hubby could make a sack cloth look good.

'Mm-hmm,' I reply, accepting a cheek kiss. I sip from my
enormous mug of tea, watching as he begins the (overly
complicated) process of making coffee with his new espresso
machine.

'So, something special on?' he asks.

I wait until the loud grinding stops to reply. 'I've got a
client coming in for an early meeting – she's had to squeeze it
in before work. Actually, she's a *former* client.'

'*Former* client?' Tristan glances over his shoulder, then resumes fiddling with the machine. 'Any idea what it's about?'

'Not really. The last time I heard from her, she'd matched through another agency. Maybe it fell through and she wants to re-engage us.'

The espresso machine starts gurgling and I take my tea and climb onto a stool at the breakfast bar.

'Meow.'

'Oh, good morning, you little minx,' I say to our cat, Saffron. 'Thanks for waking me up at two and then again at four. *So* appreciated when I had to be up at six.' Though, Tristan and I also had a late-ish night, something I can't blame on Saffron, as we're trying to get pregnant.

Saffron sniffs the air, then struts past me, beelining for Tristan, who's her favourite. He lifts her up one-handed and sips his espresso, and Saffron starts purring loudly.

'Has that happened before?' he asks, resuming our conversation. 'A client engaging two matchmakers at once? Seems a bit... unorthodox.'

'It's not the norm, but it does happen. Some clients like to cover their bases – especially if there's a time crunch or some other mitigating factor.'

'Such as having to marry in the next forty days or forego a sizeable inheritance?' he asks with a twitch of his mouth.

'That's a very specific example, Mr Fellows. Did you just come up with that?'

'Absolutely.' He snaps his fingers. 'Right off the top of my head.'

'Uh-huh.' I sip my tea, eyeing him over the rim of the mug.

'And if I follow that example through to its logical conclusion, I believe I should have engaged a second, or even a third matchmaker when I signed on with Ever After. Isn't that so, Ms Dean?' he asks, his eyes twinkling.

'Oh, absolutely,' I deadpan. 'It was grossly remiss of you to put all your eggs into one basket. I mean, it worked out for *you*.' I stare at him wide-eyed, impressed that I'm keeping a straight face.

'And for you, I would hope?' he asks, frowning.

'Other than breaking the cardinal rule of falling in love with my client and risking my career – a career that I *love*...' Tristan's frown deepens and I'm not entirely sure we're still playing. I reach across for his hand and clasp it. 'Yes,' I say quietly. 'It worked out for me as well. Better than I could have imagined.'

He breaks into a broad smile, then lifts my hand to his lips and kisses it.

'I knew it,' he says with a wink.

I snatch my hand away and he sniggers. 'You cheeky bugger,' I chide, which makes him laugh out loud.

I hold off as long as I can, giving him my best I'm-being-serious glare before I start laughing. 'Dag,' I say – my way of giving him 'the win'.

But we're not *really* one of those couples who compete. Tristan is my person – my biggest cheerleader and my safe place to land when it all goes to shit, which of course, it does sometimes. Him walking into the Ever After Agency a year and a half ago, in need of a wife and in a short time frame, was a pivotal moment in my life.

We fell in love – completely, utterly, undeniably in love.

Was it inconvenient? Was it unprofessional? Yes to both. But when you know, you know. And that's one of the aspects of matchmaking I love the most – seeing that spark ignite, witnessing a client finding everything they've ever wanted.

I'm in the business of happily ever afters – or HEAs – and it is both a privilege and a pleasure. So, if Kate Whitaker needs my help – no matter what this is about – I'll be there for her.

'Right,' says Tristan, downing the rest of his espresso. 'I'm off like a bucket of prawns in the hot sun.'

'Really?' I ask, blinking at him.

'What? Don't you loike it when I speak Strayan?' he asks, bunging on a *dreadful* Australian accent.

'No, babe. I prefer it when I'm the Aussie and you sound like *you*.'

'Which is…?'

'Like a BBC news presenter circa 1964.'

We hold each other's gaze, both smiling mischievously, then he springs into action, depositing his tiny cup into the dishwasher and checking his briefcase. I glance at the time, realising that I need to get going too. I drink another glug of tea, then quickly tidy the kitchen. After saying our goodbyes to Saffron – mine tolerated and Tristan's embraced – we leave together.

It's such a rarity, we indulge in a soft, lingering kiss in the lift as we ride to the ground floor. Outside our building, we part ways with another quick kiss and head off in opposite directions.

4

POPPY

It takes Kate Whitaker twenty uninterrupted minutes for her to explain her predicament and when she finishes, she peers at me expectantly. 'So, what do you think?' she asks.

I blink back at her, dumbfounded, as I sift through everything she's told me. It's not often I'm left speechless. I was a psychologist before I was a matchmaker and people have told me all sorts of things, some of them almost unimaginable, but this is a doozy.

I inhale deeply, buying an extra moment to respond.

'I know what you're going to say,' she says, which is impressive, because *I* don't.

'What's that?' I ask with a slight smile.

'That this sounds like one of those sensational, real-life stories you'd read about in *Women's Weekly*. Or maybe an episode of *Black Mirror*,' she adds with a dry laugh.

'It is remarkable,' I say – the first word that comes to mind.

'That's one way to describe it.' She sits back heavily against her chair. 'Poppy, the man leads a double life! How did I not spot the signs? I'm a project manager – and a good one at that.

I'm *paid* to see how the minutiae form the big picture. How could I be so utterly oblivious?'

'Because, from where you were, you didn't have access to the big picture,' I say, my professional insight finally kicking in.

'I suppose so. And now I do – well, more of it than I had before.'

'Exactly. So, all the lies you swallowed, all the niggling doubts – now you have context for them. I bet he had an answer at the ready for every question you raised.'

Pathological liars typically do, I think.

'Oh, absolutely! How about this one? I couldn't go to his house because it was being renovated and *that's* why he was living at the Langham,' she says sarcastically. 'I really should have figured that one out – living in a hotel for six months on a pilot's salary? And how long can bathroom renovations actually take? The only upside of that lie is having stayed there. It's a lovely hotel.'

She pauses, her expression wistful, but I keep quiet, letting her sort through her thoughts.

'Honestly, Poppy, I can't believe how naïve I've been. I'm *far* too trusting. I mean, *hello*! Giant red flags everywhere!' she exclaims, waving her arms about to demonstrate.

'You are being way too hard on yourself. Love can make you blind to red flags. That's one of the reasons we carefully vet everyone who signs on with Ever After.'

'You're a red-flag filter,' she says.

'I haven't heard it put like that before, but yes.'

Kate huffs noisily, then looks out the window. 'I think I know what I want to do, a way for me to move forward' – her gaze lands back on me – 'but I keep going back and forth.'

'It's a lot to process and it may take some time to figure out. It sounds like you have a good ally, though – your cousin.'

'Margot. And yes. She's exactly who you want around when everything goes tits up – no-nonsense, bolshie as anything, and utterly fearless... And you would *never* cross her. The night I told her, she threatened to cut Jon's bollocks off with gardening shears.'

I wince at the mental picture.

'Exactly,' she says with a wry smile. 'She wouldn't actually do it, but I *can* imagine her showing up on his doorstep, a giant pair of shears in hand, if only to scare him.'

She mimes a snipping action and I snigger. Margot sounds like a real character.

'Hah! Jon's doorstep. Wherever that may be,' she says, her lips drawing into a scornful line.

'Mmm.'

'I feel like such an idiot, Poppy. And I'm not an idiot. I'm clever and I should have known better. I've wasted six months of my life, which puts me back at square one. I really thought Jon was... well, you know.'

'Is that why you wanted to see me? To re-open your case?' I ask, wondering if we're getting to the crux of Kate's visit. 'It may not be wise to leap straight back into dating,' I continue, 'but I'd happily be your matchmaker again sometime in the future.'

'Hmm?' she asks, seemingly confused by my question. 'Oh, no – it's nothing like that. I'm done with romantic pursuits – at least for some time.'

Now *I'm* confused. 'Then how can I help you? Oh,' I say, thinking I might know what she's come to ask. 'Did you want me to be there when you confront him? To support you?'

'No. I mean, I'll need to face him eventually, but I haven't decided how or when – and my cousin is part lioness, part gorgon, remember. Margot will back me up.'

I have no doubt Margot would make the perfect lieutenant in a confrontation, but I'm still baffled why Kate asked to see me. Maybe she needed to talk it through with someone who's not tangled up in this mess. 'So, is there something else I can help you with then?' I prompt.

'I *think* so.' She hesitates, biting her lower lip as if she's summoning the courage to say what's on her mind. 'Poppy, you've always been so kind to me and almost immediately, I felt like you understood me and what I was looking for in a partner.'

We exchange smiles. It's good to hear that she felt as connected to me as I did to her.

'And, you know how I said I keep going back and forth on what to do next?'

'Yes.'

'Well...' She lifts her chin and looks me straight in the eye. 'I've decided. Poppy, I need you to help me get revenge on Jon.'

'Revenge?' I'm so surprised, the word pops out of my mouth before I can temper my reaction. Typically, I love a challenging case, one with a twist or an especially tricky aspect to figure out, but for the second time this morning, I'm left speechless.

The air in the room hangs heavy with Kate's request, and I can tell she wishes she could suck the words right back into her mouth.

* * *

Kate

Now that I've said the R-word out loud, it sounds ludicrous, if not improper. And judging from Poppy's reaction – she's gawping at me, her mouth hanging open – it's also improbable.

What was I thinking? I'm not Inigo Montoya and this isn't *The Princess* (Bloody) *Bride*!

'It's ridiculous, isn't it? And wrong? *Really* wrong. I mean, peace, forgiveness, and all that rubbish, right?' I say, my hands fisted in my lap.

'It's not *wrong*, Kate,' she says adamantly, finally rejoining the conversation. 'Being angry is completely understandable. *And* normal,' she adds hurriedly.

If that's meant to reassure me, it doesn't. Methinks the matchmaker doth protest too much.

'It's just... *revenge*, Kate... Is that really what you want?'

I eye her across the conference table, my resolve wavering by the second. 'Yes?' I reply, though it comes out as a question. 'Oh god, I really have no idea. Hearing myself say that...' I lace my fingers in my lap and frown out the window.

'And I'm guessing Margot's had a hand in this?' she asks gently.

Of *course*, Poppy made the connection; this has Margot's pawprints all over it. I wouldn't have even *thought* about seeking retribution had she not brought it up – save for keeping the ring and selling it.

'That's an astute observation,' I reply.

'Well, from what you've told me, this seems more like a Margot idea than something you'd come up with.'

'She can be scarily convincing.'

'I don't doubt it.'

'But it's not like she suggested it and I suddenly agreed,' I explain hastily. I may be a naïve idiot when it comes to Jon, but I'm not a total pushover.

'I don't doubt that either,' Poppy replies kindly.

'But there is a part of me – a *growing* part of me – that wants Jon to pay for what he did. And not just footing the bill for a day of pampering.' I roll my eyes at myself. 'In hindsight, it's rather juvenile that we did that – like a silly prank perpetrated by a teenager. It's not like he's going to bat an eye.'

'Maybe not, but don't knock self-care. Everyone needs to top up their own bucket from time to time. You needed it – if only to build up your emotional stamina for what's to come.'

I contemplate this for a moment, recognising that I told myself the same thing. 'All right – fair. I get a pass on the massage and the facial – *and* the bottomless Champagne.'

'Everyone gets a pass on that.' For her weak joke, she gets a weak smile. 'And, as I said, it's completely normal to wish him ill,' she continues reassuringly. 'It will take some time for you to fully process what's happened, but there are other ways to get on with your life.'

'Such as?' I ask. Poppy must have seen and heard it all when it comes to love, but right now, I couldn't feel further from 'getting on with my life'.

'Well, you've heard the adage that the best revenge is living a happy life – or something to that effect?'

I shrug noncommittally. Having never been in this situation before – none of my previous breakups involved cheating – I've never really considered the nuances of revenge.

'How about karma?' she asks hopefully. 'Do you believe that what goes around comes around, that Dunn will eventually get his just desserts?'

'Honestly?'

'Always.'

We exchange a smile.

'From my experience, people like Jon – *men* like Jon, especially – they don't get their just desserts. They simply go about life doing whatever the hell they want, not giving a rat's arse about who they hurt along the way. So, no, I don't give much credence to karma.'

'That's fair. But I'll be honest with you, Kate, our agency has vast resources we can deploy when needed but we're in the business of happily ever afters, not payback.'

'I understand,' I say. I'm disappointed, but I knew it was a long shot.

There's also a part of me that's relieved. I'm not sure what I would have done if Poppy had agreed – bought a sword and taken fencing lessons? *Hello, my name is Kate Whitaker. You lied about wanting to marry me. Prepare to have your bollocks lopped off.* Maybe I *am* Inigo Montoya – only the wronged fiancée version, Iniga.

And I'm not sure why every time I think about exacting revenge on Jon, he ends up castrated. Actually, I do, and her name is Margot.

'Look,' says Poppy, drawing my attention, 'what I *can* do is bring this to my colleagues and get their take on it.'

'Really?' I ask, suddenly hopeful.

'Really. I've never encountered anything like this before, so maybe they can provide some additional insight or...' She throws up her hands. 'Scratch that. I genuinely have no idea what they'll make of it, so no promises, okay?'

'No, no, I understand,' I say, leaning forward, my eyes locked on hers. 'And *thank* you, Poppy.'

'Don't thank me yet. There may be nothing more we can do for you – other than put you back on the books, but you've said you don't want that.'

'God, no. I pity the next man who comes within three feet of me.'

Poppy glances at her watch, which prompts me to check mine.

'Oh, sorry. I've kept you far too long and I really should get to work – especially having left early yesterday afternoon.' I stand and reach across the table and Poppy shakes my hand.

'Before you go,' she says, 'we didn't get a chance to talk about Willem de Vries.'

My cheeks instantly flush, the traitors. 'How do you mean?' I ask casually.

Poppy's eyes narrow slightly – I can tell she's onto me.

'I meant his request – to go meet his sister.'

'*Right*,' I say, composing myself. 'To be honest, I've been so fixated on Jon and how to make him pay that I've barely given it any thought. He wants me there this coming weekend – Willem, I mean.'

My cheeks heat up again and Poppy's expression transforms into one of concern. With good reason. On top of everything else, I'm attracted to my fiancé's fiancée's brother. What could possibly go wrong there?

'It's a lot to ask of you,' she says, pretending to ignore my reaction to Willem, 'but if you're hell-bent on justice, then...' She trails off, leaving the rest of the thought unsaid.

'Then I should help Adriana,' I say, finishing it. It does make sense – and I'm surprised I didn't think of it earlier. Probably too distracted by gardening shears and the god-like brother.

'Anyway, it's something to consider,' she says with an encouraging smile.

'No, no, you're absolutely right. And I *will* think about it.'

Poppy stands and indicates for me to leave the meeting room first, then walks me to reception.

'Thanks again, Poppy, for everything,' I say when we get there.

'Of course. And I'll let you know if anything changes after I've spoken to my colleagues.'

We say goodbye and as I ride the lift down three floors, I imagine Jon's face when Adriana tells him she knows about me. Or maybe I should be the first to confront him – I've been engaged to him the longest.

Like I told Poppy, I know I'll have to confront him eventually, but the mere *thought* of being anywhere near Jon again sends shivers down my spine, as if someone has walked over my grave.

'Ground floor,' the lift announces, and I return to the present with a jolt.

Thank god I have Margot on my side – and now Poppy. Even if she and her colleagues decide there's nothing they can do to help me, I'll have her moral support. And when the time comes, I'm going to need every ounce of it.

5

KATE

There's this wonderful, unexpected sense of lightness that takes hold as I walk towards the Tube station, like a weight has been lifted off my chest. Maybe it's sharing my predicament outside of my inner circle of one.

Speaking of Margot, I promised to call her as soon as I finished with Poppy. She answers right away.

'Well?' she asks, skipping formalities.

'Well, after she got over the shock, she was really good to talk to. She's an excellent listener and has this incredible insight.'

'Ouch.'

'You haven't been replaced, silly. But Poppy sees the situation more objectively.'

'So, she doesn't want Jon drawn and quartered then?'

'Ah, no.'

'How much did you tell her?' she asks.

'I told her everything, including your plan to buy gardening shears.'

'And what did she say?'

'That you need professional help,' I quip, even though I know that's not what she meant.

'Oi!' she chides, and I chuckle. 'I meant what did she say about getting back at Jon?'

'She's conferring with her colleagues, but I sense it's a no-go.'

'Oh.'

I laugh. 'What did you expect? They're matchmakers, not the Justice League.'

'Mmm, Henry Cavill.' She moans suggestively, but she's lost me.

'What's Henry Cavill got to do— Oh, right, Superman,' I say, sidestepping a dogwalker whose legs are tangled up in the dogs' leads.

'So, what did she say about going to Amsterdam?'

'She's nudging me towards it.'

'*Interesting...*' Margot responds, drawing the word out. 'I might like this Poppy woman. She sounds very sensible.'

'She is *and* she's got me thinking. If I can help Adriana see Jon for who he really is—'

'Help her escape Arseface's lies and general bastardery, you mean,' she interjects.

'Yes, *that*,' I say impatiently. 'Anyway, if I *do* help Adriana, then that could be its own kind of justice, perhaps dampen my desire for revenge.'

'Ooh, I like that,' she says, surprising me. I'd have thought she'd still be pushing for retaliation, being the poster child for wrathful women everywhere – *and* the person who planted the seed in the first place.

'I like it too, the more I think about it,' I reply. 'Even if it's only Poppy steering me away from something more sinister.'

'Which is what he *deserves*.' Ah, there's the Margot I know and love.

'Margot, I'm going,' I say, deciding this instant. 'To Amsterdam.'

'Excellent. And I'm coming with you.'

'You don't need to do that. I'm perfectly capable of going by myself.'

'Well, yeah,' she scoffs, 'but I want to meet Thor.'

I laugh again. 'You muppet. I'm not having you come along just to perv on Willem.'

'It's not just for that, Kate,' she says, her tone suddenly serious. 'Actually, it's not that at all. This is some intense bullshit and I'm not letting you go through it on your own.'

'Oh, okay.'

'Besides, I love Amsterdam, and I haven't been for ages,' she adds, slipping right back into Margot mode. And I love her for it – for her fierce protectiveness, for making it impossible to say no to her. Also, it won't be as terrifying if she's there with me. I may have decided it's the best course of action, but it still scares the absolute hell out of me.

'Okay,' I reply. 'I'll message Willem, then check the train schedule to Amsterdam.'

'Brilliant. And I'll look for someplace to stay.'

'*Two* rooms this time, Margot.'

'I don't snore.'

'You do. Two rooms.'

'Fine. Oh, have you heard from Arseface?' she asks.

'Only his daily text messages,' I reply, my stomach taking a nosedive.

So much for feeling more buoyant, but what did I expect? These past few days have been an exercise in emotional nimbleness '– I'm up one moment, down the next, and my stomach is along for the ride. It hasn't felt this rubbish since I ate a dodgy kebab after the Taylor Swift concert and spent the night on the loo.

I wish the Ever After Agency *was* the Justice League and Poppy was Wonder Woman. Maybe then I could borrow her bracelets to fend off Jon's lies like bullets.

You're everything I ever dreamed of – ping – I'm so lucky to have you – ping – I miss you so much – ping – I love you, Kate – ping – We'll have the best life together, Kate – ping, ping, ping.

Lies – every one of them. Bloody liar.

'*And?*' Margot prods.

'Oh, soz. He says how much he misses me and I—'

'You reply with two emojis – the scissors and the cherries,' she says, interrupting me again.

'Scissors and cher— Oh, I get it. Graphic – apt even – but no. I just reply "See you soon".'

'Even though you never want to see him again.'

'Even though "never" will be far too soon, yes,' I reply, my voice straining as that buoyant feeling rapidly slips away. *Focus, Kate.* 'Anyway,' I say brightly. 'I'm at the Tube now. Call you after work?'

'Okay.'

She ends the call without saying goodbye – no standing on ceremony with Margot – and I descend underground.

* * *

Poppy

I've been distracted all morning, ever since Kate Whitaker dropped her bombshell. I was absolutely useless at the staff meeting, stumbling over the updates on my other cases, even though I know them inside and out. I'm now re-examining Kate's case file, focusing on the list of potential matches I assembled months ago. Our vetting process is thorough – as Kate said, we're like a red-flag filter – but *how* thorough? Could any of these men be leading double lives like Kate's fiancé?

God, even the *idea* of matching someone with such a duplicitous liar makes me queasy.

And for the first time in ages, I'm anxious about how to proceed. I play many roles as a matchmaker: confidante, counsellor, cheerleader, conciliator, cupid... I do *not* want to add vigilante to that list.

'Shall we go in, Poppy?' Ursula – senior agent and frequent mentor – is beside my desk, her generously applied Chanel N°5 wafting in the air between us.

'Ah, sure,' I reply, returning to the here and now. I stand, picking up my tablet from the desktop. 'After you.'

I follow Ursula into our boss' office where the agency's founder, Saskia, and her co-founder, Paloma, are waiting for us. There's a bit of chatter between the other three as we get comfy on the facing sofas, but I don't join in as I'm collecting my thoughts.

As I called this meeting, they all eventually look my way, which is my cue to begin. I force a smile and walk them through Kate's situation, watching closely for their reactions.

Saskia, who we refer to as 'The Swan' for her calm and stoic nature, listens intently, nodding at certain points, her eyes narrowing at others. Paloma, who is far more forthright and easier to read, intermittently tuts, occasionally frowns, and several times, she looks at Saskia with a can-you-believe-this? expression.

When I disclose that Willem de Vries has asked Kate to go to Amsterdam and why, she asks, 'He *what*?'

But it's Ursula's reaction that surprises me the most. First, her brows lift half a millimetre, which for Ursula, who's had more work done than a certain LA-based famous-for-being-famous family, means she's intrigued; I've captured her imagination. Then, as I reveal each detail of Kate's conundrum, Ursula's complexion turns a deep shade of red and her almost immobile lips purse ever so slightly. She's obviously incensed, but is it the general awfulness of the situation, or is she simply empathising?

'So, I'd appreciate your take on this situation,' I say, yet to drop the biggest revelation, that Kate has asked me to help her get revenge. 'But there's one more thi—'

'And the name of this agency?' Ursula asks abruptly, cutting me off. 'The one that matched Kate with a prospective polygamist?'

'Perfect Pairings,' I reply.

Ordinarily, I might enjoy the alliteration of four Ps in a row, but this is not an ordinary situation.

Ursula huffs angrily. 'I thought as much. Those *cowboys*,' she spits, imbuing the word with a substantial amount of rancour.

'So, you've encountered them before?' Paloma asks.

As one of London's most prestigious matchmaking agencies, we're aware of the competition, but it's rare that we engage with another agency directly.

Ursula nods as she looks at us in turn. 'Perfect Pairings,' she says, her clipped accent hitting the Ps as though she's spitting out grape pips. 'I know exactly who they are. My former business partner is at the helm.'

Now *this* is news and I shelve my big reveal for later.

'I hadn't realised,' says Paloma. 'That you'd once been in a partnership.'

Neither had I. Ursula has been a matchmaker since the early nineties, but my understanding was that she ran a one-woman agency until Saskia persuaded her to join Ever After eleven years ago.

Ursula waves a hand dismissively. 'Ancient history and not something I like to dwell on. When Clarissa and I parted ways – as far from amicably as is possible – I decided I'd be better off flying solo.'

'Until you came to us,' says Saskia with a smile.

She and Ursula exchange a warm look.

'Yes, until then.'

'So, why did the two of you fall out?' Paloma asks, intruding on their moment.

'That list is as long as the Thames *and* just as convoluted. Suffice to say, Clarissa wanted to cut corners and I did not.'

'On such things as vetting perspective matches?' I venture.

'Precisely,' she says, her mouth milking every syllable from the word. 'Perfect Pairings is only successful because they play a numbers game. The more people through the door, the more matches they can claim to have made. Never mind the pour souls who end up with no one or – worse – someone like your client's fiancé, Poppy.'

'I had no idea they were so *reckless*,' says Saskia, her brows knitted. It's highly unusual for her to react so vehemently, but it's also understandable.

'But how have they flown under the radar so successfully?' asks Paloma. 'Surely someone's spoken out at some point? They must have had dozens of unhappy clients over the years.'

'I'd say it's in the hundreds,' says Ursula, 'but Clarissa is shrewd. I've seen a copy of the agreement her clients sign – absolutely no wiggle room for complaints.'

'I hate to be that person,' says Paloma, 'but it might be a

good thing, their confidentiality clause. If these practices got out, it could be a blight on the entire profession.'

As head of client relations, I can understand her perspective. Any distrust of the profession would impact Ever After and, by extension, our clients.

We're all quiet for a moment – me as I contemplate whether it's worth mentioning Kate's request, especially as revenge is a weighty addition to an already troubling discussion. Maybe it's better left for another time.

'Poppy?' Saskia asks. 'Do we know if the second woman used the same agency?'

'Uh, no, she didn't use an agency. She met Dunn by happenstance.'

'Hah,' snorts Paloma, and we all look at her. 'Sorry, but men like that don't meet their second fiancées "organically",' she says, her voice ripe with sarcasm. 'I can almost guarantee it.'

'Agreed,' says Ursula.

'Well,' I say, 'if Kate does go to Amsterdam to meet Adriana, she can find out more. I should also mention that Adriana's brother, Willem de Vries, is continuing to investigate Dunn.'

'Concerns about there being another fiancée?' asks Saskia. 'I suppose it's possible there's a third woman out there, also in the dark.'

'Or a fourth,' Paloma remarks cynically – although, I've thought the same thing.

'That's it exactly,' I reply to Saskia. 'Something about Dunn's supposed whereabouts not adding up – too many gaps in his stories.'

'Do you think we should bring Marie in?' asks Paloma. 'To assist the brother?'

Marie Maillot is the agency's private investigator. She's close to seventy but either she styles herself after Lisbeth Salander from *The Girl with the Dragon Tattoo* or Steig Larsson knew Marie and stole her look for Lisbeth. Studded black leather, top to toe, jet-black hair, and more tattoos than a long-shoreman. On a good day, she's curt, on a bad day, abrasive, regarding everyone with disdain, including her fellow French. But she's incredibly resourceful and when it comes to investigative skills and connections, she's in the upper echelon of her field. She'll also be the first one to tell you that.

'Uh, from what Kate's told me, he's on it, but I'll keep Marie in mind,' I say, and Paloma nods in agreement.

'Oh, this really is a right pickle your client's in, Poppy,' says Ursula, huffing out another breath. 'Through no fault of her own, of course,' she adds hastily, but I'm more caught on the assumption that Kate is my client.

I mean, she is... but she also isn't...

'About that...' I start, because I'm not sure which to tackle first – Kate's standing as my client or her unusual request.

'Was there something else, Poppy?' asks Saskia.

'Yes,' I reply, going with the easiest matter to address. 'It's what Ursula said just now – about Kate being my client. I mean, she *was* my client, of course, but she isn't interested in us finding her a new match. Not for the foreseeable future, anyway.'

'Then why did she come in this morning?' asks Paloma.

This, of course, leads us to the BIG REVEAL. I inhale deeply through my nose and meet Paloma's eye.

'Kate would like me – well, the agency – to help her get revenge on Dunn,' I state matter-of-factly, as if I'm rattling off a coffee order.

All three of them talk at once.

'I'm sorry?' asks Ursula, blinking at me rapidly.

'Did you say... *revenge*?' Saskia's eyes narrow curiously.

'Can't say I blame her,' says Paloma, her mouth bunching to the side.

Then as Paloma's words register, Ursula and Saskia's heads swivel in her direction.

'Paloma,' says Saskia with an uncertain smile. 'You're not suggesting...?'

'No,' she replies a little too quickly. 'Course not.'

All three look back at me. 'And what did you tell her?' asks Saskia.

'I made it clear that exacting revenge is not the best course of action, particularly with regards to her own wellbeing, which is why I nudged her towards going to Amsterdam. If she can help the second fiancée see sense, then that will foil Dunn's plans to either string two women along or become a polygamist. Not exactly revenge – more like justice.'

'Well said,' says Paloma with a nod, and I take the compliment with a tight smile.

'I also stressed that if she *still* wants to go down the revenge route then, unfortunately, we won't be able to help her.'

Saskia sits back against the sofa, visibly relieved. 'That's very sensible of you, Poppy. Thank you for making the agency's position clear.'

I send Saskia a smile too, but it's more of a thank-god-I-didn't-screw-that-up smile.

'Hold on,' says Ursula, and I look over. Her face may be motionless, but her eyes are alight with mischief – something's afoot. She raises her forefinger, its long nail painted a glossy red. 'If she *does* come back to us on the matter of revenge, I say we revisit this discussion.'

Saskia tilts her head, her mouth in a taut line. 'No, Ursula. We don't do that sort of thing.'

Paloma angles her body towards her co-founder and old school chum. 'Sask, think about it. If Perfect Pairing's practices get out – rather, *mal*practices – it could adversely impact the entire profession, including Ever After. *But* if we help out on this case, come up with a foolproof plan to punish this... this...'

'Weasel,' I supply.

'Yes, thank you, Poppy. Weasel. *And* we ensure Blackheart's agency is held accountable for their part in this palaver, then we kill two birds with one stone. We help the client, and we save matchmaking.'

Saskia frowns at Paloma, something I have never seen in all my years at Ever After. 'A little dramatic, don't you think, Paloma? Especially for you,' she adds, but Paloma appears unchastened.

Turning to me, Saskia says, 'You said you've guided Kate towards a more' – her eyes flick towards Paloma, then return to me – '*reasonable* solution, but if she does ask again about something more drastic, then... Well, I'll consider it.'

Paloma and Ursula clearly take this as a small victory and exchange a glance.

'Until then,' she says firmly, 'Poppy's right. Kate isn't currently her client, so we do nothing. Understood?'

It's highly unlike Saskia the Swan to caution her team this way – especially her partner and the agency's most senior agent. This may be why we reply, 'Yes, Saskia,' in unison like we're in nursery school.

We file out of Saskia's office, and Ursula and Paloma go straight to Paloma's office, talking animatedly in hushed tones. It's obvious they're already conspiring, despite Saskia's warning not to. I escape to my desk and sit heavily on the chair.

The main reason I called that meeting was to share the weight of Kate's bizarre situation and get a sense check, but it was even more successful than I'd hoped. My course of action has been endorsed by my bosses, we're not closing the door on Kate's case entirely – maybe I *will* have the chance to get Kate an HEA, after all – and I have two unlikely allies should Kate need assistance with more stringent measures.

God, I really hope it doesn't come to that. 'Poppy Dean, Love Vigilante' does *not* have a nice ring to it.

6

KATE

'Kate, have you got a sec before you head out?'

It's Friday afternoon and I'm halfway out the door, but when Mina Choi asks for a second of your time, you smile brightly and say, 'Of course.'

I roll my case back into my office, setting my handbag on top, and follow Mina into hers, where floor-to-ceiling windows look out over Tottenham Court Road. She takes a seat behind her desk, and I sit opposite her.

'I won't hold you up – you're obviously off somewhere for the weekend,' she says.

'Uh, yes.'

'Mini break with Jon?' she asks, a reasonable question that instantly sets me on edge.

'Uh, girls' trip – to Amsterdam,' I reply – not a lie, but not the whole truth.

'Sounds fun. Look, I just wanted to check... is everything all right?' she asks with a slight head tilt. 'You've seemed a little off your game this week.'

Oh god. It's far worse than I thought. After Monday's fake

migraine, I've been determined not to let the situation with Jon impact my work performance any further. I've obviously failed. Or perhaps it's Mina's uncanny ability to read people, something that has served her well at the helm of Elev8te but has now landed me in the hotseat.

Her dark-brown eyes study me thoughtfully as she awaits my answer.

Tell the truth or spin a lie? I wonder. Mina and I have an excellent professional relationship, but we're not friends. I don't want to jeopardise her faith in my abilities; will explaining my situation impact how she views me?

Sod it. I inhale deeply and take the plunge. 'Jon and I are no longer engaged,' I say – again, not an outright lie but also not the full picture.

Her eyes fly to my left hand, which is markedly missing an engagement ring. I hold it up and wriggle my fingers.

'Not having it cleaned – but I didn't want to break the news just yet.'

'Oh, Kate, I am so sorry to hear that,' she says sympathetically.

I shrug. 'Thank you. And I apologise if my work hasn't been up to snuff this week. I promise I'll—'

'Kate,' she says, interrupting. 'Please – no apologies. Honestly, you operating at eighty per cent is far better than most people at a hundred. That's not why I asked you in here. I was simply concerned, that's all.'

'Oh, well, thank you,' I say.

Surprisingly, it's cathartic telling Mina my engagement is off – and here I was worried that it would diminish her faith in me. I'm glad I was truthful. Well, *partly* truthful.

'Of *course*! We walk the walk around here,' she says, referring to Elev8te's key ethos that employee wellbeing comes first. 'Now,' she says, with her trademark grin. I can only guess from that glint in her eye what's coming. 'I know you'll have planned to be back here first thing Monday morning...'

'Because Monday is a workday,' I state matter-of-factly.

'Not for you, it isn't.'

'Sorry?' I ask, confused.

'I want you to take the day.'

'Oh, I don't need to—'

'Kate, when was the last time you took a mental health day? Oh, I know – *never*. Take Monday off. Stay in Amsterdam an extra day... go to a spa... lie on the sofa all day... Do whatever you like, but you're not to come into the office.'

'You're sidelining me,' I say, somewhat stung.

'I'm looking out for you.'

I sit back against the chair. 'So, I have no choice.'

'Nope. If I clap eyes on you before Tuesday, you'll owe me a week's pay.'

'A week? So, pulling out the big guns.'

She raises her brows at me, and I snigger softly. This conversation took a sharp and sudden turn from where I thought it would go – but for the better.

'All right, you win,' I say, standing. 'I shall see you on *Tuesday*.'

'And not before nine.'

'Any other conditions you'd like to put on this mandate?' I ask, laughing.

'Only one,' she says with a grin. 'Have a brilliant time in Amsterdam.'

'Will do.'

I leave Mina's office, now in a hurry to catch the Tube to St Pancras where I'm meeting Margot.

* * *

'You jammy cow,' says Margot when I tell her Mina's mandate. She leans across the table, punctuating her words with a light slap on my arm.

'Oi. And what makes me jammy exactly? That I'm on my way to break another woman's heart or that my fiancé is a lying arsehole?'

'You know what I mean. And it's *ex*-fiancé.'

'I wish I did. And I'm not sure it's right to call him my ex when I haven't broken things off yet.'

'Semantics,' she says dismissively. I shake my head at her, but she misses it, her gaze lifting to the departures board overhead.

'We should go,' she announces, springing into action. She downs the rest of her pre-travel champers, then barrels through the crowd, her roller case in tow, as I rush after her.

We find our carriage and climb aboard, and I trail behind her to our seats. I've sprung for Standard Premier, which includes dinner and drinks. Although Margot has already sussed out our proximity to the Café Métropole car and plans to buy us a bottle of champers – whether I like it or not.

In her mind, I'm supposed to be celebrating – *still*, as if this is some sort of month-long festival. The Fuck Me, My Fiancé's a Prick Festival. Imagine the throngs who'd attend if it were real – probably half of them engaged to Jon.

After the train departs St Pancras and Margot pops out of her seat to procure the promised bottle, I retrieve my phone from my handbag and navigate to my messages – specifically the thread with Willem. I send a quick update:

On our way.

My pulse quickens as the dancing dots appear – wildly out of order considering who's making those dots dance. Jon may be a cheating bastard, but a quickened pulse at another man's hands (so to speak) feels like a betrayal. Oh, the irony.

Willem's message finally appears:

Thank you again for coming. I really appreciate it.

I type out a quick reply:

All part of the service.

Oh no, that's awful. Delete.

She'd do the same for me.

What the hell does that mean? Adriana doesn't believe I exist – why would she do *anything* for me? Delete!

Looking forward to it.

Really? I'm looking forward to upending another woman's life? Delete, delete, delete!

Of course. See you tomorrow.

There. Simple, clear, and not even the slightest hint that I've completely lost my mind.

And I'm certain I have. Swinging wildly between opposing emotions, in a constant state of conflict and confusion... Getting caught in an endless loop of questions that beget even more questions... Mentally replaying moments with Jon, and not one of them seeming like it actually happened.

It was only a week ago when *my* world was upended. It simultaneously feels like minutes ago and ten years ago.

'They only had prosecco,' says Margot, appearing at my side, holding aloft an open bottle and two plastic cups. She sits, then pours and hands me a brimming cup, mostly froth. 'To my cousin, who is beautiful and brave and about to kick some serious arse.'

I snigger – how could I not? – then take a sip. Only bubbles go up my nose, making me splutter.

'Sorry,' she says. 'Bad pour.' She reaches over and sticks her forefinger in my cup.

'Oi, what are you doing?'

I watch, fascinated (and horrified), as the bubbles recede down the side of the cup. 'It's the quickest way,' she replies. 'I saw it on Instagram.'

'It's the *disgusting* way. Here.' I swap my cup for hers and she shrugs, taking a drink.

My phone, which is set to silent, buzzes on the small table in front of me and I flip it over to read the incoming text message. It's Willem:

Where are you staying?

I catch Margot reading over my shoulder and give her a sharp look.

'What?' she asks rhetorically. 'Just seeing what Thor has to say.' She reaches over and scrolls up.

'*Margot*,' I say, snatching the phone away.

'He's not exactly a sparkling conversationalist.'

'I'm not sure what you were expecting. It's not like we're friends.'

'Oh, I don't know – a *hint* of flirtation. Is that too much to ask?'

'Flirta— Remind me again why I brought you.'

'You didn't *bring* me. I invited myself along. And you need me.'

She's probably right but I'm starting to wish this was a solo journey. I stare at her a moment and she steadily meets my gaze. Typical Margot.

'So,' I say, holding up my phone, 'the address, please?'

Margot obliges and I send the address to Willem, having to override autocorrect four times to spell the street name correctly.

He replies almost instantly:

That's not far from my house. If you'd like to meet up later, there's a bar close by.

'Huzzah! That's *more* than a hint of flirtation. He's asking you out.'

'Not on a date. He's just being friendly,' I reply, not bothering to temper my irritation.

Margot seems unconvinced but doesn't press, and I type out a noncommittal reply. We won't arrive until late and I suspect I'll be longing for sleep. Actually, I'm longing for sleep now and the lulling movement of the train isn't helping.

'Have you heard from Arseface today?' Margot asks when I put my phone away.

I sigh heavily and rest against the seat. 'Can we please talk about something else? Or nothing?'

Margot's hand lands lightly on my leg, patting it three

times. I slide my eyes in her direction, catching her supportive expression. She gives me a kind smile and I return it. One of the things I love most about Margot is her ability to switch seamlessly from cheery distraction tactics to empathetic love.

It's probably best that she invited herself along, because if I linger on what I'm doing for more than five seconds, I break into a cold sweat.

'Thanks,' I say softly.

She pats my leg a final time, then takes out the latest book in the Mackenzie August PI series, her favourite. While Margot reads, I sip my prosecco and regard the English countryside out the window.

Seriously, what the actual fuck am I doing?

* * *

'Is this right?' I ask.

Our driver has dropped us off on a residential street that runs alongside a canal and Margot is rolling her case *towards* the water.

'It's right. Follow me,' she calls over her shoulder. She stops in front of a houseboat, crosses a walkway, and checks her phone for the code to the lockbox beside the front door. It springs open and she holds up the keys with a grin. 'See?' she asks, looking up to street level.

When I put Margot in charge of accommodation, I thought she understood that meant a hotel. This is not a hotel.

'Come on,' she says cheerily. She disappears inside the houseboat, and I follow, closing the front door behind me.

Margot is running around switching on lights as I take in the main room of the houseboat. It's *lovely* – Scandinavian-style furniture, a chunky knit throw on the sofa, a dozen or so pot plants, and pops of orange in the throw pillows, an area rug, and lamps. There's a table for two butted up against the wall, and the kitchen is compact but, as I hadn't expected we'd even have a kitchen, it's a bonus. Especially as it bears a welcome basket with tea, coffee, long-life milk, and a packet of *stroopwafels*!

'Your room's down here,' says Margot from one end of the house.

I follow the sound of her voice into a bedroom that's decorated similarly to the lounge. She's spreadeagled on the double bed, her eyes closed.

'You sure?' I ask with a mocking smile. 'You look rather comfortable.'

She cracks her eyes and peers at me through her lashes. 'The other room only has a single bed.'

'That's okay. I don't mind.'

She props herself up on her elbows. 'But what happens when you want to bring Thor back for a shag?'

'Margot!' I plop onto the edge of the bed, laughing. 'You do realise you sound like a teenager when you talk like that?'

'You do realise that it's mostly an act?'

We exchange a weighty look as she gives me a rueful smile. I'm the only person Margot is ever truthful with about her inner struggles.

'Right,' she says, hopping off the bed. 'I'm going to get settled in my room. What time are we meeting Thor?'

I'm overcome by a huge yawn. 'Sorry.'

'Very attractive.'

I give her a look, my mouth quirking, and she sits next to me. 'So, no drinks with Thor?'

'*Please* call him Willem.'

'Fine, so no drinks with Willem?'

'Am I doing the right thing?' I ask, abruptly changing the subject. I hold my breath. She'll either make another joke or understand the gravity of what I'm asking and take the question seriously.

'Jon deserves whatever's coming,' she says gravely, and I release the breath.

'I know. But tomorrow, I'm going to meet Adriana and she's Jon's *fiancée*, Margs. His *fiancée*. He's told her he loves her. They've had romantic dinners. They've walked hand in hand along the canals. They've slept late on a Sunday morning, then stayed in bed, reading and drinking coffee. He's made love to her. He's put a sodding ring on her finger! Everything I thought was ours, he's had that with her. She's the "other woman".'

'Not in the way that usually means. She's not his mistress. She's convinced she's the only one.'

'Somehow, that makes it worse. The poor woman. She has no idea what's about to happen. Maybe it was wrong to come here.'

Margot scooches closer and grabs my nearest hand, holding it in both of hers.

'Look, Adriana won't take Willem at his word – she's too blinded by love. Because Arseface has lied to her, just like he lied to you. It's the right thing to do, helping her understand who she's engaged to.'

'It may be the right thing to do for *her*, but what about me?' I ask, my voice small and hoarse. 'How am I supposed to face the woman who's been sleeping with Jon? God, even the *idea* of them together...' I shudder, desperate to dislodge the gruesome thought.

Margot stands and faces me, hands on her hips.

'Katherine Ellen Whitaker.'

My eyes snap to meet hers.

'Take it from the ex-wife of a philandering twat, no good can come of going down that path. You think scrolling Instagram reels is a time suck? You can waste a *lifetime* entertaining those kinds of thoughts – *and* they will drive you mad. Of course you're going to miss Jon – the Jon you knew. And, yes, you will get sad sometimes and, yes, you might be jealous of Adriana. But there's no going back. That Jon, the life he promised? That's a fallacy. It was never real to begin with.'

'I know,' I interject, somewhat defensive.

'Good. And now you get to be there for someone who *doesn't* know – well, not yet anyway.'

I stare up at her, succumbing to a smile. 'You're clever, you are.'

'Well, yeah.' We exchange smiles. 'But I'm also of the belief that when you learn a lesson the hard way, tell *everyone* so they don't have to make that same mistake themselves.'

'Clever *and* wise.'

'Exactly.'

I sigh, my heartrate slowing, the tangled knots in my midsection easing. I glance at the clock by the bed. It's close to midnight and I yawn again.

'Probably a good thing you're not seeing Thor tonight,' Margot teases. 'You're an ugly yawner.'

My yawn transforms into a wide-mouthed laugh. 'You muppet,' I say, smiling up at her adoringly. I really am glad Margot is with me. I can't imagine how riled up I would be if she weren't here.

'Right. I'm off to bed. You message the Norse god and tell him tonight's a no-go – a brilliant tactic, that, playing hard to get.'

'I'm not—'

'Goodnight!' she sing-songs, making her way to the other end of the houseboat.

I'm still sniggering when I unlock my phone, discovering a message:

I miss you darling

'Oh, sod off, Jon, you arse-faced twat,' I say aloud, which is *hugely* satisfying. Then I navigate to the thread with Willem and fire off a message, apologising for being too shattered to meet up. A reply comes moments later:

Disappointing but I understand. See you tomorrow.

Disappointing. How can one word have the power to make my pulse quicken? Again.

7

KATE

'I feel like I'm going to be sick,' I murmur to myself.

We're walking to Willem's house and the closer we get, the more intensely my stomach roils with nerves. I shouldn't have had that second *stroopwafel*. Or the first.

Margot stops me with a hand on my arm. '*Actual* sick or...?'

'No, it's just... Margot, what the hell am I doing?'

'You are saving another woman from Arseface's evil clutches,' she replies earnestly.

'Right,' I say, setting off again. I check Google Maps on my phone. Two minutes. In two minutes, I'll be confronted with Jon's other fiancée. *Gah!*

I've taken extra care with my appearance today, telling myself that if I look good, I'll feel good. That's been about as effective as making tea in a chocolate teapot. An outfit – even a favourite one – only has so much power.

Even so, it can't hurt that I've made an effort. I'm wearing dark-wash jeans, my one-shouldered slouchy top that Margot declared 'sexy AF', and heeled boots for an added boost – both literally and metaphorically. My hair behaved itself this morning and beachy waves fall to my mid back, and thanks to exhaustion and a decent bed, I slept well and my skin looks glorious.

If only I *felt* glorious.

We arrive at a terrace house with a dark-green door and I double check the street number, then turn to Margot.

'Ready?' I ask.

'Are *you*?'

'No.'

I turn and knock on the door. Moments later, there's the sound of heavy footsteps and a muffled, 'Coming.'

Then Willem opens the door.

Involuntarily, I inhale sharply and behind me, Margot whispers, 'Fuck me.'

I'd shush her if it wouldn't be so obvious, but she's right. In less than a second, I take in Willem's appearance and OH. MY. GOD. I thought he was handsome the night we met...

He's wearing faded, low-slung jeans, a well-worn T-shirt that drapes enticingly from his broad shoulders, and his feet are bare. His dark hair is still damp from the shower, his bright-blue eyes are creased at the corners, and (endearingly) he nicked himself shaving, a tiny spot of blood dotting his smooth, strong jawline.

Is it rude to swoon on a near-stranger's doorstep?

'*Hallo*, *hallo*, come inside.'

He steps aside and I shimmy past him – it's a very narrow entryway – emerging into a spacious combined lounge–dining–kitchen. At the rear of the room are floor-to-ceiling windows and a glass door that leads out to a small patio and a lush, compact garden with borders of daffodils. At the end of the garden is a free-standing structure that looks like it might be an office.

Willem closes the front door and we all look at each other for a moment before Margot steps closer, her hand extended.

'Hi, I'm Margot – Kate's cousin.'

'Sorry!' I say, embarrassed to have forgotten my manners. I did tell Willem that Margot was accompanying me, but I should have made the introduction. 'Margot – Willem, Willem – Margot,' I say redundantly.

Willem shakes her hand with a smile. I don't know him very well – actually, barely at all – but he seems tense. Nervous even. Well, that makes two of us. It would make three of us if Margot ever felt uneasy about any situation ever.

'Can I offer you something to drink?' Willem asks, tilting his head towards the kitchen.

'No thanks,' I say, right as Margot replies, 'Well, I see you have one of those fancy-pants coffee makers, and I could murder a latte.'

I could murder you, I think. This isn't a social call. But as Margot pointedly avoids eye contact – she knows I'd scold her for being cheeky – Willem gets started on making her a coffee.

'This is a beautiful house,' I say, mostly to make conversation – although Willem's house truly is something to behold.

'Thank you,' he replies, deftly handling the coffee machine. 'This half belonged to my parents for many years – Adriana and I grew up here – and when they retired, they wanted to downsize, so I bought their house *and* the one next door and renovated both buildings. This level is now one home – the bedrooms and bathrooms are through there' – he points to a large, wooden sliding door – 'and I turned the upstairs of both buildings into apartments, which I rent out. And there's a studio apartment at the back,' he adds, nodding towards the structure at the end of the garden.

It's an impressive undertaking and ordinarily, I'd like to

learn more, but more pressing is Adriana's whereabouts. Before I can ask, he starts heating the milk, filling the room with a screechy gurgle.

'Uh, just wondering...' I say when he turns off the milk steamer.

He glances over his shoulder, his brows lifted inquisitively.

'Is Adriana here?' I ask in a whisper.

He shakes his head. 'She's at yoga.' He glances at the clock on the oven. 'She'll be home soon.'

The relief at being given a momentary reprieve is overshadowed by yet another revelation: Adriana and Willem live together, something I hadn't expected.

Willem hands Margot her coffee. 'Please, sit,' he says, signalling for us to take a seat on the sofa.

I sit, but Margot doesn't.

'Actually,' she says, pointing outside. 'Would you mind if I had my coffee in your garden? I could use a moment to myself.'

'*Margot*,' I say through gritted teeth. For our entire lives, Margot has never once asked for a moment to herself – she's the ultimate extravert. What is she up to?

'Of course,' Willem replies. 'Just watch out for the money spiders. Ady hates them – she's always walking through their webs in the morning – but I leave them alone because they're supposed to bring good luck.'

Margot, the sceptic, grins up at him as if she believes in that sort of thing. 'I'll be careful.'

Still patently ignoring me, she excuses herself and heads out into the sunshine-filled garden, closing the glass door behind her. She'd better come back inside the moment Adriana gets home. That's the whole point of her being here –

to support me when I come face to face with Jon's other fiancée.

And it's obvious why she's left me alone with Willem – she's playing matchmaker, even though she's well aware that romance is the last thing on my mind.

'Are you sure I can't make you a coffee?' Willem asks, now back at the machine. 'I'm having one.'

Our eyes meet for a second, sending a lightning bolt straight through me. Inconvenient timing for internal thunderstorms – not to mention inappropriate.

'Oh, go on then,' I say, ignoring the heat pooling between my legs. 'I'll have a latte. Same as Margot.'

I get up and go into the kitchen, sliding out a stool and sitting at the kitchen bench. While Willem grinds the beans for our coffees, I cast my eyes around the vast room, taking in more of the décor.

'I like that,' I say, pointing to a large rectangular artwork hanging on the exposed-brick wall.

Willem glances at it, then smiles. 'I do too,' he says, and I chuckle. 'It's actually a photograph.'

'*No*,' I say, peering at it more closely.

'*Ja*. It's a close-up of that painting.' He jerks his chin towards a painting on the opposite wall and I look between the two. 'The bottom left corner – see?'

'Hmm.' I slip off the stool and walk over to the painting, my eyes roving its abstract details, then I cross to the photograph, scrutinising it.

'Wowser,' I say, mostly to myself. I straighten and return to my spot at the kitchen bench. 'That's quite the duo.'

'I would like to have them side by side, but...' He doesn't finish the sentence, but he doesn't need to. There isn't a wall that's big enough to hang them both.

He finishes making two coffees and slides one towards me. He's even made a heart design in the froth the way experienced baristas do.

'Thanks,' I say with a smile.

Willem sips from his mug and I do the same. It's *delicious* – strong, but not burnt, hot, but not scalding…

Like Willem. The thought arrives without permission, and I shush it, annoyed at myself. Or maybe it's just my mind trying to distract me.

'So, Margot…' Willem begins. 'You felt like you need reinforcements?'

'Reinforce— Uh, yes. I suppose so.'

I smile at him weakly, then sip my coffee, not wanting to explain further. Besides, I'm not sure he'd believe that I'd intended to come alone until Margot invited herself.

I look over and he's still watching me, a glint of amusement in his eyes. He really needs to stop that. It's unnerving.

And between his made-to-order coffees and Margot making herself at home, anyone would think we're here for a friendly visit. Any moment now, he'll put on a playlist and fire up the barbecue.

'I understand,' he says. For a moment, I'm not sure what he means, but then I realise we're still talking about Margot. 'I was shaking in my boots when I came to see you.'

'You were not,' I say, laughing spontaneously.

'I *was*.'

I eye him disbelievingly, my mouth quirking at his wide-eyed, innocent look. 'Mmm… like butter wouldn't melt in your mouth,' I say with a suspicious shake of my head.

His eyebrows lift – he clearly gets that I'm teasing him.

'Something's just occurred to me…' I say. 'Your English – right down to the vernacular – it's *flawless*.'

'Thank you,' he replies, as if he's not sure it's a compliment.

'I mean it and you're welcome. But why is that exactly? I know the Dutch study English at school but, seriously, yours is excellent.'

'I did a student exchange to America in high school. A lot of Dutch people do. Ady did as well.'

'Oh, wow. And where did you go?'

'So-Cal, dude. I even learned how to surf,' he replies with a remarkably good American accent. It makes me laugh again, easing the tension even further.

'I suppose there's not much opportunity for that in the Netherlands – surfing.'

'You suppose correctly.'

'And what about Ady? Where was her exchange?'

'Chicago.'

'Oh, I've always wanted to go there. I was obsessed with John Hughes films when I was a teenager. I had a massive crush on Ferris Bueller. I blame Margot for that – she led me astray, like always.'

He smiles.

'And is it really like that – high school in America?'

'Like it is in films?'

'Yes,' I say, propping my chin on my hand and leaning in.

He scrunches his nose – adorable (gah!) – and shakes his head. 'It's just normal. Although, I did like the pep rallies.'

'Oh, I bet – the cheerleaders, especially.'

His eyes narrow. 'I think you may have a distorted view of who I am, Kate,' he says, his tone turning serious.

I'm about to backpedal when there's the sound of a key in the lock. We both look towards the door, the air charged with anticipation.

Then I watch, mesmerised, as Adriana enters, a yoga-mat

carrier and calico bag slung over her shoulder. She closes the door behind her and when she turns around and sees us, she stops, standing perfectly still.

She's taller than I expected – at a guess, two or three inches taller than me – and her long, yellow-blonde hair is pulled up into a thick ponytail. She has a square-shaped jawline and pert nose, wide-set blue eyes, the same colour as Willem's, full lips, and expertly arched, light-brown brows. Even without makeup, she's beautiful.

Adriana reaches up to her ear and presses the stem of her earbuds to mute whatever she's listening to.

'*Hallo*,' she says warily. To Willem, she says something in Dutch, her tone indicating that she's less than impressed to find me here.

Wait until she learns who I am.

Willem replies, first in Dutch, then in English, which is clearly for my benefit. 'Why don't you get changed, then join us.' This isn't posed as a suggestion, more of an instruction, and Adriana's terse expression sours even more.

'I have things to do,' she says pointedly. She storms off, swinging open the patio door and heading towards the studio. She doesn't seem to notice Margot, who's curled up on a rattan armchair at the edge of the patio.

'I'm sorry about that,' says Willem, standing. 'I'll be right back.' He goes after his sister, crossing paths with Margot, who joins me inside, her face creased with confusion.

'What happened?' she asks. 'Did you tell her who you are?'

'We didn't get that far,' I reply, my eyes trained on Adriana's door.

'Well, one thing's for sure – she's even hotter than her brother.'

'Margot!' I chide, my head snapping in her direction.

'Oh, don't "Margot" me. I'm not apologising for stating the obvious.'

Before I can say anything more, shouting erupts from the studio. Unsurprisingly, it's Adriana, and Willem's low, rumbling voice fills the few silences between her rage-filled words.

'We should go,' I say, standing abruptly and sloshing coffee down the front of my jeans. Wonderful, now I look like I've wet myself.

'We should *stay*,' says Margot, tugging on my hand.

I drop back onto the stool and we wait out the siblings' argument in silence while I fish a tissue out of my jeans pocket and do my best to mop up the wet patch.

Eventually, Willem comes back inside. He lets out a heavy sigh, running his hands over his head and clasping them behind his neck, making his biceps bulge. Noticing this amid the mayhem makes me chuckle.

Realising my faux pas, I attempt to pass it off as a cough – *unsuccessfully*. Willem drops his hands, eyeing me curiously, and Margot looks over with a baffled expression.

'Sorry,' I tell them. 'A little overcome by the absurdity of the situation.' Another half-truth. I seem to be accruing them like crumpled tissues in a coat pocket.

'It is very strange,' Willem admits. 'Maybe we should—'
'*Hallo.*'

Three heads swivel towards the patio where Adriana lingers just outside the door, peering in at us with an inscrutable look on her face.

'Hi,' I say instinctively.

She studies me, her expression guarded, as she leans against the doorframe. 'Willem tells me you claim to be engaged to Jon,' she says evenly.

It stings, the accusation that I'm outright lying, but there's a vulnerability in her eyes that softens my heart. She's hurting, like I am.

'That's right,' I reply.

'You could be a *friend*, someone who's willing to lie for him.'

'Him who?' asks Margot, and we all look to her. 'Who do you think Kate's lying for? Your brother or that conniving arse-hole who's screwed you both over?'

I sigh. If there were medals for anti-diplomacy, Margot would win gold.

'Excuse me, but who are you?' Adriana asks her – a fair question.

'She's my cousin,' I reply before Margot can say something snarky. Well, *snarkier*. I shoot Margot my please-shut-your-mouth-this-instant look – one she is extremely familiar with – and she presses her lips together, contrite.

'Look,' I say, my attention back on Adriana. Her chin lifts and she openly meets my gaze, but I'm not fooled by the bravado. 'When Willem came to me last Friday,' I continue, 'I was completely blindsided and, at first, I didn't believe him either. I thought he'd got the wrong man... I thought perhaps you'd been engaged to Jon in the past... But when he told me about you and showed me evidence of Jon's duplicity, I had no choice but to admit the truth. As hard as that was.'

She swallows hard and her eyes gloss with tears.

'I promise that Willem hasn't made this up and he hasn't asked me to lie. This isn't a ruse to break up you and Jon.'

I reach into my handbag and take out my phone, then open to the photo of me and Jon at Oblix, right after he proposed. We're at our table, the lights of London visible behind us, and I'm holding up my left hand, the diamond ring glinting and both of us beaming. Without looking at the photo – it's still too raw – I walk over and show it to Adriana.

'You see, I really am engaged to the same man you are – Jon Dunn.'

'AKA Arseface,' Margot chimes in.

'*Margot*,' I say, spinning around and glaring at her.

'*What?* That's his name,' she states unapologetically. 'Jon Arseface Dunn.'

There are several beats of silence, and my breath catches in my throat, then we all start laughing at once, even Adriana – albeit somewhat reluctantly.

When the laughter wanes, Willem crosses to his sister and gently rubs her arm. 'Ady, I'm sorry for surprising you – with Kate, I mean – but I didn't know what else to do.'

Adriana sniffs, then give him a tight-lipped smile. 'I just didn't want to believe it,' she says with a shrug. Her tears start flowing, and she buries her face in his shoulder. He wraps her in a hug, his chin resting on her head and the muscles of his back straining against his T-shirt as he speaks to her in Dutch with a soothing tone.

I look away.

Amongst all the emotions coursing through me – including satisfaction at having helped Adriana accept the truth – what I can't justify is my attraction to Willem. It's terrible timing, for one thing, but it's also horribly inappropriate considering the situation.

Eventually, he steps back and looks down at her, asking her something softly in Dutch. Probably if she's okay.

She nods, then her gaze lands on me. She stares at me for a time, and I let her. I don't mind because I'm as curious about her as she must be about me.

God, she really is very pretty – far prettier than me. And I know from Willem that she's twenty-nine, teaches the Dutch equivalent of Year Four, has travelled extensively, and is fluent in three languages other than Dutch (English, French, and Spanish).

She's beautiful, clever, accomplished...

No wonder Jon fell in love with her, I think with a sharp pang of jealousy.

Although, the jealousy doesn't last. The logical side of my brain overrides it almost instantly. Because Adriana – or Ady, if she ever lets me call her that – is not my rival. I can tell, simply from the thoughtful way she's regarding me, that I have a new ally in this, this... *mess*.

'I want to ask you something,' she says eventually.

'Anything. And I mean that – ask me anything.'

She takes in a deep breath. 'How did Jon propose?'

That's not what I thought she was going to ask and my eyes widen in shock.

'You don't have to tell me if you don't want to.'

'No, I said I'd tell you anything and I meant that. Only...'

I glance at Willem and, somehow, he seems to understand without me explaining further.

'Margot, how about you and I go for a walk?' he suggests. 'There's an excellent café nearby. Great coffee.'

'But...' Margot holds up her unfinished coffee, then catches on. 'Great idea,' she replies brightly. She crosses to the sink where she deposits her mug. 'Okay, Thor,' she says, 'lead the way.'

Willem's head tilts in confusion. 'Thor?' he asks.

'Come on, it's uncanny,' she says, as if it's indisputable.

He laughs and they leave, then it's just me and Adriana. Jon's two fiancées.

'Right,' I say, 'the proposal.'

'Wait,' she says, leaping off the stool. 'Do you drink?' she asks, opening a tall cabinet.

'I do but it's, uh...' I glance at the clock on the oven. 'It's only 10 a.m.'

'So, too early for this, then?' she asks, taking out a bottle of vodka.

I laugh. 'Well, if Margot were here, she'd say no. But she lives on "Margot time".'

'Well, Kate, Margot isn't here, so what do *you* say?'

'Oh, fuck it. Pour me a drink, then we're swapping proposal stories.'

She quickly makes two vodka oranges and hands me a glass, then sits next to me at the kitchen bench.

'Tell me everything. And if that *klootzak* proposed to you the same way he did to me...'

'Is that the Dutch equivalent of arsehole?'

'Kind of. It literally means scrotum,' she replies, her brows raised sardonically.

'Right,' I say. 'Well, the *klootzak* took me up to the top of the Shard – that's the highest building in London and it has the most spectacular restaurant—'

'Mm-hmm. Sounds a lot like A'DAM Tower here in Amsterdam,' she says, and I take her word for it.

I've barely even started and already I anticipate striking similarities between our proposals.

I'm right.

8

KATE

If I thought my life was like a *Black Mirror* episode before, now it's as if Yorgos Lanthimos turned his hand to romcoms. 'Surreal' doesn't even begin to describe it.

As I listen intently to Adriana telling me about her courtship with Jon, I struggle to reconcile the Jon she's describing with the man I know. There are similarities, of course – the most notable is that he's attentive, yet loves her independence – but there are also glaring differences.

For one, *her* Jon is a diamond dealer.

I already knew this from Willem, but hearing Adriana's depiction of Jon's intricate lies is another jarring reminder that this is really happening.

And commercial pilot, diamond dealer – two professions that couldn't be further apart. From each other, or from the truth – that Jon is an idle, entitled toff, or what the Americans refer to as a 'trust-fund baby'. An extremely wealthy man, who inherited everything he has and contributes nothing to the world but lies – *and* with all his jet-setting about, a heavy carbon footprint.

'I notice you're not wearing your ring,' I say when the opportunity arises.

Adriana glances at her hand. 'Oh, I take it off when I go swimming or to yoga. It's too...' She wiggles her fingers as she searches for the right word.

'Big?' I ask.

'Yes! *Huge!* Two and a half carats! A great behemoth of a thing. That's why it was so easy to believe Jon worked at Gassan. I would have preferred something far more tasteful.'

'I felt exactly the same way about mine. Margot calls it THE MONSTROSITY – all capital letters.'

Adriana chuckles. She seems to possess a decent sense of humour, which is impressive all things considered. She's certainly run the gamut of emotions this morning – a bit like me a week ago.

'I'll be right back,' she says, jumping up from the sofa and trotting out to her studio. She returns less than a minute later bearing a ring box.

'Here,' she says, opening it and handing it over.

'Oh my god,' I say, staring at the ring. 'That's identical to mine.'

'I thought it might be. *Klootzak!*'

'I couldn't have said it better myself,' I say, meeting her eyes. I snap the box shut one-handed and return it. 'You know, Margot made some preliminary enquiries this past week. Those rings are worth around £30,000 – possibly more.'

Her jaw drops and she slowly sits, clearly dumbfounded. 'That's...' Lips parted, her gaze fixes on the benchtop. 'I knew he'd spent a lot of money on it but that kind of excess... it's *obscene.*'

'That's the perfect way to describe it. Will you return it? To Jon, I mean.'

'I have no idea. You?'

'I'm keeping mine,' I say decisively. 'I'll sell it, give some money to charity... put the rest towards my mortgage...'

She nods, a far-off look in her eyes. I can only imagine what's going on inside her head.

'Can I ask...' I say, drawing her attention. 'I know it's a lot to get your mind around, but I'm wondering if you ever had doubts?'

'About Jon – our relationship?' she asks.

'Yes.'

She nods. 'I did, yes. All the time, but I ignored them. I convinced myself it was because I'd never really dated a *man* before. Jon's older, he has this incredible career, he's worldly...' I note that she's still talking about him in present tense and I wonder how long that will take to change.

'But all my boyfriends before Jon...' she continues. 'Willem called them "bad boys" – no money, no ambition, no direction. But all *very* good looking,' she adds with a wink.

'Jon's not unattractive, though,' I say.

'No, but...' She shrugs, not saying anything further, but I get it. There are Henry Cavills and there are Simon Peggs. Jon's attractive in his own way but he's more of a Pegg than a Cavill.

'So, you were drawn to how different Jon was from the blokes you dated before,' I suggest.

'Yes, exactly. And what about you?'

Not for the first time in this conversation, I sense her reticence. Adriana both wants to know and doesn't, which I completely understand.

'I had different reasons for falling for Jon,' I admit. 'Mostly that his life dovetailed so easily with mine. I thought we had similar values, wanted similar things. In many ways, it felt simple, uncomplicated.'

'Uncomplicated!' She laughs freely at that.

'Yeah, yeah...' I say, sniggering along with her.

'There is something else...' she says when our laughter dies. 'And this must be why I convinced myself that this was a real, grownup relationship... It wasn't all about *sex*, you know?'

'Same with me!' I reply candidly, instantly wishing I could take it back.

Adriana smirks at me, her eyes narrowing.

'Sorry – too much information,' I say.

'It's okay. I get it. Jon's not the most...'

'No, he isn't,' I reply. 'But I convinced myself that the intimacy side of things didn't matter as much as everything else.'

'So, we've *both* been lying to ourselves,' she observes, her lips flattening into a line.

'I'd say so, yes.'

I'm thrown off kilter when an unnerving mental picture pops up, unbidden and unwanted – Jon and Adriana in bed together. It's like poking an open wound with a stick and I swallow hard, tamping down the rising bile.

'Are you okay?' she asks, her face etched with concern.

I look away from her potent gaze, wondering how to answer because I am very much not okay. But she's been open with me – this has been one of the frankest conversations of my life – so I may as well be truthful about everything.

'Adriana, as easy as it is to talk to you – and believe me, I'm astounded by that, almost as much as you existing in the first place... But that aside... It's difficult picturing you and Jon together, especially intimately. Even though I know up here' – I tap the side of my head – 'that Jon's whole persona is a fabrication, my heart is taking a little longer to catch up.'

'I understand,' she says, her eyes filled with empathy.

There's a profound relief in sharing my predicament with

someone who truly gets it, and I exhale slowly, the unease giving way to calm. I send her a warm smile and she returns it.

'And I want to say something, but I don't want it to come across as condescending – or insulting.'

'You can say it,' she replies.

'It's just... you seem so stoic about everything. I did *not* handle the news as well as you have.'

Her brows lift in disbelief, then she grins at me.

'That's generous, considering I got home an hour ago and you've already seen me shouting at my brother, then sobbing on his shoulder, and now I'm tipsy on vodka. At eleven in the morning.'

At the mention of vodka, I eye my half-drunk glass. With the *stroopwafels* and the heightened emotions, I don't think I should drink any more, and I push it away.

'Now can *I* say something?' Adriana asks.

'Of course.'

'When Willem first told me about you, I tried to convince myself you weren't real, only I knew he wouldn't lie to me about something like that. He never lies about anything. But I felt stupid and gullible, so I told myself he must be mistaken. Although, he's also never mistaken. It's really annoying that he's so perfect.' We share a gentle laugh. 'Anyway, I knew deep down that it was true – that you and Jon were also engaged – but I kept lying to myself. I even convinced myself it was a good idea to introduce him to our parents.'

'Willem told me about that. It was the clincher – what made me decide to come.'

'I did wonder how he convinced you.'

'He seems like a good man – *and* a good brother,' I say.

She sighs. 'He is. Willem's always looked out for me. That's why it's impossible to stay angry at him. Although, I have tried very hard these past two weeks,' she says wryly.

'He told me that part too.'

'He must like you. Willem isn't open with many people.'

He must like you.

It's an innocuous statement considering the heftier topics we've covered, but Adriana's words zip through me like the silver ball pinging around a pinball machine. I can almost *hear* the bells chime as long-dormant parts of me light up, exhilarated.

Gah! What am I, a schoolgirl with a crush? I may not be able to control how it *feels* being around Willem, but I can control my actions. From now on, no more perving on the fit brother.

'So,' I say brightly, changing the subject, 'now that we're both in the know – and are willing to admit it to ourselves – how do we proceed?' *This* is my wheelhouse – strategising and executing a plan.

Adriana groans, her head tipped back. 'I suppose we need to confront him. Together would be best – and soon. Dinner with my parents is meant to be next Wednesday.'

I hadn't planned on staying past Sunday and I have no idea when Jon is due to arrive in Amsterdam, but I suppose I could stay a little longer. Mina has already given me Monday off. She might be amenable to extending my personal leave another day or two.

'*Unless…*' says Adriana, and from her tone, I can tell something big is coming.

'Unless?' I ask hesitantly.

She sits bolt upright, clearly struck by inspiration. 'What if we got back at him?' she asks, more animated than I've seen her all morning.

'You mean *revenge*?'

I should have anticipated this, but foolishly, I hadn't thought beyond proving to Adriana that I existed.

'Yes!' She edges closer, her eyes alight with excitement. 'You and I join together and we...' She flaps her hands like she's trying to conjure the solution from thin air. 'You know...'

'Actually, I do,' I say, angling my body towards her.

After my discussion with Poppy, I accepted that revenge was off the table, that justice would prevail simply by doing right by Adriana. But now...

'In fact, I had the same idea,' I add.

Her eyes bore into mine. 'You did?'

'Yep, and there may be someone who can help us. *If* we can convince her to change her mind. But it *is* a long shot.'

Ignoring the 'long shot' part, Adriana grins, bouncing excitedly. And right as I'm about to explain who Poppy is, the front door opens and in walk Willem and Margot.

* * *

'That's *not* a good idea,' Willem says firmly. This must be his I'm-the-big-brother-and-what-I-say-goes tone. I'm not mad at it.

'*Will*,' says Adriana. 'Listen to—'

'I *have* listened and it's too...' The right word seems to elude him. 'Just break off the engagement, then never see him again.'

Adriana switches to Dutch and as I only understand the basics, all I have to go on is her imploring tone. But no matter what she's saying, it's clear Willem isn't going to waver.

This is a shame, because if I can't change Poppy's mind about exacting revenge on Jon, Willem is my backup plan. He seems like the sort of bloke with the skills – *and* the connections – to do some serious damage to Jon's life. But that vigorous head shake says it all. Hmm, maybe *Poppy* is my backup plan.

I look over at Margot, who is listening intently to the siblings, even though she knows about as much Dutch as I do. When I catch her eye, she mouths, 'What the eff?'

'Right?' I mouth back.

If anyone had told me when I woke up this morning how this day would go, I would have laughed out loud. There have been so many surprises, including my new alliance with Adriana, that I'm practically dizzy.

Adriana throws her arms out wide. 'Then he just gets away with it. What's his punishment?!'

'His punishment is losing you!' Willem exclaims. He turns, pinning me with an intense look. '*Both* of you.'

It takes me a moment to comprehend the meaning behind Willem's words. I'm little more than a stranger to him, yet he believes I'm worthy of more – more than Jon and his lies.

Willem expels an exasperated sigh and hooks his hands behind his neck again, a gesture that has more power over me – and my libido – than I'd like, especially as I *just* made a pact with myself to stop perving on him.

'So, you won't help us?' Adriana asks him.

It's unlikely a yes is coming, but I hold my breath in anticipation regardless.

'No,' he says, and I slowly exhale. *Poppy it is, then*, I think. 'I cannot support something that might end up backfiring – what if you end up in trouble, Ady, or in danger?'

'Dang— We're not having him *eliminated*, Will. It's not like we're planning on hiring a hitman or anything.'

'*No*,' I concur, jumping into the conversation. 'Nothing like that. Just some run-of-the-mill, make-his-life-miserable revenge, that's all.'

Willem's expression softens a fraction, and is that the hint of a smile I see?

'That's *all*?'

'Yeah, like "accidentally" rolling his car into the Thames,' Margot pipes in, making the air quotes.

'That's *illegal*,' Willem says, pointing at her, 'and exactly why I'm not getting involved.'

'Well, not that then,' says Adriana. 'But, Will, if we don't do *something* – if Kate and I simply end our engagements – what's to stop Jon from moving onto the next victim?'

'Or *victims*,' Margot chimes in.

Willem seems to consider this point, but from the way his arms are folded tightly across his chest (making his biceps bulge even more, damn him), he remains unconvinced.

'What about something like tricking him into donating a large sum to charity?' I ask, the idea randomly popping into my head. The room falls silent, and the four of us exchange glances, the weight of shared contemplation permeating the air.

'How would that work?' asks Adriana eventually.

'I have no idea,' I reply honestly. 'I support several charities, but I've never discussed them with Jon. What about you?'

She coughs out a derisive laugh. 'I asked Jon to contribute to a fundraiser at my school – for the performing arts program – and he refused.'

'He flat out refused?'

She nods.

'Did he give a reason?'

'Oh, yes. He said the arts are a waste of time and children

should focus on the three Rs – reading, writing and arithmetic.'

'The three— *What*?' I ask, appalled. 'Has he travelled here from the nineteenth century in a time machine?'

'He also said the Netherlands is a wealthy country and that government funding should cover the costs.'

I blink at her. 'That's horrible.'

'Yes. One of the many signs I ignored.'

'Red flags we call them in England,' I say.

'Yes, here too – *rode vlaggen*.'

'Arseholes must be universal,' Margot concludes, and Adriana and I nod our agreement. Margot turns to Willem. 'You've been awfully quiet since Kate's suggestion. What do you think?'

'It's clever. It could work. But I haven't changed my mind; I'm still not comfortable helping you. There's too much that can go wrong.'

'Argh – *Will*!' Adriana cries.

'It's okay, we might not need your help,' I tell him, slightly smug.

Surely this idea is enough to make Poppy change her mind.

9

POPPY

I'm out for coffee with my bestie, Shaz, and her girlfriend, Lauren, when I get a call from Kate Whitaker. It's not unheard of for a client to contact me on the weekend but Kate's status as my client is still in question.

That said, she's in Amsterdam right now on her mission to 'save' fiancée number two, and I'm curious about how it's going. I excuse myself and head outside into the crisp spring air.

'Hi, Kate.'

'Hello, Poppy. I'm sorry to bother you on a Saturday, but there's something I wanted to discuss with you. Is now a good time?'

'Yeah, now's fine – just out with friends, but I'm happy to chat for a bit. Is this about your trip to Amsterdam?'

She hesitates for a moment before replying. 'It *is* but it's also related to what we talked about last week.'

'Ahh.'

So, she's back on the retribution train. I expected this. I've also had Ursula in my ear all week, asking if we've heard from her. Neither seem willing to drop it.

Kate jumps in hurriedly. 'Now I know you said the agency wouldn't be able to help with that but—'

'Kate, sorry to interrupt, but it turns out that my colleagues *are* willing to discuss it further.'

'Really?' she asks excitedly.

'No promises, but we're not ruling it out. It will likely depend on what you have in mind.'

'No, no, of course. And after our meeting, I *had* put it out of my mind, I promise. But having talked with Adriana – she's here with me now – we're on the same page. It's not enough to simply end our engagements. We want Jon to *pay* for what he did.'

'I totally get it, the need for justice,' I say – and I do, but I am not signing the agency up for vigilantism; I need to set realistic expectations here.

'Justice, yes. But we're also thinking of other women out there – Jon's next victims. We want to prevent him from simply shrugging off his losses and moving onto other women.'

'Did you have something specific in mind?'

'Actually, yes.' She explains their idea and I'll admit, I could see it working. 'What do you think?' she asks, hesitancy in her voice.

'It's definitely something to consider,' I reply noncommittally. 'When are you back in London – how soon can you come into the agency?'

'Uh, I'm not sure yet, but I'll let you know.'

'Okay,' I say. 'But it sounds like your trip to Amsterdam has gone better than you thought it would.'

'It has, yes,' she replies, then lowers her voice. 'I really didn't expect to connect with Adriana, but she's lovely, Poppy. We're already firm allies.'

'That's great – one good thing to come from all this.'

'Mmm,' she replies – arguably a simple utterance but I detect an undercurrent of something else. I wonder if it has to do with Adriana's brother. 'All right, I've taken up enough of your time,' she says. 'I'll let you know when I'm heading back to London.'

We end the call, and I go back inside the coffee shop.

'So, what's the goss?' Shaz asks the second my bum hits the chair.

During the years I've been a matchmaker, I've often shared morsels from my more interesting cases with close friends – anonymised, of course. And at times, it has helped me gain additional insight into the nuances of the case – particularly from Shaz. Unlike me, she's still a practising psychologist. It can't hurt to get her thoughts – or Lauren's.

I give them the digest version, watching their expressions transform from surprise into shock.

'Fucking hell!' Shaz declares when I wrap up.

With a laugh, Lauren shushes her. 'Babe, I'm not sure the elderly women two tables over appreciate your colourful vocab.'

Shaz makes the 'eek' face, looking over and mouthing, 'Sorry,' to two tight-lipped women, who then return to their conversation.

'So, do you reckon Saskia will go for it?' Shaz asks me.

'I have no idea. If Paloma and Ursula think it will work, they may be able to persuade her. I guess we'll see.'

'And will you be involved?' Lauren asks.

I laugh. 'I hope not. For a start, I have no idea what I'd bring to the table – not with what they have in mind. We may need to get the agency's investigator involved but...' I shrug.

Lauren seems satisfied with my answer, so I return to what we were talking about before Kate called. 'Now, tell me more about your sperm donor.'

Like Tristan and me, Shaz and Lauren want to be parents, only their journey has been markedly different to ours. And, as Tristan's best friend and his wife – Ravi and Jacinda – are expecting Baby Sharma in a few months, there's a buzz of excitement in our friendship group. With any luck, we'll get to experience parenthood together and our kids will grow up as cousins.

'He's a rocket scientist,' Lauren replies. 'An actual rocket scientist.'

'No way.'

'Way,' Shaz quips, then she fills me in on the rest of their donor's profile.

Kate

'Well, that went better than expected,' I say, stepping back inside after the call with Poppy. I fill the others in, eliciting varying responses: an excited smile from Adriana, an I-should-hope-so nod from Margot, and a scowl from Willem.

'And this is the matchmaker who introduced you to Dunn?' asks Willem. If he believes that, then no wonder he's scowling.

'No, of course not,' I reply. 'It's a different one.'

'Right.'

He doesn't say anything else, but his meaning is clear:

what sort of woman has *two* matchmakers? I look away from
his scrutinous scowl. Willem and his judgement can get in
the bin!

'So, what are we all doing now?' asks Margot.

It's presumptuous of her to ask. I assumed we'd leave
Willem and Adriana to their day and head out to explore
Amsterdam. And with Willem's unsupportive, judgey attitude,
I'm inclined to make a swift exit.

'Oh, er...' mutters Willem. 'I've got a meeting to prepare
for.'

A perfect excuse to wrap this up, and I turn towards the
door.

'Boring!' Margot declares. '*And* it's Saturday. Why are you
working on a Saturday?'

'Margot!' I hiss as Willem stumbles over an explanation,
but she ignores me.

'Come on!' Margot exclaims. 'If we were in one of those
heist films, this is the part where we all go out and
celebrate.'

Adriana chuckles – she obviously finds Margot amusing –
but Willem shoots her a disdainful look. 'Celebrate *what*
exactly?'

I can tell he's about to say more but Margot cuts him off.
'Assembling the team! You know, like in *Ocean's 8*.' He stares at
her blankly and rather than dropping it, she doubles down.
'When Sandra Bullock and Cate Blanchett bring all the others
together to brief them on the heist, they crack the champers
and celebrate.'

I don't bother correcting her – they celebrate *after* they pull
off the heist – because when Margot gets like this, there's little
that can dampen her enthusiasm.

'Right,' Willem growls, his scowl intensifying. That's twice he's said that since I came back inside. It must be Willem speak for 'you are completely bonkers'.

'But you're forgetting that I'm not *on* the team,' he says sharply.

Adriana sighs, drawing attention from the rest of us. 'Sorry to interrupt this fascinating discussion,' she says, her optimism ebbing away before my eyes, 'but I've just realised something. If you and I are staying engaged to Jon until we do whatever it is we're going to do, then how do I get out of dinner with our parents?'

'Oh,' I say, 'I hadn't thought of that.'

'Exactly,' says Willem. 'There's a lot you haven't thought about – *either* of you,' he adds, his eyes sliding between me and his sister. 'And this *isn't* a silly heist film – this is real life.'

'First,' I say, leaping to my own defence as much as Adriana's, 'we *know* this is real life. We're not stupid!'

As soon as the words are out of my mouth, I recognise that we are a *little* bit stupid to have trusted Jon. Even so, my defence has the desired effect, and Willem immediately starts stumbling over an apology.

'I didn't mean to suggest—'

'Yes, you did. You absolutely "meant to suggest". Which brings me to my second point. While I can understand how protective you are towards your sister, you aren't *my* older brother. In fact, we're practically strangers, so I don't need you telling me what's best.'

Now *I'm* scowling. At Willem. To his credit, he meets my gaze and even though Margot is sniggering behind me, I don't break eye contact. Eventually, he looks away, chastened.

'I apologise,' he says quietly. 'You're right and I'm sorry.'

'Wow,' says Adriana. 'Willem never apologises – to anyone, so—'

'*Ady*,' he says, his head snapping in her direction.

She raises her eyebrows at him as if to say, 'Am I wrong?'

He expels another exasperated sigh. 'I don't believe this,' he says to himself.

'Hey,' she tells him, 'you're the one who invited Kate here, so...'

'I guess that makes you Sandra Bullock,' Margot quips. Willem's mouth twitches, but the smile doesn't take hold.

A phone chimes – it's Adriana's – and she reads in the incoming message. 'Well, I don't need to worry about dinner with Mama and Papa.' She holds up the phone, her expression hardening. 'Jon just cancelled.'

'Let me guess,' I say, my tone dripping in sarcasm, 'some sort of diamond emergency?'

'Apparently. He's been asked to go to New York to fill in for a colleague at a rare stones trade show.'

'My arse, he has,' Margot scoffs.

'I was afraid of this,' says Willem.

'Afraid of what?' I ask, looking over.

'If he's not going to be here in Amsterdam and he's not seeing you in London, then...'

He lifts his shoulders, his meaning obvious.

'Then he might already have a third fiancée,' I say, the realisation landing with a thud.

'Yes.'

Margot gasps. 'Arsehole.'

'*Klootzak!*' adds Adriana, slumping onto the nearest stool.

'I'll look into it,' says Willem.

'I thought you said you weren't on the team,' I say.

He looks at me, his jaw tense. 'This is different – this is about unearthing the extent of his deception, not about revenge. And I told you I was still investigating him.'

'Oh god,' says Adriana wanly. The poor woman – this is a lot to take in, even for me, and I accepted the truth about Jon a week ago.

'So,' says Margot, 'I'm sensing that we're no longer in a celebratory mood. Shall we postpone the champers?'

It's such an absurd thing to say that my immediate reaction is to laugh, but with the gravity of the situation, I do my best to swallow my laughter. It breaks loose regardless and when I look over at Adriana, a wry smile spreads across her face.

'You certainly have a way with words,' Willem tells Margot, reluctant amusement in his eyes.

'Thank you,' she replies, taking him at his word.

He looks over at me and I wish I could tell what was going on behind those intense blue eyes. Because despite everything that has transpired this morning – including him being an arse *and* me telling him off – I'll admit that I'm captivated by the tall, brooding Dutchman.

Inappropriately and inconveniently captivated.

* * *

'So, what are you wearing on your date?'

We're back at the houseboat and I'm sifting through the contents of my small case. I didn't pack much, as we're only here for two nights. I also hadn't expected to be going out alone with Willem, and everything I packed is casual.

'It's not a *date*, Margot. You invited yourself along on Adriana's girls' night, then guilted Willem into taking me to dinner.'

'Semantics,' she says, her default response when she can't back a flimsy argument.

'It's not semantics. That's exactly what you did and more to the point, you did it on purpose.'

'So what if I did? What's the harm in shagging the fit brother?'

'Gah!'

'I'm telling you, Kate. You and Willem together – there was *frisson* in the air.'

'Frisson? Really? You've never used that word before in your life. I doubt you even know what it means.'

'Of course I do. It's what happened between you and Willem this morning.'

I roll my eyes at her, something I've done so many times over the course of my life, I could map the inside of my head – *freehand*.

'Whatevs,' I reply, tired of the conversation. I return to my outfit conundrum, contemplating wearing my jeans with a black boat-necked top. I hold up the top and look in the mirror.

'So, if this isn't a date, why does it matter what you wear?' she asks, peering at me smugly from the bed where she's stretched out.

'It doesn't,' I reply tartly.

'Then just wear what you have on.'

I look down at the outfit I selected this morning – my if-you-look-good-you-feel-good outfit. 'You're right,' I say. 'I'll just wear this.' I start refolding the clothes I've taken out of my case.

'Perfect,' she says, 'but maybe freshen up a bit, fix your makeup.'

'I'm not— Why would I bother?'

'Because we've been out all afternoon.'

'To *museums*.'

Because I dragged Margot to the Rijksmuseum 'under duress' – or so she said – *she* insisted on a tit-for-tat visit to Madam Tussauds.

'So? Don't you want to look your best?'

'It's just dinner.'

'God, you can be so stubborn,' she says huffily.

'*I* can? Just let it go, will you.'

She sits up and crosses her legs. 'You must be forgetting who you're talking to. I am *not* about to ignore that you're attracted to Willem.'

'Did you miss the part where I told him off?'

'Oh, no, I very much remember that part. It was like season two of *Bridgerton*. You two have more chemistry than Kate and Anthony.'

I stop refolding my clothes and fix Margot with a piercing look.

'Oh, don't be all' – she flaps her hand about – 'Kate-ish. Adriana saw it too. Why do you think she suggested that I join her and her friends tonight?'

'*Suggested?*'

'All *right* – why do you think she heartily agreed when I asked if I could come? Doesn't matter. What matters is that you're into Willem and he's into you.'

I stare at her for a long moment, then cave. 'It's physical attraction, pure and simple,' I say feebly. 'Willem is objectively a very handsome man.'

'He's fucking gorgeous. Any woman who doesn't think he's hot is either related to him, a lesbian, or dead.' I drop my head into my hand, swinging it from side to side. 'Tell me I'm wrong,' she continues. 'Oh right, you can't because I'm not.'

'*Margot.*' I sigh, lifting my head and meeting her gaze again.

'*Kate*,' she counters. 'There's something electric between you two. It's obvious.'

'Not to me.'

'Then you're lying to yourself,' she says gently.

It seems that the tough-love portion of this evening's programming has come to an end, but this gentler approach from Margot is much harder to handle. Because she's not wrong. I am lying to myself. I know it and she knows it. And she knows I know it.

'Shit,' I say, perching on the edge of the bed and staring at the floor. 'Now what?'

Margot reaches over and pats my arm. 'Oh, lovely. Now you get in the shower, then make yourself gorgeous.'

When I look up, she's smiling at me encouragingly and I fall about laughing, releasing all the pent-up pressure of the day.

'You're such a muppet,' I tease.

'Call me what you like. But do as you're told and get in the shower.' She climbs off the bed. 'And shave your legs – you know, just in case...' She waggles her eyebrows.

'Oh, for god's sake.'

'And tomorrow morning, I want to hear *everything*.'

'Get out!'

She leaves, her cackling laughter following her down the hallway, and I go into the bathroom to shower – *and* shave my legs.

Just in case.

10

KATE

Willem said he'd pick me up at the houseboat, so I'm waiting outside. There's not much traffic on the road but as each car approaches, I tense with nerves.

I'm nervous. To see Willem.

Because despite assuring Margot that this isn't a date, her words have stuck – that he and I have chemistry (or rather, *frisson*) – and they've been on replay in my mind for the past hour.

I never had that sort of connection with Jon. We didn't argue, we didn't challenge each other's thinking, we didn't square off...

In contrast, there's Willem.

I recall the flash in his eyes when he scolded us about our retribution plan. I mean, he was wrong, but at least he took a stance.

All Jon ever said was things like, 'Oh, yes, I quite agree.' Upon reflection, that made for a rather dull time. And I couldn't say with any certainty what Jon stands for, what he believes.

Then again, I'm comparing him to an actual man; it's likely that Jon's entire personality is a construct the same way his fabricated life is.

It's uncomfortable viewing the Kate–Jon dynamic from the outside, seeing it for what it really is – or was. How did I convince myself that what I wanted from a relationship was constant time apart and picture-perfect, film-montage-style dates?

I've been a fool.

'*Hallo!*' Willem's voice draws me from my dark thoughts as he rides up on a bike, stopping next to me.

'Oh, hi,' I say, surprised he's not in a car. 'You're riding a bike.' The moment the words are out of my mouth, I recognise how stupid they sounded.

He looks down, pretending to be shocked. 'So I am!' When he looks up, his eyes are creased at the corners.

'Sorry, that was a silly thing to say. It's just... How are we getting there exactly?'

'You don't have a bike?' he asks.

'Not on me,' I retort.

'I mean with your accommodation. Margot said your host left bikes for you to use.'

More surprises – that Willem expects me to ride through Amsterdam, something that terrifies me after spending the afternoon dodging speeding cyclists, *and* that he and Margot discussed this evening's transportation without me knowing.

I haven't responded, and Willem dismounts, rocking his bike onto the kickstand. He walks over to the houseboat, stopping next to the two bikes parked out front. I've passed them several times and it has never once occurred to me that they're for us to use.

'These are probably the ones. Do you have your keys?'

'Oh, right,' I say, delving into my handbag.

I hand over the keys and in no time at all, he has unlocked one of the bikes. He walks it over to me.

'How tall are you?' he asks, running his eyes from my head to my feet.

Heat floods my insides. I can't remember the last time a man looked me up and down like that – especially one as good-looking as Willem.

'Uh, five-eight,' I reply.

He nods, then raises the seat a couple of inches.

'Try this,' he commands and without thinking, I comply, climbing on. Though I can't quite reach the ground with my feet and the bike wobbles. I'm about to topple off it when Willem catches me around the waist one-handed, his other hand reaching for the handlebars. For a moment, I'm pressed against him and he smells so damned good, I have to stop myself from nuzzling his neck.

After a few long moments, he gently releases me. I ease off the seat and stand, straddling the bike frame.

'Sorry about that,' he says gruffly.

He reaches behind me and adjusts the seat again while I attempt to ignore each of the *five times* his hand bumps against the back of my legs. *Is he doing that on purpose?* I wonder, hoping like hell he is.

'Try it now,' he says, stepping back.

I look up at him and he's watching me intently. *Frisson*. The word pops into my head and it instantly strikes me how right Margot was. There *is* frisson between us.

I climb back onto the bike seat, now able to reach the ground. Willem nods, satisfied. 'Oh, you can ride a bike, yes?'

'Well, *technically*,' I reply. 'But it's been a while.'

'Don't worry,' he says with a grin, 'it's like riding a bike.'

'Ha-ha, hilarious,' I say, sniggering despite myself. I couldn't say if he deliberately made me laugh to dispel my rising anxiety, but it has helped.

He goes to his bike and climbs on.

'Follow me,' he says. 'I will use hand signals to show which way we are going and if we come to an intersection, I'll make sure you're close behind me, so I don't lose you. Okay?'

I nod. 'Um, shouldn't I be wearing a helmet?' I ask.

'Most people don't but...' He reaches behind him, retrieving a helmet from his left saddle bag. I take it from him and clip the strap under my chin. It's a small thing, but it does make me feel more secure about riding through a bustling city. I only hope we're not going far.

'And don't worry – it's not far,' he says, somehow reading my mind. 'Only two and a half kilometres.'

'Brilliant,' I say brightly, trying not to let on that I'd much rather be travelling by car.

Willem sets off and I follow, a little wobbly at first, but within a couple of blocks, I get the hang of it – just like he said I would. Willem takes it slowly as we zigzag through the neighbourhood, riding along canals and crossing bridges.

It's such a beautiful city, particularly at this time of the evening with the lights from the tall, narrow houses reflecting on the canals and the streaks of pink in the dusk sky. A handful of boats move languidly through the waterways and people of all ages are sitting outside enjoying the early spring weather – some on benches by the canals, others in front of their homes.

It's a different pace of life here from London – calmer, as if people are more present in their lives than Londoners. Sometimes, it strikes me how frantic my life is – with my daily commute into Central London and constantly navigating the hoards, even to do something as simple as food shopping. I do love living in London – and my job – but there are times when I long for something else – a quieter life, a slower pace. Somewhere I can exhale and just *be*.

Amsterdam feels like that, and I've been here less than twenty-four hours.

'We're going onto a main street now,' Willem calls over his shoulder. 'Stay close.'

'Okay!' I call out.

We turn onto a busy bike path, and I narrowly avoid colliding with an oncoming cyclist who has overtaken someone. Right as I brace myself for impact, he slips back onto the correct side, his expression unfazed.

More cyclists fly straight at me, careening out of my path at the last second, and others zip past us, their handlebars only inches from mine. This is the bike path from hell. One wrong move and I'll go arse over tit, land in the road, and get squashed by a lorry.

So much for Amsterdam's Zen-like serenity. If I survive this bike ride, I'm buying a lottery ticket.

* * *

'Well, that was horrible,' I say as I dismount.

'You did great,' Willem replies with a laugh. He leads the way to a crowded row of parked bikes, beaming at me.

'I did *fine* – not great,' I retort. 'And I'm *this* close' – I hold up my thumb and forefinger a millimetre apart – 'from dumping this bike in the canal and catching a cab back to the houseboat.'

'They tend to frown on that – deliberately throwing your bike into the canal. Enough end up in there by accident.'

I peer into the murky water. 'Really?'

'Around twenty-five thousand a year.'

'Twenty-five *thousand*?' I exclaim.

He nods.

'Well, then what's one more?' I ask cheekily.

But he's onto me, giving me a sly, narrow-eyed smile.

We slot our bikes into the haphazard row and lock them. 'How will we remember where we parked?' I ask, looking around for a landmark to help mark the spot.

'Years of experience,' he replies, that smile firmly in place. It's sexy and I look away.

'So, which way?' I ask – an obvious question, but I'm distracting myself, ignoring that one look from Willem can turn my insides molten.

He jerks his head towards the right, and we head off. There are too many obstacles in this part of the city to walk side by side – people, bikes, tables and chairs outside restaurants, the occasional tram – so mostly, I trail behind him. Every so often, he glances over his shoulder.

'Still here,' I say after the tenth time, and he nods. God, I hope he didn't catch me staring at his arse. Some men – like Jon – have a flat arse, but Willem's fills out his jeans perfectly.

Eventually, he stops outside a corner bar called Bar Feijoa. 'I thought we could have a drink here before dinner.'

I squint into the darkness. The bar is quiet at the moment, but it seems like the sort of place that ramps up at night. The sort of place I used to frequent in my late-teens and early-twenties – usually with Margot. There was a time when I did shots off the bar and kissed strangers and danced until I was a sweaty mess.

Then I discovered other ways to have fun, more *adult* ways. *Then you got boring, Kate.*

The thought comes out of nowhere, an emotional slap to the face, and I swallow hard then step inside the bar, Willem close behind me. The bartender looks up from the cutting board where he's slicing limes and grins.

'Willem,' he says, firing off a greeting in Dutch. There seems to be a chastising tone to his words, which is confirmed when Willem switches to English and apologises.

'Yeah, I know. Sorry, but I've been busy with work. This is Kate.'

'Hello,' I say.

He reaches across the bar, presumably to shake my hand, and I place mine in his. Then he presses his lips to the back of my hand, eyeing me through his lashes.

'Okay, okay,' says Willem. 'I didn't bring her here for that.'

The bartender releases my hand, then raises both of his. 'Can't hurt to try,' he says, and he and Willem exchange a loaded look.

'And do *you* have a name?' I ask him.

'I do, m'lady,' he says, a wide grin splitting his face. 'I'm Kwame.'

'Nice to meet you, Kwame. So, what's your specialty?' I ask. 'You like cocktails?'

'I do, but it's been a while since I've had one.'

'What do you like?'

It's an innocent question, but my traitorous mind instantly conjures a less-than-innocent reply. *I like tall, broad-shouldered, brooding Dutchmen with intense blue eyes and sardonic smiles.*

'Uh...'

He gives me a funny look. 'Fruity drinks? Sour? Spicy?'

'Whatever you'd like,' I say, feeling foolish. It's obvious my thoughts were written all over my face. I need to stop entertaining salacious ideas about Willem.

'I'll surprise you,' says Kwame. 'And what are you having, my man?'

'Grolsch IPA.'

Kwame looks at me, rolling his eyes at Willem's simple order as if we're in cahoots, and I relax a little. I climb onto a barstool as he gets to work, and Willem slides onto the one next to me.

'So, you haven't ridden a bike for a while, and you haven't had a cocktail for a while…' he says, his low, rumbling voice reverberating through me. 'What *have* you been doing, Kate?'

My heads snaps in his direction and he's watching me closely, his eyes questioning, teasing. Only, this isn't being teased. This is being judged, as if I am somehow lesser than my younger self simply because my priorities have changed.

'I've been working,' I reply evenly. 'I have an incredible job – I love what I do.'

'That's great but what's the saying? All work and no play makes—'

'Oh, I play. I play *hard*, don't you worry,' I retort with a snorting laugh.

I have no idea what I meant by that. It's also largely a lie. Unless I count shopping for homewares online, or trawling real estate sites for country cottages, or the odd weekend away with Margot.

What about visits to Mum and Dad in the Midlands? Those can be enjoyable. Mum and I go to the garden centre, have a coffee and buy some paperbacks. And Dad and I walk their Border Collie, Steel, through the nearby forest.

Oh god, have I forgotten how to have fun – actual, proper fun?

Willem's staring at me, his mouth twitching, but I won't

look away first. I made that ridiculous statement; I'm standing by it.

'Right,' he says eventually.

His stern gaze lands on the bar and he picks up a cocktail napkin and starts folding it into triangles, precisely creasing the edges. I observe the methodical movements of his hands, then tear my eyes away.

I don't know where to look and I don't know what to say. Where is that bloody cocktail?

'Here you are, m'lady, a Paloma,' says Kwame, placing a highball in front of me. The cocktail is a pale pink and garnished with a dried grapefruit slice. I take a sip and it's delicious.

'You like it?' he asks.

'It's lovely, thank you.'

He beams at me and I take another sip right as Willem holds up his beer. '*Prost*,' he says.

'Oh, sorry. Jumped the gun there. *Prost.*'

I tap the rim of my glass against his and he gives me a tight-lipped smile, then downs a mouthful of beer.

Kwame resumes his preparations, and Willem and I stare straight ahead, drinking in silence. There's a mirror across from us and I catch his eye in the reflection, but he looks away a second later.

Right when there was an ease developing between us, we've ended up in a cul de sac of miscommunication, resulting in stung feelings. Namely mine.

But does it matter? Willem's not my friend. He's not even my ally in all this. His stance is clear: pursuing justice and making Jon pay for what he's done is a mistake – a *folly*, even.

I can't believe I shaved my legs for this – what an idiot! This is so far from being a date, I could have worn a dressing gown and fluffy slippers, and one of those gloopy facial masks that come in a foil packet.

Willem's only here with me now because Margot strong-armed him into spending the evening with me. If I didn't need his help navigating back to the houseboat, I would finish this cocktail, try and find my loaner bike amongst the thousands lining the nearby roads, then return to our accommodation and order takeaway.

Or forget about the bike and catch a cab, like I said before.

'So, do you want to hear where we're going for dinner?'

I meet his eyes in the mirror, then turn towards him. 'Do you *really* want to go to dinner with me?' I ask.

'Yes, why?'

'Because...' I don't finish answering. Maybe Willem's experience of this evening is vastly different to mine. Maybe to him, this is normal, friendly conversation.

'Because we keep bumping heads?' he asks, his expression softening.

'I was going to say "locking horns" but yes.'

'Look, the way I see it is this: I showed up at your apartment unexpectedly and dropped a bomb. Then I asked you for a huge favour and you agreed. We may... *lock horns* but I like you, Kate. I can tell you're a good person; you have integrity and you're kind. And I'm grateful that you came here and helped me – helped *Ady*. The least I can do is buy you dinner.'

I gulp. Willem's words are not only thoughtful, but for the first time in I can't say how long, I feel *seen* – by someone other than my immediate family.

So, how can I say no to dinner now?

'Okay. So, where are we going?' I ask.

'You'll see,' he says with a grin.

'You just offered to tell me maybe *ten* seconds ago.'

'And now I've decided it will be a surprise.'

'Oh, great. I *love* surprises. Like when a strange man shows up at my door to give me bad news.'

'Strange?' he asks, giving me a side eye.

'Not like that – strange as in not known to me – a *stranger*.'

'Ahh.'

'Although, from what I can tell so far, you're also a little odd.'

His eyes widen and he starts laughing.

I make a show of sipping my drink and ignoring him as he chuckles beside me.

11

KATE

Dinner is at a restaurant called The Pantry, which is about as old-school Dutch as it can get, from the décor (I've never seen such an extensive collection of Delftware) to the menu to the waitstaff, who bustle about with warm smiles and funny quips like kindly aunties.

I ordered the *boerenkoolstamppot* with a sausage and when it arrived, I did my best to smother a laugh – unsuccessfully, mind you. Because the enormous sausage looked exactly like a penis. That it was balanced between two large scoops of mashed potato and kale made it worse.

As it was placed before me, I sniggered, my hand hiding half my face. When I was brave enough to meet Willem's eye, he was chuckling softly.

'Welcome to the Netherlands,' he said, 'where our national dish is also an anatomy lesson.'

At that, I laughed loudly and Willem joined in, the shared joke doing the trick. Any lingering strain between us melted away and conversation turned to far less harrowing topics than a cheating fiancé.

'So, how did nine-year-old Willem cope with becoming a big brother?' I ask.

He smiles thoughtfully. 'I was a boisterous boy – loud, active, sometimes destructive...' We exchange smiles. 'You'd think it would have been a huge shock to have this tiny baby girl come into my life, but...' He smiles gently, his gaze unfocused. 'I loved her the moment I saw her, and I knew that no matter what, it was my job to protect her.'

'Wow,' I utter breathlessly. This speaks volumes about why he's reacted the way he has. He simply wants to protect Adriana. And seemingly, by association, *me.*

His gaze snaps back into focus as I contemplate whether I *want* his protection.

'And you?' he asks, keeping the conversation going. 'You haven't mentioned siblings...'

I shelve my internal musings to probe another time and launch into an explanation of my relationship with Margot – how we grew up more like sisters than cousins.

'She's an interesting person,' he says, clearly choosing his words carefully.

I laugh. 'Margot is... Let's just say there's no one like her. For one, she's older than me, yet most of the time she behaves like a naughty teenager. I'm constantly chastising her – in a playful, loving way, of course,' I add.

'Of course,' he says with a knowing half-smile.

'But she's had a lot of hardship in her life, so it's easy to forgive her behaviour. Plus, she's good for me.'

'In what way?'

'Well, she's my closest friend. And she doesn't judge me – she may *nudge* me from time to time to get me out of my comfort zone – but it comes from place of love. She can also be a lot of fun.'

'Oh, I don't doubt that,' he says, his eyebrows raised.

I realise too late that I've circled back to the subject of fun, something I'd like to avoid delving into deeper, especially having admitted to myself that my life is markedly devoid of it.

We're quiet for a moment, and I contemplate whether I want one last bite, or if I should listen to my protesting stomach. I set my cutlery across my plate, deciding I've had enough. Willem, however, has scraped his plate clean. Impressive considering it was a full ham hock and a mountain of chips.

'Would you like to order dessert?' the nearest 'aunty' asks me cheerfully. 'We have *poffertjes*.' She nods encouragingly and although I've yet to try the enticing tiny pancakes, there is no way I'd fit in even one.

'No, thank you,' I reply with a smile.

She looks to Willem, and he orders an espresso. 'Would you like a coffee?' he asks.

'Oh, I can't drink coffee this late. I'm amazed you can. Won't you be up all night?'

There's an amused glint in his eyes as he shakes his head, alerting me to the unintended double entendre. I look away.

You two have more chemistry than Kate and Anthony. Margot's words blare annoyingly in my head as I struggle to think of something innocuous to talk about.

'So, it seems there *is* the possibility of a third fiancée,' I say, instantly regretting it. I was supposed to switch to an innocuous topic, not a *noxious* one.

'Maybe,' he replies, his expression suddenly serious. He steeples his fingers, lightly tapping them together – a tell that he's uncomfortable talking about this, perhaps? 'I did investigate further after I saw you in London, but as far as I could tell, he wasn't engaged to anyone else – for now, anyway.'

'Okay.' It's hardly a relief to learn that I'm currently one of only two when there's every chance Jon is in New York shagging some poor, unsuspecting American.

Willem's coffee arrives and he doctors it with a packet and a half of sugar.

'But, as I told you, I work in cyber security. I'm not really an investigator; I could be missing something.'

'Oh, right.'

'I'll do my best, Kate, I promise.'

'I know.'

I trust him, but as he's just said, we may be bumping up against the limitations of his expertise. I wonder if there's some way Poppy and the Ever After Agency can help.

Willem tips his head back and downs his espresso, setting the empty cup on the table. 'Shall we go?' he asks, and I nod. He signals for the bill and taps his phone after waving away my offer to pay half.

We head towards the bikes in silence.

'Kate?' he says after we've walked a few blocks.

'Yes.'

'Thank you – *really*, I mean it.'

'For what?' I ask with a gentle laugh. '*You* paid for dinner.'

But he doesn't laugh. Instead, he stops, reaching for my hand to lead me out of the foot traffic. It's like I've been plugged into an electrical socket. Energy surges from his hand to mine, then through my whole body, pulsing between my legs. He releases my hand and looks at me intently, and I reluctantly shove aside the desire to reach up and pull his mouth down to meet mine. He clearly has other things on his mind.

'Thank you for coming to Amsterdam,' he says, 'and for talking with Ady... I fear this will get harder for her before it gets easier. I can tell she likes you and she's going to need you on her side – I hope that's okay.'

'Of *course*. I am on her side. And as difficult as all this is, I need Adriana too. Look, Willem, I had no idea what to expect coming here. I knew it was the right thing to do – and that it might help me in some way – but it was terrifying. Right up until the moment Adriana stopped glaring at me as if she wanted to skin me alive and toss me into the canal.'

He sniggers. 'She can be... formidable.'

'That's one word to describe her.' We share a smile. 'And there's something else... I get that you're not keen on our plan – or *any* plan to get back at Jon.'

He sighs.

'But I need it. I know that now. And it seems like Adriana does too.'

'But she—'

'No,' I say with a shake of my head, and he stops talking. 'I understand you being protective, but Adriana needs *you* on her side as well.'

'I *am*.'

'You are – but not about this. Please give it some thought, all right? It'll be easier on Adriana if you support her on this.'

'Okay. I'll think about it.'

Now that I've said my piece, my libido pops its head up again, and my eyes land on Willem's lips. I just *know* he'd be a good kisser. Jon's kisses were always on the chaste side. He never kissed me passionately.

'We should go,' says Willem and, once again, I'm back in the present, embarrassed by my errant thoughts and mentally giving myself a slap.

I have a lot to deal with before I should even *entertain* thoughts of this nature, let alone act on them. Part of me is looking forward to returning to London, where I'll go back to being Sensible Kate.

The other part wishes I could climb into bed with Willem and let him do whatever he wants to me for as long as he likes.

The ride home is less harrowing than the ride into the city – although, I'd be okay with never having to ride a bike around Amsterdam again. I park mine in front of the house-boat next to its twin and turn towards Willem.

If this *were* a date – a successful one – we'd be coming together for a goodnight kiss. But despite our candour and the shared laughter – and the moments of frisson between us – this is *not* a date.

This is simply two people with a vested interest in the same outcome – that Adriana and I extricate ourselves from our engagements and come out reasonably unscathed.

If only I could stop staring at his mouth.

'Well, goodnight,' he says.

And before I know what's happening, he smacks a kiss on my cheek, climbs back onto his bike, and cycles away.

I stare after him for a while, the spot where his lips met my cheek tingling. This isn't France, or Spain, or Italy where cheek kisses are de rigueur. A handshake would have been a perfectly acceptable way to say goodnight. So why the kiss, abrupt as it was? Did it mean something more than a friendly farewell? And should I mention it to Margot?

I only realise when he turns the corner that we didn't make plans to meet tomorrow. We also didn't say if or when we'd speak again.

Maybe that's a good thing, I tell myself as I fish the keys out of my handbag and go inside.

* * *

Monday morning, back in London, I'm like a Mylar balloon that's lost its helium.

I didn't stay in Amsterdam an extra day, as there was no point – Margot has work today, Adriana is teaching, and Willem went to Bruges yesterday afternoon to meet with a client – so I returned to London with Margot as planned.

When we got to St Pancras, we parted ways with a tight hug and me promising to keep her up to date. I'm not expected at the office today – rather, I'm forbidden from showing up – so I've arranged to meet Poppy at the Ever After Agency.

But even the hope that the agency can help isn't enough to make a dent in my gloomy state. Because I wish I was across the Channel, staying on a houseboat in a quiet neighbourhood of Amsterdam with plans to see Willem.

'Oh, Kate, you muppet,' I mutter to myself, throwing an arm over my face.

It can't be healthy fixating on the tall Dutchman. It's obvious I'm only doing that because it's easier than dealing with the fallout from Jon's actions.

Poppy once told me she was a psychologist before she was a matchmaker. I wonder if she can help me make sense of all this. I could ask her if it's normal in a situation like mine to transfer romantic feelings from one person to another.

Normal – hah! Nothing about this situation is normal. And there's a massive difference between what I once felt for Jon and what I now feel for Willem.

I've never wanted Jon to lay me down on a bed, pin my arms above my head one-handed, and crush his mouth to mine while his other hand slides between my legs and—

My phone chimes with an incoming message – a shame because there was a lot more to that fantasy – and I reach for my phone, hopeful that it's Willem checking in.

But it's not from Willem. It's from Arseface:

Hello beautiful. This is your daily reminder that I miss you. So sorry I've had to stay in Stockholm longer than expected. I promise to bring you some lingonberry jam. xxx

'Yeah, you do that, Jon,' I say, disgusted by the three kisses as much as the lie. And I don't want any more lingonberry bloody jam! Bloody psychopath. Or is he more of a sociopath? I should ask Poppy about that too.

As I do every morning, I reply:

See you soon. *smiley face*

He never seems to twig that I have *literally* replied with the exact same words for over a week now. Or maybe he has and he either doesn't care or he thinks I'm so grief-stricken at not having seen him for two weeks that I can't think of anything else to say.

Moron.

* * *

When I arrive at the Ever After Agency, I'm greeted by their receptionist, Anita, a woman who possesses a magical quality that instantly sets me at ease. She must be like this with everyone, but with her warm smile and self-deprecating chitchat, it's like reconnecting with an old friend.

After I decline a beverage, she leads me to the meeting room where Poppy and her colleagues are waiting – two women who couldn't be more distinct from each other.

One is dressed and coiffed immaculately and is of indeterminate age, her face so smooth, she either has a plastic surgeon on the payroll or an ageing portrait in her attic. The other looks like a seventy-year-old goth – head-to-toe black leather, cropped jet-black hair, and sharp, observant eyes lined heavily with black liner.

'Hi, Kate, come on in,' says Poppy when I hesitate in the doorway.

I enter and take the seat on her left.

'This is Ursula Frayne,' she says, introducing the first woman. 'She's the senior matchmaker at the agency.'

'Hello, Kate. I hope you don't mind me sitting in on your meeting, but I have a vested interest in your case.'

'No, no, of course not,' I say, my curiosity piqued. *What does she mean by 'vested interest'?* I wonder. 'Nice to meet you,' I add politely.

'And this is Marie Maillot, the agency's investigator,' Poppy says.

Investigator? I hope that means what I think it means. Why else would they bring her in?

'Hello,' I say with a smile.

Marie's mouth purses into a tight knot and she nods at me curtly. Right, so not much of a talker.

'Cutting to the chase…' says Poppy, capturing my attention. 'We've considered your request, and we've decided to help you.'

For a moment, I'm too shocked to speak, then her words sink in. They're going to help me!

'Oh, *thank* you, Poppy,' I say, flooded with relief. Like I said to Willem, I've come to realise how much I need this. I need Jon to pay for what he's done so I can move on.

'Don't thank me just yet. There's a lot that needs to happen before we put a plan into action.'

'Of course,' I reply, sobered by Poppy's cautionary tone. 'And before we get started, there's something you should know – pertinent information that recently came to light and may impact how we proceed.'

I may be in the midst of a messy personal situation, but nothing beats project-manager speak to give me a boost of confidence and make it sound like I've got a handle on the situation, even if I don't.

'Oh?' asks Poppy.

'Yes, after I spoke to you on Saturday, Jon cancelled on Adriana. He was supposed to meet her parents this Wednesday, but he spouted some lie about a trade conference in New York. Meanwhile, he's been telling *me* he's in Stockholm. We suspect there may be a third fiancée.'

Poppy's eyes widen in surprise.

'If so, she *could* be in America,' I say, 'but with Jon, she could be anywhere.'

'*Not* a fiancée,' says Marie in a thick French accent, and all our heads swing in her direction. She retrieves a packet of cigarettes from the pocket of her leather jacket and for a second, I think she's about to light up. Instead, she takes out a cigarette, then sucks on it as if it *is* lit.

How bizarre. And when is she going to expand upon the 'not a fiancée' comment? I can't say I'm particularly impressed with Marie thus far.

'Sorry, Marie,' says Poppy. 'What are you saying?'

After exhaling a non-existent plume of smoke, Marie trains her beady eyes on me.

'Her name is Lucia Rossi and she's a British-born, half-Italian artist living in Verona. He hasn't proposed yet, but he *has* bought the ring.'

This revelation stuns the rest of us into silence.

12

POPPY

I've worked with Marie for years now and I've never doubted her ability to deliver – like she just has – but I'll also never get past how frustrating she can be. Why didn't she tell us this *before* Kate got here?

'Very helpful information, Marie,' I say with a clenched jaw.

Ursula and I exchange a look of solidarity; I can tell she's frustrated too.

'Uh... sorry...' Kate splutters. 'How do you know all this – about the third woman? Lucia... um...'

'*Rossi*,' Marie supplies pointedly. 'When Poppy contacted me yesterday, I looked into your Jon Dunn. Pfft, *quelle espèce de fils de putain*,' she says with a disdainful jerk of her head.

'*Marie*,' I caution. My French may be lacking but I understand 'son of a bitch' and there's every chance Kate does too. We do *not* use profanity in front of clients at Ever After.

Marie shrugs like a bored teenager and it takes all my resolve not to growl at her.

'Sorry,' says Kate again, clearly perplexed. 'I meant *how* –

as in, how did you uncover the identity of Jon's um... *girl-friend*?' she asks, faltering on the word. 'And so quickly?'

'Marie is one of the top investigators in this part of the world,' says Ursula, leaping in before Marie can give one of her typical dry retorts.

'Kate,' I say, redirecting the conversation, 'you have thoughts on how to seek retribution against Dunn. Could you please explain what you had in mind to Ursula and Marie?'

'Oh, yes, of course,' she says, visibly composing herself.

To her credit, Kate may have been caught off guard by Marie's revelation, but she switches seamlessly into her explanation as if she's in a professional setting, outlining her idea clearly, articulately, and thoroughly. And she's obviously given it more thought since we spoke on Saturday.

'Now, Jon is legitimately wealthy, but it's inherited wealth,' she says. 'He hasn't worked a day in his life.'

'*Oui, c'est vrai*,' Marie concurs, capturing our attention for a second time. 'The family's wealth is generational. The last Dunn to work was Dunn's great-great-grandfather. He owned a shipping company that was very profitable from the 1920s. All the first-born males since... *lazy*.'

'All the more reason to get him to donate a large sum to charity, don't you think?' Kate asks, a bitter edge to her words.

'It's a compelling argument,' Ursula replies. 'But there's wealthy and there's *wealthy*. What's a "large sum" to Jon Dunn? Marie, do you have any indication of his net worth?'

Marie consults a page in her tiny Moleskin notebook. 'A hundred million pounds – approximately.'

'Oh my god!' Kate exclaims. She stares at Marie, wide-eyed. 'Then I'm definitely keeping the ring!' she declares with a scoffing laugh.

Marie sniggers at that – a rare occurrence – and I curb my own laughter.

'Hmm,' says Ursula, tapping a fingernail on the table, 'it might be challenging to make a significant dent in that sum.'

'Or we simply up the ante,' Kate suggests with a wry smile, and Ursula nods approvingly. 'To that point, the *amount* of the donation is not all of it,' she adds, getting to the crux of the idea. 'It's the chosen charity. Apparently, Jon has a particular disdain for arts' education. According to him, children should study the three Rs and nothing more.'

'He sounds like an utter moron,' says Ursula. She momentarily presses her fingers to her lips. 'I am so sorry – that was incredibly unprofessional of me.'

'Please, no apologies,' says Kate. 'He *is* a moron. A conniving, manipulative, arse-faced moron. Anyway,' she says with a quick shake of her head, 'I doubt it will be difficult to choose a worthy cause – *if* we can find a way to make this work.'

'Actually,' I say, realising something, 'I should have thought of this before, but there's a program called Creative Futures Fund here in London that my husband donates to. It's for underprivileged children.'

'Ooh, that might be perfect,' says Kate, her eyes lighting up.

'I'll send you the information,' I reply. 'But now the hard part: how do we get Dunn to agree to the donation?'

'*That's* where we need the most help,' Kate replies. 'I mean, if I *have* to see Jon, I will but...' She appears apprehensive, shuddering as if a goose walked over her grave.

'Actually, I don't think that will be necessary,' says Ursula.

'Oh good. Wait, you're not thinking about putting Adriana in the firing line, are you? I'd like to keep her out of this as much as possible,' Kate says earnestly. 'We've been messaging and she's had a wobble since I was in Amsterdam. This is hitting her quite hard.'

'No, no, I quite agree that we should keep you both out of harm's way,' says Ursula. '*And* Ms Rossi – though what to do about her is a whole other kettle of fish.'

'What did you have in mind, Ursula?' I ask, steering her back to the most pressing matter.

'Actually, Poppy, it would involve *you*.'

'Me?'

'Yes. What I propose is a *sting*.' There's a mischievous look in Ursula's eye that's starting to make me nervous.

'A sting?' I ask.

'Mm-hmm. We honeypot Dunn with you as the bait.'

'Wait, *what*?'

'Yes, we set up a happenstance meeting, you get close to the mark, draw him in, then convince him to donate a sizeable sum to charity.'

'That's a bit of a leap, don't you think?' I ask. 'What makes you think I can convince him of *that*?'

'Years of matchmaking experience,' she replies. 'I can *guarantee* he's the type of man who will gladly flash his wealth about to impress a prospective love interest. I've encountered Dunn's type before many times – *too* many.'

She may have, but I remain unconvinced.

'Are you su—'

'*Then*,' she says, talking over me, 'once the donation is finalised, we'll gather the others, including Ms Rossi, and reveal that we're onto him.'

'And that his donation has gone to arts' education,' Kate adds with a satisfied smile.

'Precisely,' Ursula replies.

A dozen thoughts fly through my mind at once, including that Ursula's description of this caper is so well-versed, she must have done this sort of thing before. But the stand-out detail is that she wants to use me as bait to hook a three-timing, lying bastard.

She wants me to become fiancée number four!

'Uh...' I murmur. I look to Marie, helpless, but she seems as bewildered as I am.

'It all sounds brilliant, Ursula,' Kate gushes. 'Just like *Ocean's 8*,' she adds, a reference that baffles me further. We're not robbing the Metropolitan Museum of Art. We're trying to find a commensurate punishment for a wannabe polygamist!

'Before we wander too far down that path,' I say calmly, finding my voice, 'I'm not sure this is a good idea.'

Kate and Ursula speak at once, their voices blending, but their meaning clear. They are both fully on board with this bonkers plan.

Wonderful – now what?

'Marie,' I say, turning to my would-be ally, my fingers mentally crossed, 'what do *you* think?'

Her expression shifts and her eyes flash with excitement. 'I think it sounds fun.'

'*Fun?* For whom? Not for *me*, that's for sure,' I respond adamantly.

She gives me her signature shrug and draws from her unlit cigarette. Okay, so Marie isn't going to help me.

'*Please*, Poppy...'

Kate's pleading tone breaks through my thoughts, and I look her in the eye.

'The only way to stop Jon is to turn the tables on him. And

Ursula's plan does that. It will hurt him in the hip pocket, totally piss him off, *and* we'll all get to confront him together – say our piece.'

I exhale through my nose, resigned. When it's put that way, this plan *does* have merit.

'If our bosses sign off on it, I'll do it,' I say, resigned.

Unsurprisingly, she ignores the 'if' part and beams at me.

'But like I said before, no promises, okay?'

'Okay,' she agrees.

'I'm sure it will be fine,' says Ursula dismissively.

I could throttle Ursula right now. For years, she's been a mentor to me, and I've always looked to her to be a beacon of sense and professionalism. Now she's behaving like an evil mastermind.

'Oh,' says Kate as if she's suddenly remembered something. She turns to Ursula. 'You said you had a vested interest in my case. What did you mean by that?'

'Well, just as you want Dunn to pay for duping you into an engagement, I'd like my former business partner to pay for compromising my professional reputation.'

'And how does that concern me?' Kate asks.

'She owns Perfect Pairings.'

'*Oh*, I see.'

'*Mm-hmm*,' Ursula replies.

Marie clears her throat and we all look her way. She taps twice on her phone, then lifts her head and addresses us. 'Dunn has a reservation at the Langham on Wednesday for two nights.'

'So, *not* in New York then. Imagine my surprise,' says Kate sarcastically. 'Wait – did you determine that while we've been sitting here?'

'*Mais, oui*,' Marie replies as if it's a stupid question.

'Wowser,' Kate says to herself.

'Well, Poppy, it looks like we have the mark's known whereabouts in two days hence,' says Ursula. 'Kate, we'll need you to brief Poppy on all things Jon Dunn. Marie, keep digging – determine if there are any other women he's romantically involved with.'

Marie nods her acceptance of her assignment and just like that, I've been usurped. Not only am I now positioned at the centre of this case, but Ursula's issuing commands as if it belongs to *her*.

'There's something else we need to consider,' I say, commandeering this discussion before Ursula volunteers me for anything else. 'Do we continue to involve Adriana's brother, Willem de Vries? He's been instrument—'

'Yes, yes, we should definitely keep working with him,' Kate interjects.

I catch her eye and she looks away, lips pressed together and her cheeks flushing. She must recognise what her outburst has revealed. And while Kate may believe she's ready to leap into a new relationship, I truly hope she takes some time to heal.

'It's that he's been really helpful, you see,' she adds feebly. 'So, it's only fair to keep him in the loop.'

She does have a point – about keeping Willem informed. 'Marie,' I say, 'would you be willing to liaise with Mr de Vries? He may have pertinent information to share.'

She regards me for a moment without speaking, and I have no idea how she'll respond. Marie is a lone wolf, but she's also been known to surprise me.

'I've heard of him. I will contact him.'

Case in point: Marie already knowing who Willem is – *and* being willing to work with him.

'Great,' I say. 'Now, the last thing to discuss is Ms Rossi. She may not be our client, but she is associated with this case. How do we go about informing her of Dunn's duplicity?'

I look at the others in turn. Marie won't want the task – she's about as far from a people person as one can get. Ursula seems too caught up in her honeypot scheme. And Kate is way too close to it.

I suppose that leaves me.

'I'll do it,' says Kate.

'Are you sure? It's a big ask.'

'No, I want to. I know how it feels to be in that position.'

'If you're sure?' I ask again, and she nods. 'I s'pose you could ask Adriana to go with you.'

'I don't think she's up to it, though.'

'Oh right, of course,' I reply.

'But I'll talk to Willem, and we'll figure something out.'

Now I'm more convinced than ever that Kate's hoping for something to happen between her and Willem de Vries, and I'm not sure what to do about it.

'Excellent,' says Ursula. 'I love it when a plan comes together.'

'Hah!' barks Marie – her version of a laugh. '*The A-Team*. I love that show.'

'It's a classic,' Ursula agrees.

If I wasn't already reeling from everything else that's happened in this meeting, I'd die from shock at Ursula Frayne and Marie Maillot fangirling together over an eighties TV show.

* * *

'Tris? I'm home!'

'Hello, darling,' he calls out. He comes out of our bedroom, having already changed into his typical post-work outfit of jeans and casual button-down shirt.

We may have been married for a year-and-a-half, but the sight of my husband's washboard stomach beneath semi-sheer white linen and his denim-clad muscular thighs is enough to set my body alight.

As soon as I tell him my news, I'm dragging him back into the bedroom to have my way with him and get on with our baby making. Especially as my parents are visiting from Tassie soon. It would be extra special to break the news that they're going to be grandparents while they're here.

Tristan crosses to me as I deposit my handbag on the hall-stand, then step out of my shoes. 'Welcome home,' he says, capturing me around my waist and dipping his head to kiss me.

I snake my arms around his neck as the kiss deepens, and it's soon obvious that I'm not the only one thinking about sexy bedroom antics. But thoughts of today's meeting keep intruding, ruining the moment.

'Tris,' I whisper against his lips.

'Mmm?'

I lean back, breaking the kiss, and his eyes slowly open.

'Something on your mind?' he asks.

'How can you tell?' I ask, feigning disbelief, and we share a soft laugh. He watches me, patiently waiting for me to tell him what's going on, and I gently ease out of his embrace.

'Okay, here goes,' I say. I take a deep breath. 'You remember that case I told you about – the one with the guy who's engaged to two women?'

'I do, yes.'

'So, it turns out there's a *third* woman and I've been volunteered to become the fourth.'

Tristan blinks at me in surprise. 'Am I going to need a whisky before you tell me the rest?' he asks, and I can tell he's only half-joking.

'Probably. Actually, *definitely*. And I'll join you.'

Tristan goes to our drinks trolley and pours two hefty slugs of his favourite whisky – Tomatin – and I climb onto the sofa, sitting cross-legged. He joins me, handing me a tumbler, and we clink the rims together, then take a drink.

'Right, now that I'm suitably *lubricated*,' he says with a sexy smile, 'tell me why my wife is about to take a lover.'

'Eww!' I backhand him lightly in the chest and he pretends that it hurt. 'I am not "taking a lover" – and if you knew anything about this guy... Just, *no*, Tris. *Blech*,' I say with a shudder.

'Duly noted,' he says, landing a peck on my lips.

'But I will have to *pretend* to be interested in the slimy weasel.'

'Sounds, er... challenging.'

'Well, yeah. And I'm going to need your help.'

'My help? Wouldn't this be more Shaz's domain? Or Jacinda's?'

'No, because our mark is a toffee-nosed, lazy git from old money, and I'll need your advice on how to charm him.'

'Because *I'm* a toffee-nosed, lazy git from old money?' he asks with a laugh.

'No! But you did grow up around people like that,' I reply, and he eyes me with amusement.

Tristan is from old money – and he did inherit millions from his grandfather – but unlike Jon Dunn, Tristan has worked extremely hard since he left uni. His professional accomplishments are testament of his tenacity and work ethic. He also donates a huge sum annually to an array of causes – including, of course, an arts' education program.

'There's something else,' I say.

'Some other way to insult me?'

'Hardly. You know you're my favourite person.'

He winks at me.

'No, it's about that arts' program you donate to, Creative Futures.'

'*We* donate to, darling,' he says, correcting me. But as much as Tristan refers to his considerable wealth as ours, I still struggle to get my head around it sometimes.

'Right – *we* donate to. Anyway, listen to this…'

As I fill Tristan in on the rest of the sting operation, including how it could boost the foundation's coffers, he gets more and more excited.

'What do you reckon?' I ask.

'I *reckon* that it's brilliant. And even if means helping my wife get engaged to someone else, I'm in.'

'Thank you, babe,' I reply. I take another sip of whisky.

'Just one more question,' he says.

'Mmm?'

'Any chance this will be wrapped up before your parents arrive?'

'Oh, right.' Mum and Dad land in less than a month. How likely is it that the honeypot scheme will be behind me by then?

'Judging by your expression, I take it that's a no then?'

'Not necessarily – maybe it will play out quickly.' As soon as the words are out of my mouth, I realise how unlikely that is. '*Ugh*,' I groan, feeling the full weight of this assignment.

'Honestly, of all the things I've had to do as a matchmaker, this may be the hardest.'

'Well, a good thing you have a toffee-nosed, not-so-lazy git on your side,' he teases.

Knowing I have Tristan's support downgrades my dread to mild trepidation – even though it's a lot to ask of my husband, supporting me while I ostensibly seduce another man.

13

KATE

I nibble on my lower lip as I place the call to Willem. He's not expecting to hear from me, and I have no idea if he'll answer. And the longer it rings, the more I wish I'd sent a text message instead.

'*Hallo*, Kate,' he answers eventually, his face filling the screen. From the shaky image he's obviously on the move.

'Is this a bad time?' I ask. 'I can call back later.'

I catch sight of myself in the thumbnail and lift my phone, instantly erasing the slight double chin. I've refreshed my makeup for this call, giving myself the dewy, natural look that actresses in romcoms 'wake up' with. I haven't spent any time examining *why* I've ensured I look my best; I already know the answer and I'm not exactly comfortable with the reason.

'This is fine,' he replies. The motion of his camera starts making me queasy and I look away. 'I'm just about to board the train. One moment while I find my seat.'

I should have messaged him instead. This is the same fluttery anxiousness I'd get when I called a boy I liked and his mum would shout for him to come to the phone.

'*Hallo*,' Willem says again and when I look at the screen, the image has stabilised. He's smiling, making the tummy flutters intensify.

'Hello,' I reply, also with a smile. 'Sorry to bother you – you're obviously in transit – but I have some news.'

'Is it about Lucia Rossi?' he asks.

'It *is*, and how do you already know that?'

'Marie Maillot called an hour ago. She told me about your meeting.'

'Wowser, she's *fast*.'

'And direct. It was a very short call,' he says, clearly amused.

'I can't say I'm surprised. She's not much of a conversationalist. Had you heard of her – before she called?' I ask. 'She mentioned she knew who *you* were.'

'She did?'

I nod.

'Well, that's unexpected,' he says, his brows lifted in surprise. 'And I had heard of her, yes. Everyone in cyber security has.'

'Really?'

'Mm-hmm. In the early 2000s, she wrote a malware detection program that we still use today.'

'Ahh, that explains a lot – her being techy. It barely took her two minutes to uncover Jon's whereabouts later this week.'

'I hear there's a plan involving your matchmaker.'

'Poppy's not my matchmaker any more,' I say, a terse edge to my voice. I don't want Willem thinking I've re-engaged Poppy's services.

Because you want to make it clear that you're available, says the voice inside my head. It's not wrong but it's also not helpful.

'Sorry,' he says, his brows knitted.

'Doesn't matter,' I say, making light of it. 'Anyway, the agency's managing that side of things – I've spent the last two hours with Poppy, filling her in on all things Jon – but I've raised my hand to go to Verona and inform Lucia.'

'Really? Are you sure that's best?' he asks, which is a little irritating. 'You could call her, send an email...'

'Your own sister didn't believe you until I fronted up at your house.'

'True,' he acknowledges with a slow nod.

'And do you think *I* would have believed you if you hadn't shown up in person with irrefutable proof? If you'd called me or emailed, I would have thought you were a scammer,' I continue, driving home my point.

'I understand.'

'Even then I was dubious. I googled you, you know. Before I met you at the pub.'

'I would expect nothing less,' he retorts with a smirk, and I can't tell if he's teasing me. 'Kate, I can come with you – to Verona,' he adds, catching me by surprise.

I'd hoped he would offer, but I didn't expect it, and I didn't dare ask.

Especially not after I spent the entire Tube ride home from Ever After imagining being in Verona with Willem. Only we weren't there for Lucia – we were *together*.

This fantasy climaxed in a rather steamy scene beneath Juliet's balcony where, surrounded by a crowd of romantic pilgrims, Willem held me close to him, his fingers splayed against my stomach, while his other hand surreptitiously slipped beneath my skirt and worked its magic between my legs.

Highly unsuitable thoughts for the Tube. The woman

across from me must have been a mind reader. When I snapped out of my steamy fugue, she was staring at me with a knowing smile. I got off at the next stop even though it meant I had to walk half a mile to get home.

'You're not saying anything,' he says. 'You don't want me to come?'

Are we still talking about travel plans? As well as chiming in at inopportune moments, it seems my inner voice also has a dirty mind.

'It's not that,' I reply.

'So, you *do* want me to come with you?'

I do, but not for the reason he thinks, and I sigh. 'Look, Lucia deserves the truth, and I think it should come from me – or Adriana, but it's a lot to ask of her.'

'It's a lot to ask of you too.'

'Well, yes, but she's— Never mind.'

I was going to say that Adriana's having a harder time with all this than she may be letting on – a girls' night out only has so much healing power – but I'm not sure she'd want me say anything.

'Kate, you might be right about Ady sitting this one out. Most of the time she seems okay, but last night she called me crying.'

Ah, so he does know about Adriana.

'I'm so sorry to hear that.'

And I am sorry, especially as *I* haven't cried over Jon since the night Willem showed up and Margot came over to console me. My pragmatic mind taking charge, I suppose. No sense in crying over someone who doesn't exist.

'Mmm,' he murmurs, his expression pained. He sighs. 'It's a big mess,' he concludes, and I chuckle wryly.

'Astutely put. It is a big mess, but it's not yours to clean up,'

I say, as much for myself as for Willem. I may want him to accompany me, but it's for ulterior motives and that's not fair on him.

'Kate—'

'You've already helped so much...' And he has. He may have shown up unannounced and dropped a bomb, as he said the other night, but I would much rather know about Jon now than have married him and *then* discovered I was one of three.

'Will you think about it – me coming to Italy with you? Marie Maillot and I have already agreed to share our findings, so I'll have access to all the information you require.'

I snigger softly. 'Trust you to be all *logical*,' I tease.

'It is my specialty,' he quips.

He smiles and even though there's a body of water between us, that smile warms me from the inside out. It also ignites an inferno between my legs. It's a good thing I'm no longer on the Tube and safely ensconced in my flat.

'I'll think about it,' I say.

It *does* make sense, him coming with me, but it may be difficult to concentrate on the core purpose of the trip if I'm constantly fantasising about Willem slipping his hand inside my knickers – *extremely* difficult.

'Ahem...' I clear my throat, staving off the inappropriate thoughts. 'So, um... I'll let you know?' I say, posing it as a question.

Ugh. I sound exactly like my fourteen-year-old self and not at *all* like a mature woman with oodles of life experience. If this weren't a video call, I'd roll my eyes at myself and slap my forehead.

Instead, I plaster on a bright smile and ring off before Willem cottons on that I am, in fact, a blithering idiot.

* * *

'How was Amsterdam?' Mina asks, popping her head into my office.

'Good, yes! Productive,' I say without thinking.

'Productive?' She steps inside, folding her arms across her chest, a furrow appearing between her brows. 'I thought you were going away to have some fun. Oh god, Kate, you weren't *working*, were you?' she asks with mock horror – at least I *think* she's joking.

'No, no, nothing like that,' I say, forcing a laugh. 'Sorry, I meant it did the trick – helped kickstart the healing process.'

'Oh, good.' She sits in the chair opposite me, a rare occurrence. Almost every time we meet, it's in her office or a meeting room. She also has an odd expression on her face, which makes me uneasy. 'And how's your day going so far?' she asks with a concerned head tilt.

'Ah, good, yes. I got in early and put my head down, and I'm already caught up,' I say brightly, hoping to reassure her that a day off hasn't impacted my work.

'I'd expect nothing less from you, Kate. As I told you last week, you at eighty per cent is far superior to most people at a hundred.'

It's a nice compliment, but where is she going with this? 'Thanks, Mina,' I say with a smile. 'Your confidence in me means a lot.'

'Listen, I've been thinking...' she starts, her expression hinting at something intriguing.

Ooh, maybe she's broaching the possibility of me moving to Europe. We'll be opening a satellite office later this year, and I'd definitely consider being part of the advance team.

'Since you announced your engagement,' she continues,

instantly quashing my mounting enthusiasm, 'I've had it in mind to gift you a fortnight's leave for your honeymoon – so you didn't have to use your holiday entitlement. As my wedding gift to you.'

'Okay,' I say. God, I'd rather be discussing pap smear results with Mina than my broken engagement.

'And now that you're no longer *engaged*...'

In a professional context, Mina Choi is confident and articulate, regularly conversing with some of the most influential people on the planet – billionaires, CEOs, magnates, and even heads of state. So why is she struggling to express herself with *me*?

And then I get it.

'Oh, no, that's fine,' I say. 'A very generous gift – thank you – but I'm not expecting you to honour it. Not now, and until thirty seconds ago, I didn't even know about it, so...'

'But that's the thing. I'd like to give you the time off regardless.'

'Really? But why?' It's rude of me to speak to Mina so abruptly, but I can't fathom why she would want to give me time off for something that's no longer happening.

It also occurs to me how fortunate I am that Jon and I hadn't set a date yet. This whole situation would be infinitely worse if I were having to cancel wedding plans and a honeymoon! But then again, that's probably because Jon planned to string me along indefinitely while he collected fiancées like charms on a bracelet.

'Because you've earned it, Kate,' Mina says, and my focus returns to our conversation. '*And* because...' She looks over her shoulder, then gets up and closes the door. She returns to the chair and sits, her eyes boring into mine. 'It happened to me.'

There's a beat of silence as I unpack the meaning of her words – or attempt to.

'Sorry, *what* happened to you?'

'I had a broken engagement. About fifteen years ago. Actually, it wasn't just a broken engagement. He left me at the altar.'

'Oh my god. I'm so sorry.'

'Yes, well, it was an awful time – a blessing in disguise in the end, of course. Because a year later, I met Jeff.' She and Jeff recently celebrated their twelfth wedding anniversary.

She smiles and I return it, even though I'm finding this conversation extremely uncomfortable. Does Mina *pity* me? It's a horrifying thought.

'Still, it's horrible that happened to you, Mina,' I say evenly. 'I can only imagine how difficult it must have been, but my situation with Jon... It's nothing quite that, er... *dramatic*.'

Now that is an out-and-out lie. Multiple fiancées in different cities undoubtably trumps a runaway groom, but I'm not about to reveal the real reason I'm not with Jon. I'm not even planning on telling my parents.

'Of course, I understand,' she says, 'but in case you find yourself out of sorts while you get over him – and it doesn't matter if it's a week from now or a month or even a year – please come to me. That time is yours, Kate, whenever you want to take it. You've been paramount to Elev8te's success and whatever I can do to help... just say the word.'

Her timing is uncanny – perhaps I could use some of the gifted days to go to Verona – but when she punctuates her offer with an empathetic smile, tears prick my eyes. I'm instantly mortified – I have never cried at work and I am not going to start now.

But I can't ignore the way Mina's words have permeated

the professional boundaries we've established. She's seeing me as a woman, not an employee, and her empathy and kindness mean the world to me – despite the discomfort they bring.

'Thank you, Mina. I really appreciate that and I promise I'll come to you if and when the time comes.'

'Brilliant,' she says, beaming at me. 'Well, I'll leave you to it.'

She departs and I'm still sifting through our conversation when Margot strides into my office. With the early start, an intensely busy morning, and Mina's bizarre visit, I'd forgotten we arranged to have lunch together.

'Hiya,' she says, coming around to my side of the desk to hug me.

'Hiya.' I pat her on the back with one hand.

She straightens and looks down at me. 'Well, come on, chop chop. I have to be back by one-thirty and I want to hear everything.'

I regard Margot with affection as I collect my handbag from my desk drawer and slip on my jacket. There are countless times when she drives me bonkers, but there are many more when her cheery presence is enough to clear my mind of troubled thoughts, like now.

And it doesn't matter that I've already updated her on the latest by text message. I know exactly how lunch will go. Margot will ask countless questions – How was it when you found out about Lucia? Do you really think Poppy can snare Jon? How did Willem look when you called him? – and I will do my best to remember every nuance and detail and report it accurately. Anything less and she won't be satisfied.

'So, sushi, soup, or that new sandwich shop on the corner?' I ask as we leave the office.

'Not sushi. Remember last time?' She grimaces.

'Oh right,' I say with a laugh. We'd stopped at services on one of our mini breaks and Margot thought it was a good idea to have discounted, nearly out-of-date sushi for lunch. The results were not pretty and it's a minor miracle that the hire car came out of that trip unscathed.

She hooks her arm through mine as we head towards the lobby, then leans closer. 'Now, you may not have shagged him in Amsterdam, but *please* tell me you're going to shag him in Verona?'

'Margot!' I chide in a loud whisper.

'Oh, come on,' she says quietly as we wait for the lift. 'He doesn't *need* to go with you – and he knows that – yet he's insisting.'

'So?'

'He fancies you, Kate. Frisson, remember?'

'He doesn't—' I stop myself, because a small part of me thinks she's right. 'Anyway, it's irrelevant,' I continue, lowering my voice further. 'Sleeping with someone new is the last thing on my mind.'

'Hah!' she barks, breaking into loud laughter. 'Good one, Kate,' she says, pretending to wipe tears from under her eyes.

The lift dings and the doors open, and I usher her inside, stabbing at the button for the ground floor. 'You're incorrigible,' I tell her when the lift starts to descend.

'Yep, and you're deluding yourself.'

I blow out a sigh but I'm not sure who I'm more annoyed with – Margot for speaking the truth or me for denying it.

14

POPPY

I've spent two days intensively swotting up on Jon Dunn and it's left such a bad taste in my mouth, it's as if I've gargled with curdled milk.

It's calculated, what he's done, creating two distinct personas – two *lives* – with zero overlap. With one fiancée in London and one across the Channel, there is no chance of running into one while with the other. The same with his 'professions' – zero overlap between a pilot and a diamond dealer.

And who knows what he's told the third woman, Lucia. Maybe he's also an astronaut.

Cleverly, he's carried some specifics across his dual personas, likely to avoid slipping up. His favourite drink is a Negroni, for one. I've always steered clear of Negronis – far too potent for me – but tonight, I will pretend to try one for the first time, then make it my fave too.

I've created a persona named Penny for this 'chance meeting', a bubbly and effusive, wide-eyed woman I compiled as a stark contrast to Kate's stoic, pragmatic nature.

I've also been coached extensively by the odd duo of

Ursula and Marie. I swear, if Ursula were my age, she'd have raised her own hand for this assignment, rather than volunteering me. She seems to get a kick out of schooling me on various ways to 'bag the mark' – her words, not mine. Either she's watched a lot of film noir, or matchmaking was a whole different ballgame when she started back in the nineties.

Marie's advice has been on the subtle art of 'choreographed bumping', AKA how to make running into someone seem natural. And I mean that in the literal sense. If Dunn doesn't show up to the hotel's bar around 8 p.m. per his typical MO, I will need to fashion a clumsy interlude in the hotel lobby. This afternoon, I've practised crashing into someone and dropping my handbag so the contents spill onto the floor so many times, I could get a role in slapstick comedy.

I'm now at home getting ready, ripe with nerves as Tristan hovers nearby. It was all very well us joking about my assignment a couple of nights ago, but now it's actually happening, we're both on edge.

'Can I get you something to drink, darling?' he asks.

I turn away from my makeup vanity and give him a smile. 'That's okay, babe. I should probably keep my wits about me.'

'Are you sure you don't want me to come with you?' he asks, frowning.

'He's not *dangerous*. I'll engage him in conversation, charm him with "Penny", and get him to exchange contact information. Think of it as an acting gig.'

He exhales a long breath and runs one hand through his hair. 'Sorry,' he says. 'I just... I didn't expect to feel like this.'

'I know. Me neither.'

'You look pretty, by the way,' he says, his frown deepening. 'Maybe too pretty – even though you don't exactly look like *you*.'

'It's just a *role*, Tris. You are the only man I want to look pretty for, okay?'

He nods sharply. Though we both know this isn't entirely true, as the common thread between Kate, Adriana, and Lucia is that they are all very attractive women. Kate is a classic beauty like Saoirse Ronan and Emily Blunt, Adriana is a tall, blonde goddess, and Lucia is petite and dark-haired, and reminds me of Imogen Poots.

I need Dunn to be attracted to me – well, *Penny*.

I've played up my grey eyes with lashings of mascara to appear particularly wide-eyed and have pulled my reddish-brown hair into a high ponytail. I'm wearing a floaty, floral chiffon dress and my ubiquitous ballet flats, the one thing Penny and I have in common besides my Aussie accent. She will be sweet, slightly naïve, and splurging on the Langham after a stint in London for work.

It's a risk dangling an Australian in front of Dunn. Will he go for it, or will he think Melbourne is *too* long-distance for a romantic undertaking? If he balks, I'll switch gears and tell him that Penny is moving to Munich with her job.

I check the clock on my bedside table. The car is due soon. 'Want to walk me down to the lobby?' I ask.

Tristan's smile is tight-lipped. 'Of course.'

A few minutes later, we're in the lobby waiting in tense silence when a town car pulls up. Tristan has asked his regular driver to take me to the Langham and wait for me.

He turns towards me, running his hands down my arms and clasping mine in his. 'I love you,' he says.

'I love you too, and as nervous as I am, I'm not off to war, Tris. I'll be back in a couple of hours, okay? Maybe sooner.'

He smiles again, this one reaching his eyes. He lays a soft kiss on my cheek and I head out into the cool evening.

'Good evening, Ms Dean,' says the driver, opening the car door.

'Hello, Nigel.'

I slide onto the backseat and buckle up while Nigel closes the door and goes around to the driver's side.

The drive from our flat in the financial district to the Langham doesn't take long, and before I know it, Penny Mullings is in action.

* * *

I'm buzzing with adrenaline when I slip out of the Langham, cross the road, and open the backdoor of the town car. 'Hi, Nigel,' I say, climbing inside.

'Sorry, Ms Dean. I would have opened your door had I known you were on your way.'

'All good, Nigel – thanks though,' I reply, buckling up. 'Home, please.'

I consciously steady my breathing as I cast my mind back over the past hour.

The stand-out memory was Dunn's expression when I sidled up to him at the bar and asked if the seat next to him was taken. He was *delighted* to be approached, swiftly engaging me in conversation. As he asked questions and listened to Penny's potted history, his eyes never left mine and he nodded and smiled in the right places. Textbook active listening techniques, no doubt designed to reel me in. Hah!

When I faked a yawn and said I needed to get up early to fly home to Melbourne, he leapt into action and asked how he could contact me. Apparently, his role as a geological surveyance consultant for the mining industry brings him to Australia 'all the time'. Never mind that the mining hubs are nowhere near Melbourne. I suppose when you're pulling a new profession out of your bum, you might flub the details. Penny simply smiled at him and gave him her Aussie contact number, then left before Dunn could make any physical overtures.

I message Ursula and Marie on our new chat thread:

Hook line and sinker

I'll fill them in on the details tomorrow, but they will be dying to hear if phase one of our plan worked. Ursula is the first to reply:

Excellent. Well done, Poppy.

It amuses me that Ursula always punctuates her messages correctly. I wait for a response from Marie, but none comes – not really that surprising. She's the least communicative person I've ever worked with. Next I message Tristan:

Heading home babe. Keep the ponytail or lose it?

He responds immediately:

Keep it. We can roleplay. *winking face*

'Hah!'

Nigel's eyes briefly meet mine in the mirror, then return to the road.

'Sorry. Just something funny Tristan said.'

'Of course, Ms Dean.'

I stare out the window as we pass through Central London

and start fleshing out Penny Mullings' naughtier side. My husband wants to roleplay? Well, he's about to have a night he'll never forget.

Kate

'Hi, Poppy.'

I'm in my office with the door closed, and Poppy has called right on time. 'So, how did it go?' I ask, a tad trepidatious. It's not every day you chat with the woman who spent the previous evening chatting up your fiancé.

'The gist or all the gory details?' she asks.

'Uh, the gist is fine.'

I may never want to lay eyes on Jon again – even though I'll have to at some point – but I also don't want to hear the ins and outs of his and Poppy's encounter (so to speak).

She walks me through a summary of their meeting, including that when 'Penny' pressed Jon on details of his life, he patently avoided answering her. Sounds familiar.

'Did he say what he does for a living?' I ask, curiosity over-riding reticence.

'He did,' she replies, clearly amused. 'He's in mining – essentially a geologist.'

I laugh. I can't help it. 'You mean one of those people who works on mining sites, where it's dusty and loud?'

'Apparently.'

The thought of Jon, who has regular manicures and hasn't done a day of manual labour in his entire life, on a mining site wearing work boots and a hardhat is hilarious. I'd wager that the heaviest machinery Jon has ever operated is his electric toothbrush.

'And how did you leave things?' I ask.

'I gave him an Australian phone number that Marie set up for me.'

'Has he contacted you yet?'

'Yes. A simple nice-to-meet-you message, and I've replied.'

'Okay.' I heave out a loud breath. 'I'm not going to lie, Poppy, it's surreal talking about this.'

'I can imagine. It's surreal on this end too.'

'I can imagine,' I echo. 'I appreciate it, though. Adriana does too,' I add, thinking about our recent exchanges. Though, if Adriana had her way, retribution would include public shaming. I've had to sell her on the agency's plan multiple times, as she deems it far too lenient.

'It's all part of the service,' Poppy quips.

Only it isn't. This is well beyond what she typically does, and I can tell from her voice that she's not entirely comfortable with it. Understandably so.

'So, what happens next?' I ask – both wanting and dreading the answer.

'I'll keep up the communications, increasing the amount of contact over the next few days, then ask for a video chat.'

'Oh god, that sounds...' I can't bring myself to finish the point.

'Yeah, not fun, but we think it's the best way to fast-track a long-distance relationship, especially as we want him to donate to Penny's organisation. That's bound to take a lot more on my end than a few text messages.'

'Right.'

'But then, once he's well and truly invested, Penny will ask about the donation.'

'Poppy... Are you sure you want to go through with all this?'

She laughs. 'Uh, nope. But here we are.'

I appreciate her candour, but I also feel guilty. When I approached her about getting back at Jon, I had no idea she'd have to go undercover to get close to him.

'So, what about you?' she asks. 'When do you go to Verona?'

'I leave tonight.'

'It's all happening very quickly, isn't it?'

'Yes,' I reply, 'which is good. We need to get ahead of Jon's plans for global domination...'

She chuckles at my poor joke.

'But it's also a lot – mentally, I mean.'

'And emotionally,' she adds.

'Yes, that too.'

'And is Margot going with you?' she asks, an innocent enough assumption.

'Uh, no.'

'Oh, are you sure you want to go alone? I could come—'

I interrupt her. 'That's lovely of you to offer, Poppy, but *way* beyond what I could possibly ask of you. You're already doing so much.'

'Sure, no worries.'

Do I confess now or let Poppy find out through other means? No, I should be upfront. Poppy has always been transparent with me, something I value, especially considering my current situation, and she deserves the same respect.

'Actually, I'm flying via Amsterdam. Willem's coming with me to Italy – Adriana's brother,' I clarify needlessly.

'Oh, right,' she says, drawing out 'right' with her Australian twang.

'He insisted,' I add hurriedly, shifting in my chair. I don't want Poppy thinking I've arranged some sort of romantic tryst. And hopefully she can't tell that my libido has kicked into high gear at the mere mention of his name.

'I'm glad you'll have someone there to back you up,' she says with an obvious undercurrent of doubt.

Bugger, she's onto me.

'And you have everything you need from Marie – information-wise, I mean?' she asks.

'Uh, yes, thank you. I've got Lucia's address, and the address of her gallery.'

'So, you're just showing up out of the blue?' she asks with a tinge of surprise.

'That's the plan,' I say cheerfully.

'Ahh.'

'You don't think it's a good idea? That's how Willem handled it when he broke the news to me. He showed up unannounced.'

'And how did that make you feel?' she asks. Poppy must be wearing her psychologist hat right now, but it's a fair question.

'Honestly? Blindsided, *but* – as I said to Willem earlier this week – I wouldn't have believed him if he'd approached me any other way.'

'Hmm, okay.'

'How would you do it?' I ask, now curious.

'I'm not sure. Maybe contact her and ask to meet in a neutral location.'

'Under what guise, though? Tell her we want to buy some art, then when we meet say, "Just joking. You're dating my fiancé"?'

She chuckles. 'Okay, okay... There's no good way to break this kind of news.'

'No, there isn't. At least Willem's had experience. Lucia will be number three.'

'I hadn't thought of that,' she concedes.

'And as far as bearing bad news goes, Willem was reasonably good at it,' I add. *He's probably good at lots of things*, says my inner voice, which has been getting more unruly every day.

I clear my throat, shifting in my chair again. These thoughts are not only unhelpful, they *could* derail this trip to Verona. Hard to deliver bad news sensitively when you're distracted by how sexy your travel companion is.

'Anyway, I should probably get back to work,' I say.

'Me too. Good luck with it all, Kate. And if you want to talk while you're in Italy – about *anything*,' she says, loading the word with more meaning than I'm comfortable with, 'then I'm only a phone call away, okay?'

'Thanks, Poppy. And keep me informed? About Jon, I mean.'

'Of course. Travel safely.'

'You too,' I say, which doesn't make any sense, something I only realise when the call ends.

I tut at myself as my gaze lands on the small case sitting in the corner of my office. Inside that case, amongst carefully selected outfits and my toiletries and makeup, is an unopened packet of condoms and newly acquired La Perla lingerie.

I'm not sure who *this* Kate Whitaker is – besides wanton and horny – but the woman who packed prophylactics and a lacy teddy is not the same woman who's convinced she's being altruistic by going to Verona.

The question is: can I be both Kates this weekend?

15

KATE

'Hello, love,' says Mum when she answers my call. 'You all right?'

'Hi, Mum. Yes, good thanks. How are you and Dad?'

'Oh, you know, love – feeling my age, but otherwise can't complain.' It's her typical response and it makes me smile. 'As for your father... he's the same as always.'

'That's good.'

'He *has* gone on a bit of a fitness kick of late, however.'

'So *not* the same then,' I say with a laugh.

She chuckles. 'I suppose not. He's *running*, Kate.'

'Running? *Dad?*'

'Yes. He's joined the local park run group for over sixties.'

'Oh, that's... surprising.' My dad has always made fun of runners. He can't understand why you'd want to ruin a perfectly good walk by going faster.

'It's a bloody shock is what it is,' says Mum. 'But Charlie roped him in.' Charlie is my dad's best friend.

'How long do you give it?' I ask.

'Oh, I don't know, love. If I've learned anything after nearly forty years of marriage it's that your father can still surprise me. He'll probably train for a triathlon next.'

This makes me laugh out loud, which feels glorious. One of the many, many reasons I love my mum – she can always make me laugh.

'Where are you, Kate?' Mum asks. 'It sounds busy.'

'Er, Heathrow. I'm flying to Italy tonight – for the weekend.'

'Oh, lovely. It's on the bucket list, Italy, but your father would rather stick closer to home.'

I've known this about my parents my whole life – that Mum longs to travel and Dad is a homebody whose idea of a 'grand adventure' is a train ride into Birmingham to shop at the big M&S. I keep prodding him to take Mum on a proper holiday – somewhere romantic in Europe – but he always counters with, 'Oh, Mum and I don't go in for fancy holidays, love.'

If he ever *listened*, he'd realise that Mum would very much go in for fancy holidays.

'Kate?'

'Sorry, Mum, I got distracted.'

'That's all right, love. So, are you off on a mini break then? Oh, is Margot with you? Say hello from me.'

'Margot's not here. I'm going by myself.'

'Oh,' Mum exclaims. She'll wonder why, so I'll tell her before she asks.

'It's, um... a meeting. I've got a meeting with an artist.' Not a complete lie.

'That sounds interesting,' says Mum, 'but you're not working too much, are you? I mean, having a meeting over the weekend *and* abroad...'

'I promise I'm not working too much. In fact, Mina's said she's giving me some time off soon. Two weeks.'

'Oh, that's good. Will you be going somewhere nice? And I'm assuming it's with Jon?'

The way Mum's voice sours when she says Jon's name speaks volumes. Well, she's going to love what I'm about to say next.

'Actually, that's why I called, Mum – I've got news. Jon and I… we're no longer engaged.'

There's shocked silence on the other end of the call and I just *know* Mum is trying to find a diplomatic way to respond. She and Dad only met Jon once and it was a rather tense meal during which my parents exchanged a dozen loaded looks, interspersed with lengthy silences. Jon attempted to charm them but, in retrospect, my parents saw right through him.

And of course, Margot has shared what my parents truly think of Jon – that he's pretentious, smug, and superior and they have no idea what I see in him. *Saw*, I remind myself yet again.

'Oh, well, that's a pity,' Mum says eventually.

'Mum, it's okay. I know you didn't like him.'

'I wouldn't say we didn't *like* him, Kate – just that we didn't think he was good for you.'

If she only knew.

'Yes, well, it turns out you were right.'

'Well – and I'm sure your father would agree – I'm just happy you realised before you married him.'

'Me too, Mum.'

'Oh, Kate,' she says, suddenly emotional. 'We love you so much and we're so proud of you. We only want you to be happy, love.'

'Thanks, Mum.'

What goes unsaid is that my parents believe I can only truly be happy if I am loved up – with someone deserving, of course.

'I should go. We're about to board,' I say. 'Will you break the news to Dad for me?' I ask, even though I already know she will – and happily.

'Of course. And have a brilliant time in Italy.'

'I will. I'll bring back something Italian for you.'

'As long as he's handsome and has a full head of hair,' she quips, and it takes me a moment to grasp what she's said.

'Mum,' I say with a laugh. 'I said *something* Italian – not *an* Italian.'

'Oh, well. A woman can dream, can't she?'

'Who are you and what have you done with my mother?' I deadpan.

Mum laughs heartily, a sound that warms my heart. 'Bye, love. Speak soon.' She hangs up before I reply, leaving me grinning.

Dad had better be careful – if he doesn't ramp up the romance soon, Mum might take *herself* off to Italy. Though, he's running now, which is as much of a shock as Mum joking about taking an Italian lover.

Maybe both of my parents are embarking on new horizons.

Next time I visit Rugby, I'll be more forceful about encouraging them to take a romantic holiday together. Or I could book it for them. They're both retired now – Mum from being a librarian and Dad from a career as a carpenter – so their schedule is wide open. And Dad can hardly say no if everything's booked and paid for, can he? Especially if it's my gift to them for their upcoming fortieth wedding anniversary.

It's decided. I'm sending my parents on a romantic holiday.

* * *

'*Hallo.*'

I turn around with a start, spilling my coffee on the tabletop.

'Sorry,' says Willem.

'That's okay,' I say, mopping up the spill with a napkin. 'I was expecting you – I'm not sure how you managed to startle me.'

He sits opposite me, his broad shoulders shrugging. 'How was your flight?' he asks.

'Uneventful.'

'Those are always the best ones,' he says, a cheeky twinkle in his eyes.

'Yes, I suppose they are,' I say with a laugh.

He looks around. 'Nice place,' he comments.

I've been here before – I have international lounge access through work – but to me it's simply another airport lounge that happens to be in Amsterdam.

'Er, yes. They have a full bar, if you'd like something,' I say, pointing over my shoulder.

'Actually, I'd love a beer.' He stands. 'Can I get you anything?' His eyes dip to my half-empty, now-cold coffee.

'Sure, thanks. Gentleman's choice,' I add with a smile.

A funny look passes over his face, then he goes to the bar.

'Gentleman's choice?' I say to myself. If I *am* going to make a play for Willem, I'll need to brush up on my flirtation skills. I sound like the heroine from one of Mum's old Mills & Boons, the ones Margot and I used to steal from her bedside table and read under the covers when we were eight and nine.

Willem returns with two pints of beer and hands one to

me. I don't generally drink beer, but when I do, it's a half-pint not a full one.

'Brewed by women,' he says.

'Oh, great.'

'That's the name of the brewery,' he clarifies. '*Gebrouwen door Vrouwen*. Excellent beer – this is their Tricky Tripel. *Prost.*'

'*Prost.*' I clink my glass against his, then take a sip and it's delicious. 'Oh, that is good.'

'And potent – nearly twice the alcohol as most beer.'

He sips, raising his brows at me over the rim of the glass. How is it possible to be drinking a cold beer and about to melt at the same time? And is he flirting? He did just hand me a pint of potent beer – does that mean something? Something more than 'Hey, I thought you might be thirsty'? I suppose I *am* thirsty, but not for a beverage.

I look away, wishing I could fan myself without giving anything away. It's suddenly very hot in here.

'How was the rest of your week?' I ask instead.

'Busy. I've been back to see my client in Bruges – I only returned this morning.'

'Oh, I didn't realise. You could have cancelled. It can be exhausting travelling for work.'

He shrugs again. 'I'm used to it. It's only three hours by train.'

'So, your clients, are they companies, individuals...?'

'Both – and everything in between. We've worked with multi-national companies, government agencies, celebrities...'

'Wowser. Anyone I'd know?' I ask, leaning close. I'm not really one to follow celebrity news, but it is rather intriguing.

'Probably, but I wouldn't be a very good security specialist if I told you now, would I?'

I lean back, laughing. 'No, I suppose not.' We exchange smiles. 'You obviously enjoy what you do,' I say.

'Mostly,' he replies without further explanation. 'And you? You enjoy your work?'

I nod, breaking into an involuntary grin. 'I do. Mum says I was destined to become a project manager from when I was little. I was always the organiser – my classmates, my friends, even Mum and Dad. I ran the family calendar from when I was seven.'

Willem smiles.

'And in primary school, I'd finish my work early and my teachers would give me administrative tasks. They probably weren't supposed to do that, but it kept me engaged.'

'And that's what you studied at university?'

'Yes. I finished my degree, then went straight on to earn a master's in project and program management and innovation.'

I don't mention that I was awarded an academic scholarship, nor that my parents secured a bursary to help fund my studies. I also lived at home to save money and had a part-time job in a local gift shop. All these factors contributed to me developing a strong work ethic and an appreciation of fiscal responsibility. I never took my education for granted and I was more likely to be found in the library on a Friday night than at the pub.

My so-called fiancé once told me how much he admired this about me – how hard I've had to work and what I've achieved. Ironic, really, when he *hasn't* worked hard and he hasn't achieved anything. Unless spending his inheritance and conning innocent women counts.

'Anyway,' I say, continuing before I give in to thoughts of Jon, 'I'd say I'm most fulfilled when I've got oversight of the big picture and see how all the pieces fit together. I'm one of those strange people who genuinely loves a dynamic spreadsheet,' I add with a dash of self-deprecation. Though from what I've seen of Willem so far, I'm not the only one who gravitates towards order.

'What's not to love?' he asks, playing along with mock-seriousness.

'Right? Dynamic spreadsheets can be *very* sexy.'

Oh my god, I did not say that.

'I'm not sure I've heard of that sexual inclination before, not even in Amsterdam. And we're very progressive here.'

His mouth twitches, making me wish I could rewind to the moment right before I referred to project management software as 'sexy'.

Although, it's better than saying *he's* sexy, which he *is* – and which I've been trying to ignore since he showed up wearing worn-in jeans and a white, loose-weaved dress shirt with the sleeves rolled up.

I take a mistimed sip of beer, and pro tip from me: it's impossible to swallow and gasp at the same time. I cough and splutter, banging on my chest. Eventually, the beer goes down the right way, but not before the embarrassment kicks in.

'Sorry,' I say, peering at him, then immediately looking away. Concerned Willem may be the sexiest Willem yet.

'Oh.' The way he says it draws my gaze. 'We've had a gate change.' He's looking up at the departure board. 'And it's down the other end of the concourse. We should go.'

He stands, downing half his beer in one go, but I won't bother matching him. Even the little I've had has gone to my head and he's got several stone on me. I take one more sip – it really is delicious – then stand and gather my belongings.

'And I'll take this,' he says, indicating my luggage.

I'm used to wheeling my carry-on case around airports, but

it doesn't seem negotiable, and I can't say I mind this small kindness. It's another reminder that there are decent men out there and Willem is one of them.

He downs the rest of his beer, stifles a burp behind his hand, which is somehow endearing, then breaks into a smile. 'Ready?' he asks.

'Ready.'

We depart the lounge, Willem indicating which way to go, and I fall into step beside him. As we make our way to the gate, half the people we pass do a double take when they see Willem and the other half outright stare. I glance up at him, and he seems oblivious to the attention – another tick in his ever-growing 'plus' column.

Sometimes when I was out with Jon, it was like he craved attention from others, especially attractive and well-dressed people. He'd raise his voice or gesture wildly – occasionally, he'd laugh loudly out of the blue. At the time, I thought it was an indication of his confidence. Now I recognise that he was starved for attention, a sign that he actually *lacks* confidence.

Whereas Willem exudes it, which is incredibly sexy. Pretty much everything about the man is sexy. And I'm about to spend the weekend with him. My eyes drop to the handle of my case, which is enveloped by Willem's enormous hand. If only he knew what's inside it.

My phone notifies me of a message, and I fish it out of my tote as we walk. It's from Margot:

Did you pack condoms?

Horrified, I look over at Willem, but his eyes are trained straight ahead. I slip the phone back into my tote. Margot may be right on the money, but I don't want to admit to her that I've planned ahead, just in case.

Like it matters. She'll either tease me relentlessly until something happens between me and Willem or tease me relentlessly because nothing ever eventuates. Either way, Margot is invested in me having rebound sex. With Willem.

'Kate?' Willem calls.

I stop, realising I've been so deep in thought, I strode past the gate. I backtrack and join him in the queue.

'Sorry. I'm a little distracted.'

His concerned face makes another appearance. 'I can imagine. It's big.'

Please tell me he's bragging about the size of his penis...

'Uh...'

'Remember, I've gone through it, so I know,' he continues, cutting through the noise inside my head. He reaches out and runs his hand reassuringly down my arm. 'But don't worry, I'll be there with you.'

Jesus – this bloke is too good to be true – there's got to be *something* wrong with him. Oh, that's right. He's the brother of my fiancé's other fiancée and getting involved with him would make a messy situation even messier.

I wish my libido would get the memo.

'It's a nice-looking building,' I say, regarding the modern, four-storey façade in the dim light of a nearby streetlamp.

Willem, who has been around the corner retrieving the key from a lockbox, joins me on the stoop and looks up. 'It's nice,' he says, 'but I prefer that.' His gaze goes to the building next door, its crumbling stucco a dark salmon-pink.

'Then why did you book us accommodation in a brand-new building?' I ask with a laugh.

'Because I thought you would prefer it,' he replies matter-of-factly.

'Oh.'

He unlocks the front door and motions for me to go first. I do, and an automated sensor floods the white marble lobby with bright light, making me blink. It's stark, sleek, and so modern, we could be anywhere in the world.

For some reason, Willem believes this is my preference, but when I knew I was coming to Verona, a city that was founded two thousand years ago, I had something more traditional in mind.

'It's on the first floor,' he says, stooping to pick up my case then jogging up the stairs, his case in the other hand. I follow, eyeing the lift longingly, bone-weary after a long evening of travel. I want a shower, then to climb into bed and pass out.

Not even the close proximity of a god-like travel companion will keep me awake.

Willem unlocks the large front door of the flat and swings it open, stepping aside so I can enter first. I quickly take in the large entry, the sleek, modern kitchen, the combined lounge and dining room, which is decorated in 'IKEA chic', and the bathroom that boasts a bidet (I still don't know how you're supposed to use those) and a ginormous shower.

Perfect for two people! shouts my inner voice.

Ignoring it, I walk further into the flat, scouting for the doors to the bedrooms but instead, come face to face – or is it face to bookcase? – with a divider that separates a super king bed from the rest of the flat.

'*What?*' growls Willem. I turn to face him, and he's clearly confused. He spins around and strides the length of the flat, then returns seconds later. 'It's supposed to sleep four people. I thought that meant there were two bedrooms.'

There are patently *not* two bedrooms. Technically, there isn't even one.

He takes his phone out of his pocket and jabs at the screen, his face contorted with frustration.

'Fuck,' he says, as he reads his phone screen. His head swivels to the sofa. '*That* becomes a bed.' He meets my eye, his countenance uneasy. 'Sorry, Kate. I've completely messed up. I thought it would be simpler to rent an apartment... *and* that we'd have two bedrooms... I'll go check into a hotel.' He turns to leave.

'Wait.' I reach out and stop him, my hand landing on his forearm. 'It's past eleven, we both worked today, and we've been in transit for hours... We can stay here together. It'll be fine.'

'Are you sure?'

'Yes.' *No.* Not one of my imagined seduction scenarios began with an accommodation mix-up and a pissed-off travel companion.

And I could kid myself that sharing a flat was perfectly normal when there were going to be *bedrooms*, but now the only thing between us will be an IKEA bookcase – one with a clear view of the other side.

Oh, Margot is going to *love* this when I tell her.

16

KATE

I had a rubbish night's sleep – unsurprising, really. By the time we'd squabbled over who got the super king – against my protestations, Willem insisted it be me, as he was the one who'd messed up the accommodation – *and* converted the sofa to a bed, making it up with the extra bedding, it was nearing midnight.

I used the bathroom first and while Willem was in there, I slipped beneath the covers and tugged them up to my chin like a child who's afraid of the dark, then reached over and turned off the lamp.

So much for the sexy temptress who'd packed lingerie.

Willem emerged from the bathroom a few minutes later, and before the flat was plunged into darkness, I got a peek of him in his boxer briefs through the bookcase. There was a rustle of bedding, then a deep, husky, 'Goodnight, Kate. Sleep well.'

'Uh, goodnight,' I replied, instantly embarrassed by how squeaky my voice sounded. Willem either didn't notice or was too polite to comment. Then I lay awake for a good hour while my monkey brain swung from one thought to the next, intermittently landing on questions I already knew the answer to.

Why did you agree to share a flat with Willem, rather than getting a hotel room?

All the better to 'accidentally' tumble into bed together...

Did you actually *come to Verona for altruistic reasons?*

Yes... No... Sort of.

Is it really *a good idea to seduce the Norse god?*

Probably not, but I'm entitled to a little fun.

How can this situation with Willem possibly turn out like you want it to?

I'll never know if I don't try.

And then the clincher, the thought that tormented me for the rest of the night:

He's a decent bloke, Kate – kind, supportive, thoughtful... You can't just shag him for a lark – despite what Margot says. One of you could end up hurt – you both could.

That's the thing about self-truths: they have a way of working their way to the surface, no matter how hard you try to kid yourself.

And I can no longer ignore that I'm drawn to Willem for more than his looks. Which complicates this situation even further.

I'd lie here examining this conundrum further, but I'm desperate for the loo and I can't tell if Willem's awake. Will passing by his bed or closing the bathroom door wake him? I wait a few minutes longer, listening out for signs he's awake, and when I can't stand it any longer, I climb out of bed and tiptoe around the end of the bookcase into the lounge.

When I glance to my left, Willem is scrolling his phone, one arm behind his head. His eyes fix on mine and he smiles.

'Good morning. I wasn't sure if you were awake yet, so I was careful not to make any noise.'

'Me too,' I confess, 'but I... uh...' I point towards the bathroom. 'I'm just going to...'

I rush across the room, conscious that I'm only wearing a nightgown – a *short* nightgown – and close myself in the bathroom. After weeing, I wash my hands and splash water on my face. I dry my hands and face and regard myself in the mirror. Not bad, I'll admit. I've certainly looked worse in the morning. But before I go back out there, I quickly run my toothbrush around my mouth and rinse. It's unlikely that Thor and I are going to lock lips any time soon, but if morning breath can be avoided, it should be.

When I open the bathroom door, I'm confronted with the aroma of coffee. I round the corner into the kitchen and Willem is at the coffee maker, wearing the jeans he had on yesterday and nothing else.

Fuck me – and I mean that both figuratively and literally, because even in profile, I can tell he's got a muscular V that points to his groin.

As if you need directions, Kate.

'That smells good,' I say, passing by him to go to the fridge. Our host has been generous, supplying us with milk, cheese, and eggs.

'They only have pods,' he says apologetically, and I recall that he has a proper coffee machine back in Amsterdam.

'That's okay, I don't mind. I could make some breakfast? There are eggs.'

He turns, and the full force of his potent gaze nearly knocks me off my feet.

'I thought we could get an early start – have a quick coffee here, then stop somewhere for breakfast. Maybe get some *real* coffee,' he adds with a slightly superior smirk. So, a coffee snob then. Honestly, I'm happy enough with Douwe Egberts. That's all I have at home.

'Oh, okay. Sounds good.'

He hands me a mug of coffee and I busy myself with adding milk, then offer it to him. He declines, instead adding some cold water from a bottle and drinking his black.

'What time do you think Lucia will be at the gallery?' I ask, purposefully avoiding looking anywhere below his neck. Though, he's so handsome, it turns out to be a rubbish tactic for keeping my libido in check. Or my heart, which is now fluttering faster than a hummingbird's wings.

'Her website says 12 p.m. but...' He lifts a shoulder in a half-shrug.

'Time is a little more fluid here than in the Netherlands?' I ask.

'That's my experience. But, since you've never been here before, I'd really like to show you some of my favourite places before we go to the gallery.'

'That's— You don't need to do that.'

'Oh.' His face falls. This obviously means more to him than I thought.

'But, if you're offering, then I'd *love* it. I mean, *appreciate* it. It's such a beautiful city – from what I saw last night, and I've seen pictures and videos online, of course. And a couple of films that were set here.'

I sip my coffee, more to shut myself up than for the caffeine. I can tell he's watching me. Probably wondering why I've suddenly been afflicted with verbal diarrhoea.

'Good,' he says, flashing a lipless smile. 'Did you want to take the first shower?' he offers.

'Yep, great.' I leave my half-drunk coffee and beeline to the bedroom area, where I quickly check the forecast, then cast my eyes over the contents of my case. Which of the outfits I've brought will be most suitable for sightseeing with a gorgeous Dutchman, then breaking a stranger's heart?

I opt for light-blue linen palazzo pants, a white linen T-shirt, and espadrilles, which should be comfortable enough for walking on cobblestoned streets.

Twenty minutes later, I've showered and dressed, and as I apply my makeup, I try not to think about the naked man showering at the other end of the flat.

'*Kate*,' I say to myself in the mirror by the bed, 'you're here to break the bad news to Lucia. This isn't a romantic getaway, you muppet.'

'Sorry, were you talking to me?' Willem calls out.

'No, I uh…' *GAH!* 'Ready to go?' I ask, hoping like hell he didn't hear what I said.

'Almost – just need to put my shoes on.'

While he does that, I quickly slick some gloss over my lower lip and press my lips together, then drop it into my handbag. I grab one of the two scarves I've brought and tie it around the bag's strap, then slide my sunglasses onto my head like a headband. I slip the bag over one shoulder and join Willem in the lounge area.

Annoyingly, he looks great – and he's only wearing jeans and a T-shirt. Faded jeans and a white T-shirt. I look down at my outfit, then back at him. Obviously realising the same thing, he starts chuckling.

'We match.'

'We do,' I say.

'Want me to change—' He lifts the hem of his T-shirt.

'*No.*'

God, if I have to look at his bare torso for a second longer, I won't be responsible for my actions.

He lets go of the T-shirt and eyes me curiously.

'Sorry. It's fine – let's just go.'

I lead the way out of the flat into the crisp morning air. I really need to get a grip. Before meeting Willem, I was calm, articulate, measured... Now I sound like I've forgotten how to form a coherent sentence.

He must think I'm a moron.

That makes two of us.

* * *

After stopping at a local trattoria for espressos and ham and cheese *polpettes* – delicious savoury balls – we've spent the rest of the morning roaming the city, Willem in the lead and me following, open-mouthed.

It's beautiful here.

Even something as simple as a row of houses, their cracked and patched brick and stucco façades a testament to the centuries they've endured, and their window boxes bursting with bright-red geraniums, is a thing of beauty.

I must have stared at the Duomo for a good five minutes, drinking in its imposing stature and the intricate tableaux of the stained-glass windows. And the view from Castel San Pietro was breathtaking – literally, as it sits atop a steep hill and we climbed the steps instead of taking the funicular. Verona is even more striking from on high, its centre densely packed, with a dozen spires dotting the skyline.

And the Adige River! Fast-flowing, icy-blue water spanned by the most incredible bridges. Pont Pietra, visible from the vantage point at the castle, was built two thousand years ago, with dozens of additions and fixes over the centuries. Up close, it's a patchwork of stone and brick and it seems miraculous that it's still standing.

Everything about this morning has been incredible. We've skirted through side streets, marvelling at the weathered wooden doors – or maybe that was just me – and wandered through piazzas, gazing up at marble statues, palatial staircases, and ornate balconies.

Every moment has been an excellent distraction from obsessing over the moment I will come face to face with Lucia.

Now we're outside her gallery, both dumbstruck as we stare at the handwritten sign. Even in Italian, it's easy to make out what it says – essentially, that the gallery is closed for the week, because Lucia is on holiday.

'My Italian isn't great – actually, it's practically non-existent,' I admit, 'but that says what I think it says, right?'

'Yes.'

We exchange a look, then Willem walks over and cups his hands against the glass door to peer inside. 'Definitely closed,' he says, stepping back.

'So, what do we do now?' I ask.

'We go to her house.'

'We can do that' – I point to the sign, specifically to where it says 'Mykonos' – 'but I doubt she's going to be home.'

He expels a frustrated sigh. 'You're right.'

'I suppose there are some things that even a tech genius can't foresee.'

He gives me an odd, almost shy look. 'I'm hardly a genius.'

'I was talking about Marie.'

'Oh.'

'But you clearly have skills as well.'

'Thank you – I *think*,' he teases, his blue eyes twinkling.

Oh god, here comes another heart flutter. I'll need to see a cardiologist if this keeps up.

'Look, we've been on our feet for hours,' I say, trying to ignore my telltale heart. 'What do you say we find somewhere to have lunch and figure out what to do next?'

'Okay. But I *would* like to go to her house. Just to be sure.'

I stare at him a moment. The chances that Lucia is having a staycation and lied on her sign to throw people off her scent are almost nil. But we did come all this way. We might as well check her other known address.

'All right, let's go.'

He takes his phone out of his pocket and a moment later, looks up and says, 'This way.'

'Is it terrible that I'm relieved?' I ask after we give our order to the waiter – a gruff man with a salt-and-pepper moustache and an obvious disdain for tourists.

'That Lucia's not in Verona?' asks Willem.

I nod. 'Although, it's just kicking it into the long grass, isn't it? I'll have to come back at some point.'

'*We* will have to come back.'

I regard him closely, at war with myself. Do I want to spend more time with Willem? Absolutely. Should I be sorting out my disastrous love life before I even *entertain* thoughts about another man? Absolutely times two.

Was it therefore ridiculous of me to pack lacy knickers and condoms for this trip? Absolutely times a million.

'Look, Willem, I really appreciate all your help, but you've already done so much. And that's not counting showing me around Verona,' I add with a smile, hoping to soften my words.

He studies me intently, his incredible blue eyes boring into mine. I almost lose my nerve and call for the bill. Right now, I'd like nothing more than to drag him back to our accommodation and use every square inch of that super king bed.

I clear my throat. 'What I'm saying is—'

'Kate, I'm not going to abandon you.'

'Abandon me? Letting me handle this myself isn't abandoning me, Willem. I'm perfectly capable of breaking the news to Lucia by myself,' I retort crossly.

His lifts both palms to placate me and I clamp my mouth shut before I give him a right bollocking.

'I know you can do this by yourself, Kate. You're intelligent and capable—'

I scoff, cutting him off with a grunt.

'What?' he asks. 'Is something funny?'

'No, not funny – just you calling me "intelligent".'

'You are. You're other things too, but your intelligence isn't in dispute.'

'He says to the woman who was duped by a con man.'

'That's not...' He sighs. 'I would like to go back.'

'To the flat?'

Maybe he wants to ravish me on that giant bed. Gah, bloody inner voice – shut it!

'No,' he replies, 'to the part of the conversation where you got angry with me.'

'Oh, well, I wouldn't say *angry*, more annoyed.'

His lips disappear between his teeth for a moment, and he stares at me intently before releasing them. 'Kate, I want you to see this situation through my eyes.'

'Sorry,' I say. 'Go ahead.'

'A couple of months ago, Ady told me about Dunn – that she'd met this man, that he was older and different from the men she'd dated before – actually, they were more like "boys",' he says with a snort, and I recall what Adriana told me about her exes.

'Anyway, at the time, I didn't think much of it – Ady's her own person. But then a few weeks ago, suddenly they're engaged. Now *that* raised my suspicions. I hadn't met him, our parents hadn't met him... And they'd only been together, for what? Two months? That's strange, right?'

I nod, even though Jon and I hadn't been together long when I agreed to marry him – a little over three months. But even that was considered fast by most people's standards. My parents apparently thought so, and Margot certainly did. She's never shut up about it.

'But when I initially looked into him,' Willem continues, 'I didn't expect to find anything.'

'Really?' I ask.

'Well, no, nothing like this. It was simply due diligence, a way to set my mind at ease. Like I said, I've always been protective of Ady, so I planned to conduct a cursory search, appease any concerns I had, and never mention it to Ady.'

'And then you found me,' I say quietly.

'And then I found you. You may not *need* my help, Kate, but I wish you'd let me give it. Just like with Ady, I feel protective of you. Dunn is a horrible man, and I hate what he did to you – to both of you – and I want to play my part in exposing him. I want to make sure he never does this again.'

My breath hitches and I swallow the lump in my throat. I had no idea when I first laid eyes on Willem that he might become someone I felt emotionally safe with, but that's what's starting to happen.

'That's... I appreciate that, thank you.'

'So, you'll accept my help?' he asks.

'Sure,' I reply.

One word, but it speaks volumes. *Sure, Willem, I'll let you adopt the role of big brother, vigilante, and protector of foolish women everywhere.*

It's probably for the best, him seeing me that way. Now I won't be distracted by lustful thoughts of Willem – *or* romantic ones – while I excise Jon from my life.

Hah! If only that were true.

17

KATE

Lunch was absolutely delicious. *So* delicious, I set aside my wayward thoughts and feelings so I could properly enjoy the *brasato all'Amarone*, beef that's been slow-cooked in Valpolicella, a regional red wine – accompanied by a glass, of course. That's after devouring two slices of thick-cut bread I drizzled with olive oil.

I am full as a tick, as my dad would say. Willem may have to give me a piggyback ride after that meal.

Also, something occurred to me over lunch and after the waiter clears our plates, I broach it. 'I was thinking,' I begin, and Willem drags his eyes from our river view. 'We planned on being here the whole weekend in case Lucia wasn't around today, but with her in Greece, we don't have any reason to stay. We could change our flights and leave this afternoon?'

'You don't want to go to the opera?' he asks, that cheeky glint in his eye.

'The opera?' I ask with a mocking smile. '*You* like going to the opera?'

He leans back in his chair and laughs. 'What? A man like me isn't supposed to like opera?'

'It may not seem like it, but I didn't mean to be insulting. I'm surprised is all. You seem like the type of bloke who— Never mind,' I say, cutting myself off.

'Oh no, you need to finish that sentence. The type of bloke who what?'

'I only meant that you seem like... well, more of a man's man.'

His brows lift a full inch. 'And what exactly is a man's man? I'm not sure I'm familiar with that English expression.'

'Hah!' I retort. 'As we've previously established, your English is flawless, so I don't buy that for a second. You know exactly what I mean.'

He doesn't reply; he just stares at me with that tractor-beam gaze and a faint smile. Does he know the power he has, making my breath catch and my heart pound simply by setting his eyes on me? Maybe he's oblivious – some men are.

And there's the (not-so) minor matter that he's protective of me like a brother would be. Nothing sexy about that. Well, the protectiveness part is sexy, the brotherly part... not so much.

I return Willem's gaze, wondering what's really going through that mind of his. Maybe this is him flirting. Maybe he doesn't think of me as a sibling, after all.

God, I wish I knew for sure, but I'm a little rusty in this area. Jon and I never flirted with each other. In retrospect, our relationship was rather perfunctory.

'So, the opera...' I say, steering the conversation away from Willem's man's manliness.

'It's really spectacular here,' he replies lightly, letting me off the hook. 'They perform in the Arena di Verona. We didn't get to that part of the city, but it's worth seeing – with or without the opera. The Romans built it.'

'Oh, that does sound incredible. I guess I would like that.'

'Should I get tickets?'

'Sorry, I meant *someday*.'

'Why not tonight?' he asks.

Because that would be too much like a date and then we'd return to the flat that doesn't have any walls and I'm not entirely sure you're as into me as I'm into you and I don't want to launch myself at you and have you reject me.

What I *say* is entirely different. 'Because the past two weeks have been... well, exhausting. And with Lucia away, I really do think we should leave Verona today.'

He stares at me again, which is equally thrilling and unnerving, and I look away.

The waiter comes outside and starts fussing with the other tables, pushing in the chairs and gathering the place settings. I look around, realising we're the last people here and they must be closing for siesta.

'*Scusi, il conto, per favore?*' I call out.

He nods curtly and disappears inside.

'I thought your Italian was practically non-existent,' says Willem.

'Other than the basics, it is – and there are probably more polite ways to ask, but I've never had an aptitude for languages. Not for want of trying.'

The waiter returns, and when I unlock my phone to pay, Willem protests. 'You got breakfast,' I say.

'That was coffee and *polpettes* – a few euros.'

I tap my phone and the transaction goes through. 'You can buy lunch next time we're here,' I say. *And* now I've agreed that he can come with me when I return.

'Okay,' he says, backing down.

I stand and slip my handbag over my shoulder. 'Ready?'

Willem gets up and slides his chair under the table, and I do the same.

'Where to?' he asks.

'We should probably go back to the flat and look into changing our flights.'

He regards me for a moment, then puts his sunglasses on. 'Okay, Kate,' he says, and it's hard to say if I'm relieved or disappointed. 'This way,' he says for the tenth time today, and I rush to catch up.

'I meant to ask…' I say, falling into step with him. 'How is it you know Verona so well?'

Without breaking stride, he replies, 'My ex-girlfriend lived here.'

'Your ex-girlfriend? You never said anything.'

He looks down at me, his eyes hidden behind the dark glasses. 'Maybe one day I will.'

Right, that's me put in my place then. Just when I thought there might be more between us than a mutual dilemma.

* * *

'You're back in London already? And what do you mean she wasn't there?' asks Margot incredulously.

'Exactly that. We went to her gallery and there was a hand-written sign on the door saying she was on holiday in Mykonos.' I take the phone away from my ear and swap to speakerphone so I can unpack while I talk. It's after 10 p.m. and all I want to do is fall into bed, but I won't be able to sleep until I've put everything in its place.

'Who does that? Who sticks a handwritten sign on the door, then leaves for a week?'

'Jon's new girlfriend, that's who. And apparently, it's not uncommon – although Willem said it's mostly in August when half of Europe is on holiday.'

'So, what's happening there?' she asks.

'Happening? What do you mean?' I reply cagily, not wanting to go into it.

'Stop pretending,' she chastises. 'You know exactly what I mean.'

'Nothing happened – exactly as I'd intended,' I add hurriedly.

I deliberately haven't told Margot about the sleeping arrangements because she'll only harp on about it.

'Uh-huh,' she replies, and I can clearly picture her look of disbelief.

'So, what did you get up to last night?' I ask. I'm becoming a master at changing the subject.

'Book launch – for my friend, Gayle. You remember her?'

'Oh, yes, the illustrator.'

'And satirist – brilliant gal.'

'Is this the picture book about divorce?'

'That's the one – it's *hilarious*, Kate.'

'How can it *not* be? I mean, the topic alone – that's a laugh a minute, right there.'

'Yep,' she replies, missing my sarcasm. 'I bought you a copy – Gayle signed it.'

'But why? Isn't it for women who are divorced – or *getting* divorced?'

'It's for all of us, every woman who's been wronged. There's an entire section on cheating bastards.'

'Oh,' I say, suddenly deflated. I stop what I'm doing and sit heavily on the edge of my bed. 'I suppose you're right about that. God, Margs, I'm a woman scorned.'

'Well, don't get all maudlin on me. You're not Tess of the bloody d'Urbervilles.'

'Tess—' I wave my hand, even though she can't see me. 'Doesn't matter. It's just that now I'm one of those women who—'

'Who was in a relationship with a narcissistic arsehole. *Yes*, yes, you are. Welcome to the club. And it's a massive bloody club!'

Wonderful – Margot's on one of her all-men-are-bastards rants.

Run away, run away! I shout in my head, conjuring John Cleese from my dad's favourite Monty Python film.

'So, it was a good book launch?' I ask brightly.

'Oh, Kate, it was brilliant,' she replies, seamlessly reverting to supportive-friend mode. 'I'm so proud of Gayle. This book is going to fly, you know.'

'I'm sure it will. And thank you for getting me a copy. I can't wait to read it.'

'It's one of those if-I-don't-laugh-I'll-cry things,' she says, likely to be helpful but failing miserably.

'Great!' I exclaim. 'Look, I should crack on with unpacking, then get to bed.'

'Okay, but brunch tomorrow?' she asks.

'Sure,' I reply. I do have a lot to catch her up on, including that I've told Mum and Dad that the engagement is over.

'Good. I want to hear all about why you didn't sleep with Thor.'

'Margot!'

'Byeee,' she chirrups, leaving me sniggering to myself.

* * *

When I wake on Sunday morning, there's already a text message from Jon. I read it sleepily then bolt upright.

Hi beautiful. I'm unexpectedly back in London. Can I take you to lunch?

'*Bugger*,' I exclaim aloud.

Ignoring that he's probably been in London this entire week, considering Poppy met him at the Langham on Wednesday, how do I get out of seeing him when it's been *weeks*? As far as Jon's concerned, we're happily engaged. And until the agency's plan to fully ensnare Jon comes to fruition, including the collective confrontation, Adriana and I are not supposed to let on that we know about each other.

BUT I DO NOT WANT TO SEE HIM. It will be difficult enough facing Jon with Adriana by my side.

Poppy! Poppy will know what to do. Is 8.47 a.m. too early to call someone on a Sunday? If it were Margot, that would be a resounding yes – any time before 10 a.m. is considered an afront to her very being. When she said 'brunch' last night, she meant no earlier than noon.

I decide to call Poppy at 9 a.m. – surely that's a reasonable enough hour – then scroll socials while the minutes click over, which they eventually do, even though thirteen minutes feels like an *age*.

'Good morning, Kate,' she answers cheerily and not at all like I've dragged her from a lazy lie-in.

'Hi, Poppy, I am *so* sorry to call you at the weekend – *again*. And I promise I won't make a habit of it.' It's probably an empty promise – this makes two weekends in a row.

'It's okay,' she says with a trilling laugh. Maybe she's used to clients bothering her outside of work hours. 'What's up?'

I tell her about Jon's message and she sucks her breath through her teeth, which does *not* instil confidence.

'And where is he supposed to be right now?'

'Bangkok. Or Stockholm. Madrid maybe. So many lies, I've lost track.'

'Right. Hmm.'

'Poppy, I really don't want to see him. I was hoping I could fob him off with text messages until all this gets sorted.'

'No, I understand. You *could* tell him you're busy.'

'It'd be a dead giveaway that something's up. It's been weeks since I've seen him and any time he's "unexpectedly" shown up before, I've dropped everything. Oh... I've just realised how that sounds, how it makes *me* sound.'

'Don't be so hard on yourself.'

'You don't understand, Poppy. I've always prided myself on being independent. It's one of the traits Jon said he was drawn to, my independence, but now I'm realising I was essentially at his beck and call.'

'His deception was comprehensive and multi-layered, Kate. You can't be blamed for being blinkered by it. You don't think any less of Adriana because it happened to her, do you?'

'No, definitely not. I don't know her very well, but she seems like she has her head on straight.'

'Exactly, so why not afford yourself that same level of compassion?'

'Okay, I take your point.'

'Don't worry – lots of people are harder on themselves than on others. I do that sometimes,' she adds, and I wonder if it's only to make me feel better.

'Thanks for understanding,' I reply.

'Course, no worries. Now, what are we going to do about Dunn?'

Something comes to mind but I'm reluctant to ask – it's big.

'Uh, Poppy… Do you think maybe *you* could have lunch with Jon today?'

'Me?'

'Never mind – it's way too much to ask.'

'It is a lot, but the main problem is that Jon thinks Penny's already back in Melbourne.'

'Oh, that's right. I forgot.'

'Yeah. I've been messaging him since Friday about how bad the jetlag is.'

I snigger. 'Is it terrible that there's some satisfaction in that?'

'In me lying to him?' she asks.

'Yes.'

Now she laughs. 'Not at all. And if you consider the extent of our plan – particularly that you're having to fly back to Verona next week – then lying in a few text messages is no biggie.'

'Hmm… fair.'

'Now, getting back to today's problem…' she says. 'What if you're not in London right now? Your parents live in the Midlands, right?'

'Yes, they live in Rugby,' I reply.

'So, you're visiting your parents and you're so, *so* sorry, but you can't meet for lunch today.'

'That's good, I like it. But what about tomorrow? He'll know I need to be back in London for work. What if he suggests lunch – or worse, *dinner*?'

'Does Elev8te have clients outside of London? What if

you're on a work trip for once?'

'Of *course*. How did I not think of that? It's as if any time I'm in Jon's orbit – even peripherally – I lose ten per cent of my intelligence.'

'That's you being hard on yourself again. We all have blind spots when it comes to the people close to us.'

'Thanks, Poppy. And I think this will work. I'll tell him I'm at my parents today and that I'm working from the Birmingham office for the rest of the week.'

'Oh, Eleva8te has an office in Birmingham?'

'We don't, but Jon doesn't have a clue. Thinking back, he showed very little interest in what I do.'

'So, what if he decides to come to you?'

'He won't. Jon's a total snob when it comes to the Midlands – there's no way he'll show up uninvited. And he's typically on to the next destination within a week, so...'

'Hopefully it's not Verona.'

'Oh, fuck. What if it is?'

'Yeah... I'll get Marie onto it – determine his travel plans for the next few weeks. If he's off to Verona next weekend, then you should probably postpone.'

'But what if it's to propose? Marie said he's already purchased another ring.'

'Oh, that's right. Well, let's cross that bridge when we come to it. If we determine that Jon *does* plan to propose to Lucia next weekend, then we'll have to regroup. Leave it with me?'

'Okay.'

'And, Kate...' I can tell she's hedging and I'm almost positive I know why.

'Yes?'

'Look, I know I'm not technically your matchmaker now

this case has taken a left turn, but do you have romantic feelings for Willem de Vries?'

Oh god.

'Why do you ask that?' I ask, deflecting like a novice.

'If I'm totally off-base...' she says, giving me an out even though she is very much *on* base, 'then I apologise. But if I'm not, then please take care. You've gone through a lot with Jon, and it can take time to heal from something like that.'

'Okay,' I reply wanly.

Poppy's cautionary words only amplify the doubts I've had while playing the does-he-doesn't-he? guessing game when it comes to Willem's feelings. Even if he *does* see me in a romantic light, Poppy clearly thinks it's a bad idea to embark on something new – with anyone.

'Anyway,' she says, cheery again, 'I'll get onto Marie, and you enjoy your Sunday.'

'Thanks, I'll try.'

After we ring off, I sit with my phone in my hands for a few moments.

If Jon *is* planning on proposing to Lucia next weekend, then we need to intervene beforehand. If there's one thing Jon is good at besides lying, it's proposals. I'd hate for him to tell Lucia she's the love of his life – and for her to believe it – then drop the same bombshell on her that Willem dropped on me. That cannot happen. I may not have met Lucia yet, but she doesn't deserve that. No one does.

And as for Poppy's warning... If I discover that Willem de Vries feels the same way I do, it will take all my willpower to turn him down.

18

POPPY

'Tell us absolutely everything,' says Lauren, her eyes alight with curiosity. Lauren is obsessed with celebrity gossip and seemingly anything that resembles it, like a case about a con man who collects fiancées.

'I told you about it in the group chat,' I reply with a laugh.

'I want *details*, Poppy. Geez.'

'Okay, but I'm not sure what else to tell you.'

We've invited our friends around for Sunday lunch and Tristan's making one of his signature dishes: roast beef with all the trimmings. While Ravi's keeping him company in the kitchen, we women – me, Jacinda, Shaz, and Lauren – are stretched out on facing sofas, sipping drinks and catching up.

'Start with when you approached him,' says Lauren. 'What was that like? Was it strange?' she asks, her eyes narrowed with curiosity.

'Well, yeah. I mean, I've been undercover for cases before, but that was me pretending to be a journalist. This was hitting on a stranger.'

'A *dodgy* stranger,' Shaz interjects.

'*So* dodgy,' I agree.

'And?' Lauren's twirling hand signals for me to expound.

'*And* I arrived at the hotel, I saw him in the bar – which is where we expected him to be – and I climbed onto the stool next to his. After that, he did most of the heavy lifting.'

'Meaning?' asks Jacinda. Jacinda loves a clarifying question – must be the barrister in her.

'*Meaning*, he looked over as soon as I sat down, then started talking to me. He even bought me a drink. All I had to do was answer his questions as Penny – oh, and pretend to enjoy a Negroni.' I make the 'blech' face.

'And did you ask about him?' Lauren probes.

'Well, yes, it was a *conversation*, not him interrogating me,' I tease. 'But he was elusive – I didn't get much out of him. Just that he lives at the Langham when he's not travelling for work.'

'As a geologist,' Shaz scoffs with a snort.

'And what's he like?' Lauren asks, not acknowledging Shaz's interjection.

'He's...' I stop talking as I ponder the best way to answer – because what Lauren's *actually* asking is: how does he get all these women to fall in love with him?

'He's attentive and charming – obviously intelligent. And he asked all the right questions – ones designed to make me believe he was genuinely interested. Although, according to Kate, that wanes as soon as he's sure the woman is invested.'

'Arsehole,' mutters Shaz.

'And is he attractive?' Lauren asks.

I tilt my head from side to side. 'He's not *un*attractive. But he's not—'

'Not like Tristan?' Lauren whispers, and I chuckle.

'No, nothing like Tristan.'

My husband is the sort of handsome that must have landed Brad Pitt his first role. And his second, possibly even his third.

'So more like Ravi then,' says Jacinda, and my head pivots sharply in her direction.

'Jacinda Sharma!' I chide. 'Your husband is very handsome, and you know it.'

She glances towards the kitchen, breaking into a wide grin. 'He is, isn't he?'

'Yes!' the three of us chorus.

'What's that?' Tristan calls from the kitchen.

It's unlikely he can make out what we're saying over the range hood but in case he can, I bust out a big grin.

'Nothing, babe,' I reply loudly.

With a slight smile, he turns back to Ravi. Hmm. Maybe he *can* hear us.

'So, who's this bloke's celebrity comp then?' asks Lauren.

'Celebrity comp?' I ask.

'Yeah, as in who does he remind you of? Someone famous.'

'Uh, he's kinda Tom Hiddleston-ish.'

'Tom Hiddleston's *proper* fit,' says Jacinda. 'So sexy.'

'Okay, granted, but that's because he's Tom Hiddleston,' I retort. 'He's talented, he plays all these suave characters – and he's hilarious in interviews... But if he wasn't an actor, if he was some random guy you saw on the street, would you fancy him?'

Jacinda nods slowly. 'Oh, absolutely. It's that impishness.' She makes a growling sound in the back of her throat.

'That's what makes David Tennant hot,' says Shaz. 'That lopsided grin, that swagger.'

'Right,' I say, wanting to talk about something other than work, 'have we fully exhausted the topic of the lecherous lothario?'

Shaz sniggers. 'Good one.' She raises her half-drunk glass of wine in my direction.

'Hardly!' Lauren declares. This may be the most animated I've ever seen her – usually, she's the calm one and Shaz is the one bouncing off the walls. 'What's the latest?' she asks. 'Has he been in contact?'

'Oh, yeah. I'm getting two or three messages a day, some-times more.'

'Can I see?'

'Actually, I wouldn't mind taking a peek either,' says Jacinda, typically the most level-headed amongst us.

'Okay,' I say, relenting. I grab my phone off the coffee table and navigate to the messages from Dunn. 'Here,' I say, handing the phone to Lauren. 'Scroll up.'

'I'm coming over,' says Jacinda, getting up from the sofa opposite us. 'Oof,' she groans as she lands between me and Lauren. 'I swear if this baby gets any bigger...' She lays a hand on her considerable bump.

Lauren catches my eye and we share a smile. Jass is always going on about how huge she is and she looks exactly the same as she always has, but with a baby bump.

'Pretty sure that's gonna happen, Jass,' quips Shaz. She pops a chunk of cheese into her mouth. 'Still three months to go yet,' she says through her mouthful.

'Don't remind me – *and* over the summer! I'm already waddling about like a whale.'

'Whales don't waddle,' says Shaz, reaching for more cheese.

'You're not waddling,' I add. 'You're beautiful.'

'If you tell me I'm glowing, I may have to murder you,' Jacinda says dryly. 'I've promised myself I won't be one of those mothers who lays guilt trips on my child for what I went through during my pregnancy, but I'm reconsidering.'

I rest my hand on top of hers. 'I can't wait to meet Baby Sharma,' I say wistfully, and Jacinda smiles at me, her expression softening.

'Me neither,' she replies.

'Oh my *god*,' says Lauren, startling us both. 'Listen to this: "I can recall the exact colour of your eyes. Like a moody London sky on winter's day".'

'Ba-ha-ha-ha-ha.' Shaz's laughter rings out across the flat. I can't blame her. I had the same reaction when that message came through. So did Tristan.

'Are you reading messages from Poppy's new boyfriend?' Tristan asks from the kitchen.

'Oi!' I scold, pointing at him. 'We talked about that. I'd rather my husband *not* refer to Jon Dunn as my boyfriend, thank you.'

'But, darling, if I have to share you with someone else, then shouldn't I at least get a good laugh out of it?'

'Well, I've been sharing you with Saffron for over a year – I've yet to get a laugh out of *that*.'

At the sound of her name, Saffron struts into the lounge, blinking at us sleepily.

'Oh hello, little minx,' I say.

'Saff-yyy,' coos Shaz, making kissing noises at her. Saffron, who has never once come when I've called her, trots over and jumps onto the sofa, then climbs into Shaz's lap.

Everyone, including my husband, thinks this is just as hilarious as the soppy message from Dunn.

'Yeah, yeah, you lot will keep...' I say, smothering my own laughter.

Ravi comes over to refresh our drinks, and I get up and go into the kitchen. 'Hello, you,' I say, snaking my arms around Tristan's waist. I tip my face for a kiss and he presses his lips to mine. He tastes like the Pinot we've been sipping on. 'Smells good in here.'

'Thank you. I'm letting the meat rest for a bit, then I'll serve up. And I was thinking,' he says, leaning closer, 'what do you say to shooing everyone out the moment we finish pudding? Get on with our baby making.'

'Oh, I am completely on board with that,' I reply.

What goes unsaid is that we've been trying for months now. We both understand it will take as long as it takes – or we may eventually need help – but we're so excited about becoming parents that we're hoping for sooner rather than later.

* * *

'*Bonjour*, Marie,' I say when she answers her phone.

The only indication that she heard me is a soft grunt.

'There's been a development in the Kate Whitaker case and we need your help.'

'*D'accord.*'

I explain how Kate and Willem went to Verona to inform Lucia Rossi about Dunn, but she wasn't there. And that we're now concerned Dunn might be planning to propose to Lucia this coming weekend.

'Is there any way you can find out?' I ask.

'Pffft.'

In this context, that's Marie for 'duh, of course'. It can also mean 'I don't care', 'I have no idea', 'maybe', and 'I'm surrounded by morons'. After years of working with Marie, I've learned to tell the difference.

'Good, now how long do you need?'

'An hour or two.'

'Excellent!' I enthuse, but she ends the call before I finish the word. 'And you have a lovely day too, Marie,' I say to myself.

'Was that Kate Whitaker?' I look up and Ursula is standing beside my desk, her eyes boring into mine. 'How did it go in Verona?'

'It wasn't and it didn't.'

'Is this one of your Australianisms? I swear, half the time I have no idea what you're saying.'

I doubt Ursula *means* to be insulting so I let that slide. 'I meant that it wasn't Kate – it was Marie – and nothing happened in Verona because fiancée-to-be number three wasn't there. She's in Greece until Thursday.'

Ursula's expression sours, evidenced by the slight pursing of her lips, invisible to the naked eye unless you know what you're looking for.

'And Marie?' she asks.

'Marie is looking into Dunn's movements over the coming weekend.'

'Ahh, yes, he might be planning to propose.'

'Exactly.'

'Juicy case you have here, Poppy.'

Is that a hint of jealousy I detect in her voice? Although, I'm not sure what she has to be jealous about. She's been co-piloting this case since the beginning.

'Ah, yep.'

'And how's our fish? Still hooked?'

'Two or three messages a day, and look...' I quickly unlock my phone to show Ursula the photo Dunn sent this morning. She squints at the screen.

'Why is he pouting like a little boy?' she asks with obvious distaste.

'Because he misses Penny. See?' I tap on the screen to reveal the message:

You're all I can think about. Any chance I can lure you back to London?

'Are they all like that, the messages?'

'You mean soppy and ridiculous? Yes.'

'And how are you replying – what sort of things are you saying?'

I show her my reply:

Me too. I hardly got any work done today. And I'd love to but work won't send me to London any time soon and it's $$$. *shrug emoji*

'And check this out.' I scroll down to reveal the next part of the exchange:

I'll pay for the flight. I'm desperate to see you. Jon xxx

And my reply:

I wouldn't feel right about that. And hard to get time off anyway. End of financial year soon – very busy trying to get enough donations to meet our target. *sad face emoji*

Ursula looks up from the screen. 'You clever clogs,' she says, clearly impressed.

'Thanks,' I say, beaming. 'No answer yet, but hopefully that will get the wheels turning. If I can get him to offer the money... *way* better than having to ask for it.'

'Does he know which not-for-profit Penny works for?' she asks.

'Nope. He never asked and when I talked about work, I kept it vague.'

She nods appreciatively. 'Excellent work, Poppy. I had a sense you'd be good at this sort of thing.' She pats me on the shoulder, then heads towards the kitchen.

'Uh, thanks,' I say to her back, unsure how to take that. I'm happy to be called clever – not so happy to be told I'm a good liar.

My job is weird sometimes.

'Hey, Kate, it's Poppy. I have news.' I do my best to sound upbeat, but it's difficult when delivering bad news.

'You said "news", not "*good* news" – should I be sitting down?' she asks with a lilt of wry laughter.

'Probably,' I reply, dropping the pretence.

'Okay, hang on a moment.' There's the rustle of papers, then murmuring as if she's pressed her phone to her chest and is talking to someone. 'Hi again. So, I'm guessing Jon *is* planning to propose this weekend?'

'It seems so. He has a flight booked to Verona for Saturday morning and reservations at a place called Ristorante Il Desco that night.'

'No doubt expensive,' she says tartly.

'Yes, and one of the best restaurants in Verona.'

'I'd expect nothing less.'

'There's more.'

'Oh, go on then.'

'He's booked a suite in Hotel Gabbia d'Oro. I think I'm saying that right,' I say, consulting my notes.

'So expensive, opulent, and one of the best hotels in Verona?'

'Yes, yes, and yes.'

'And Marie discovered all this?'

'Yep. It only took her an hour.'

Kate snorts out a soft laugh. 'She's quite something, your investigator.'

'She is.' Now comes the pressing question. 'So, what do you want to do? Do you want to beat him to the punch? You'd have to arrive in Verona Friday night at the latest, then track down Lucia. Are you up to it?'

Her mood has markedly deteriorated since the start of this call and if I had to guess, I'd say she isn't. But I'm not inside Kate's head.

She breathes out noisily. 'I *was*. If you'd asked me yesterday, I would have said yes. But…'

I think I know what she's getting at. 'Is it because it feels more real now?'

'Yeah,' she replies quietly. 'And that keeps happening – right when I've got a handle on it, the rug gets pulled out from under me all over again.'

'That's understandable.'

She's quiet for a moment. 'But even so,' she says, audibly perking up, 'I stand by what I said yesterday morning. Lucia deserves to learn the truth before she's dragged into this even further. I'm going back. I'll take Friday afternoon off, fly straight there, and track down Lucia on Friday night. I just need to let Willem know.'

'So, he's going with you?'

'Yes, he's insisted on seeing this through.'

Kate hasn't told me anything about what did or didn't happen between her and Willem de Vries during their time together over the weekend – and nor did I expect her to – but it's clear she's interested in him romantically. And given how much time they've spent together, *and* his insistence on accompanying Kate, there's every chance he might reciprocate.

If there weren't the possibility that it might interfere with the case, I'd be cheering them on from the sidelines. Something tells me they'd be a great match. I only hope they hold off until everything is wrapped up and Kate has had a chance to heal.

'Well, that's good – you'll have someone there to support you,' I say, affecting a positive tone.

'Hiya, yes, what can I do for you?' Kate asks – she must be talking to someone else. There's murmuring, then, 'Oh. Right now? Uh, okay – thanks. Poppy, I've got to go. I think Jon's here.'

'What? At your office?'

'Yes. Oh god, I feel ill.' Her ragged breathing is audible over the phone.

'Okay, take a slow, deep breath. What did your colleague say, Kate?'

'That there was a man in reception asking for me. He didn't give his name.'

'Well, then it could be anyone. But if it *is* Dunn, tell him he's come at a bad time. Tell him he pulled you out of an important meeting and that you'll contact him later.'

'But I'm supposed to be in Birmingham – I told him I was in Birmingham this week,' she says, her panic rising.

'You were called back to London unexpectedly,' I say, rattling off the perfect alibi.

'Okay.' She exhales loudly. 'Oh god, I'm not ready to face him, Poppy.'

'I know. Call me back if you need to, okay?'

'Yep.' And then she's gone.

'What are you playing at, Dunn?' I ask myself quietly.

19

KATE

I plaster on a smile as I walk from my office to the lobby. Inside, I'm reeling as troubling thoughts ricochet around my mind, making my stomach plummet.

What is Jon doing here? Has he figured out that I've been fobbing him off? Is he here to confront me? And how does he know I'm not in Birmingham?

I round the last corner, my forced smile bordering on maniacal, but it's not Jon who's waiting for me. It's Willem.

'What are you doing here?' I blurt instinctually. 'Sorry, that was rude. I mean, hi.'

But what is *he doing here?*

'Hi,' he says hesitantly. 'Is this a bad time?'

I glance to my left where the receptionists are staring at us – Casey with their mouth hanging open.

'No,' I say brightly, 'not at all. Would you like to come through to my office?'

Without waiting for his reply, I spin and stride down the hallway, my pace decidedly faster than when I thought I'd have to face Jon. The sound of Willem's muffled footfalls behind me is somehow soothing, and I exhale mindfully. Hopefully, by the time I get to my office, the adrenaline coursing through my body will have started to abate.

I get to my office door and cast a smile over my shoulder. 'Here we are.'

I skirt around my desk and perch on the edge of my leather chair, indicating for Willem to sit in one of the two club chairs opposite me. His eyes don't leave mine as he takes a seat and I lean my wrists on the desk, steepling my fingers to keep from fidgeting.

'So...' I begin, hoping he'll leap in to explain why he's here.

'Are you okay? You seem... agitated.'

'I thought you were Jon,' I reply candidly – no sense in pretending when he's obviously got a good read on me.

Willem's eyes widen. 'Dunn? Why would you think that?'

'Oh, I don't know. There's a strange man at reception and he wouldn't give his name...'

'I wasn't trying to be deceitful. I wasn't asked my name.'

'Oh. Sorry.'

'No, *I'm* sorry I worried you,' he says, his concern evident.

I give him a reassuring smile. 'Not to worry. I'm just on edge when it comes to all things Jon. He wanted to take me to lunch yesterday and I made up a lie about visiting my parents, then working from a satellite office for the week. I thought he'd caught me in the lie, then shown up to confront me.' I expel another slow breath, my gaze fixed on my desk blotter. 'Sorry, I'm just a little worked up.'

'It's okay.'

I look up. 'So, why *are* you here?' I ask again, though more politely this time.

'To ask you to lunch.'

Now *my* eyes widen in surprise.

'You came all the way to London to ask me to lunch?'

He sniggers and, feeling foolish, I join in.

'No,' he says. 'I'm here for work. I'm meeting a prospective client later this afternoon and I thought you might be free for lunch.'

'And you know where I work because you have a full dossier on me,' I say, arching my brows at him.

'I wouldn't say *dossier*.' He brings his thumb and forefinger together. 'It's more of a thin file.'

I lift one corner of my mouth, giving him a tight smile. 'Nice distinction.'

He tips his head, then smiles. 'So, can I take you to lunch or are you busy?'

'I have ninety minutes until my next meeting,' I say, standing.

'Good,' he replies succinctly.

He stands and repositions the chair so that it lines up with the one next to it. I've seen him do this before – aligning objects so the edges or angles match up. He catches me watching him and seems embarrassed.

'But not Italian,' I say cheerfully to take the focus off him. 'Verona has ruined me for eating Italian food anywhere outside of Italy.'

He chuckles at that, the tension in his face disappearing. 'There's a good sushi place close by – how does that sound?'

'It sounds great – lead the way.' I gesture towards the door, but I should know by now that Willem will insist I go first, and he does.

I head out into the hallway, Willem following, and when we emerge into the airy lobby, both receptionists look over, then whisper amongst themselves.

They probably think this is Jon. It's a jarring thought and I'll be sure to correct them when I return.

'It smells delicious in here,' I say. 'Like puffed rice and teriyaki sauce.'

Willem sniffs the air. 'The puffed rice smell is genmaicha tea. We'll have to order some.'

We're in a hole-in-the-wall sushi restaurant in Soho, seated at a tiny table on short wooden stools. While my knees are tucked under the table – *barely* – Willem's are practically under his armpits. I press my lips together to suppress a smile. The waiter brings us menus and water, then disappears, and I sneak a furtive glance at Willem as he takes a sip of water, his eyes scanning the menu. Unable to hold it in any longer, I snigger and he looks up, a quizzical expression crossing his face.

'Sorry, but are you comfortable like that? We can go some-place else.'

'I'm fine,' he says with a reassuring wave of his hand. 'Their sushi is worth it, trust me.'

Two more people enter and now the restaurant is full. I look over my shoulder and people are starting to queue up outside.

The waiter reappears, seemingly impatient to take our order, but we've only just got here and I haven't even looked at the menu yet.

'You must know what's good here,' I say to Willem. 'Why don't you order for both of us?'

'Sure,' he says with a smile. He quickly rattles off the

names of four sushi rolls and adds a pot of genmaicha tea to the order.

'How is it you're so familiar with London?' I ask when the waiter leaves. 'I would never have found this place on my own.'

'My business partner is from here.'

'I didn't realise you had a business partner.'

'Probably because I never mentioned it.'

'Well, obvs,' I tease. 'So, who is he? Or she? Or they?'

'*He* is Max. We studied at the University of Twente together, became good friends... And after university, both of us worked in large corporations for a while – him here and me in the Netherlands – and when we both got tired of the limitations, the corporate *bullshit*, we decided to work together.'

'How long ago was that?'

'Hmm,' he murmurs, his eyes narrowing, 'seven years ago. Wow.' He shakes his head as though he can't quite believe it's been that long.

'Well, you're clearly smashing it,' I say, instantly regretting my choice of words when he gives me a funny look. From what I've seen so far, Willem de Vries is a proper grownup who never uses colloquialisms like 'smashing it'.

'What makes you say that?' he asks, his eyes glinting with amusement.

'Let's see...' I begin, hoping to redeem myself. 'Your business straddles the Channel, you've got clients across Europe... Even Marie Maillot knew who you were and she's something of a legend in your field.'

Nicely done, Kate – a proper, grownup (i.e. Willem-like) response.

'Well, if those are your metrics for "smashing it", I'll take the compliment.'

Right on cue, the heart flutters arrive, intensifying as we regard each other for a long moment. His gaze drops to my lips for a fraction of a second, then lifts to meet my eyes. *Frisson*, I think – just like Margot said.

Maybe this *isn't* one-sided. Only every time I think that, something happens to make me doubt myself again.

A platter of sushi rolls appears on the table with a thud, breaking the spell. Willem pours soy sauce into a small ramekin, then uses chopsticks to load up his plate with sushi, and I do the same.

'And is Max still a Londoner or has he moved to the Netherlands?' I ask.

'He's here, but we see a lot of each other. Most clients prefer to meet with both of us, especially in the initial stages.'

'Mm-hmm,' I murmur as I chew on a piece of sushi. It's delicious. I'd bring Margot here if it wouldn't traumatise her. 'So, Max lives here...' I begin. 'Don't suppose you have a London-based ex-girlfriend lying about as well?'

What on earth possessed me to say that?! I'd give anything to turn back time, especially as Willem looks as horrified as I am, his sushi-laden chopsticks suspended between his plate and his mouth.

'Er, no. No ex-girlfriend in London,' he says, setting the sushi down.

'I'm so sorry. That was rude of me, which makes twice today.'

He doesn't respond right away, cryptic thoughts dancing behind his eyes, disquieting me. Should I apologise again?

'Kate...' he says eventually, only he trails off, leaving me none the wiser about what he wanted to say. We stare at each other a moment longer, then I look away.

'So, tell me about this prospective client,' I say brightly, changing the subject. 'Unless it's Victoria Beckham and you're sworn to secrecy.'

I glance up and his troubled expression dissolves, his mouth quirking. 'I told you, I'm always sworn to secrecy.'

'Go on, I promise I won't tell anyone – not even Margot,' I retort, playing along – anything to make up for that mortifying faux pas. 'You can trust me,' I add.

'Oh, I know *that*, Kate,' he replies pointedly, loading his words with meaning I can't quite divine.

I look down, moving sushi about my plate. My heart, once prone to fluttering in Willem's presence, hammers away, making it hard to breathe.

'Kate...' When I don't meet his eyes, he reaches across the small table and lays his hand over mine. I lift my gaze. 'There's no *current* girlfriend either. Not in London, or in Amsterdam... Not even in Verona.'

I'm positive that last bit was to make me smile, and I do, but not because of Willem's weak joke about Jon. But because Willem just made a big to-do of clarifying that he's single.

If only I didn't have Poppy's voice in my head telling me it's a bad idea to get involved with Willem this soon after Jon.

He sits back, taking his hand away.

'So, how long are you in London for?' I ask, once again changing the subject.

'Until tomorrow, then back to Amsterdam.'

'Oh!' I say, suddenly realising I've forgotten to tell him the news. 'I'm so sorry. This completely slipped my mind. Jon's flying to Verona this coming Saturday. It looks like he's planning to propose to Lucia.'

It's baffling that I forgot about this until now and unsurprisingly, Willem seems to be caught off-guard.

He leans back, fishing his phone out of his pocket. 'One

moment,' he says, the vertical lines between his brows deepening. 'I should have heard something from Marie Mai— Oh, she just emailed.'

His eyes scan the screen, then his cheeks puff out and he expels a loud breath before lifting his gaze to meet mine. 'So, back to Verona then?'

'Yes. I was going to fly there on Friday afternoon, then try and track down Lucia before Jon arrives.' I hedge before asking the next question. 'Did you still want to—'

'I'm coming with you, Kate. I told you that before and I meant it.'

'Oh good,' I say, relieved to have Willem as backup.

Not only relieved*, Kate. You're excited about spending the weekend with him – especially now he's made it clear he hasn't got a girlfriend.*

'And I'll book us a hotel this time,' he adds. 'Two rooms, of course.'

'Of course,' I reply, nodding numbly.

But what I really want to say is, 'Forget the hotel! Let's book that IKEA-filled flat and this time, you don't have to sleep on the sofa!'

Thankfully, I'm able to restrain myself and we spend the rest of lunch making small talk while I bat away romantic thoughts of Willem like flies at a picnic on a summer's day.

* * *

'*Please* tell me you're going to seduce Thor when you're in Verona this weekend.' Margot bustles into my flat, a carry bag slung over each shoulder.

'Hello, Kate, how are you?' I say. 'Fine, Margot, and you?'

Calling out Margot on her lack of manners is simply an

evasion tactic. I do not want to discuss Willem with Margot, especially as she'll harp on about using him for a shag. And he means more to me than that now I've got to know him.

Though, of course I *do* want to shag him eventually. He's the most gorgeous man I've ever laid eyes on.

'Yes, yes, yes. Hello and other niceties,' says Margot, deftly dodging my reprimand. She kisses me on the cheek, then pushes past me and heads into the kitchen. I follow.

'What did you *bring*?' I ask, rummaging through the carry bags. I start decanting items onto the benchtop, trying to make sense of such an eclectic array of ingredients. What is she planning on cooking? 'And you know there are only two of us, right?'

'I couldn't decide between spag bol or lamb kofta, so I bought ingredients for both. And look!' She holds up two bottles of wine: a red and a rosé. 'But the rosé needs to go in the freezer,' she says, handing it to me.

'Margot,' I say, going to the fridge and swinging it open. I wave my free hand in front of the middle shelf with a flourish worthy of a gameshow host. 'I have three bottles of wine already chilled, including a rosé.'

She stops what she's doing and faces me. 'Of *course* you do – forgot where I was. You're the only person I know who has a fully stocked pantry and fridge – at *all* times.'

'I've told you, buy staples in bulk when they're discounted and always—'

'And always add something to the shopping list before it runs out. I *know*.'

'Well, then why don't you do it?' I take out the cold rosé and replace it with the one Margot brought.

'Because I *enjoy* running to Tesco Express for tampons in the middle of the night, Kate – *obvs*!'

We crack up laughing and while Margot regards the pile of ingredients on the benchtop, I pour two generous glasses of wine. 'Here,' I say, handing her a glass.

She raises hers high above her head. 'To Kate, who is *finally* going to sleep with the Norse god.'

I should have known she wouldn't let this go. And it will take more energy to keep steering the conversation away from Willem than to admit my true feelings.

I take a deep breath. 'All right, I want him, Margot. And not just because he's... well...'

'The word you're looking for is "fit", Kate. The man is straight-up fit – on any scale, by any measure. He is one hundred per cent, empirically hot.'

'All *right*, yes, okay. He's hot. But he's far more than that. Willem's *principled* and kind and thoughtful. And we've had these conversations... He's a nice man, Margs – *decent*.'

'My darling cousin,' she says, placing a hand on my arm, 'you don't need nice *or* decent right now. You're on the rebound from Arseface. You need a man who will lift you up, pin you against the wall, and screw you so royally, you see stars.'

I gawp at her.

'Oh, don't look at me like that. You need sex – *great* sex – and you need it ASAP. Trust me, it's the best method for exorcising the demons of a bad relationship. I could write a *book* about it.'

I don't doubt that and, uncannily, she's described my latest fantasy about Willem almost to the letter. But I'm not comfortable reducing his value to what he can do with his penis. He *is* a decent man, and I've now admitted to myself – and Margot – that what I feel for him is more than just lust.

'Kate.'

I snap out of my stupor to discover Margot peering at me, an odd expression on her face.

'Does that conclude your lecture on using sex to get over a shitty ex?' I ask.

Her eyes narrow. 'Almost – one last point and then I'll be quiet.'

'Ladies and gentlemen, behold, an actual miracle!' I call out to an imaginary audience.

She smiles tersely. 'I'm being serious.'

My smile falls away. 'Okay, what is it?'

'Maybe now isn't the time to be falling in love.'

'What?' I say with a scoffing laugh. 'I never said anything about falling in *love* with Willem.'

'Only that he's decent and kind and a good bloke – all the things that Jon isn't. He's also acting as your champion...'

'But you just said, not two minutes ago, that I should shag him.'

'Shag, not fall for. Just be careful with your heart, okay?'

Margot's words echo in my ears, underscored by what Poppy said earlier.

'I will,' I say quietly.

Even though it may be too late for that.

20

POPPY

'And, Poppy, we'll conclude with your update on the Kate Whitaker revenge case.'

I don't like it being labelled a 'revenge case', but at least Ursula hasn't insisted on naming it after a fairy tale, like she usually does. Anyway, it's a minor quibble, so I smile serenely, then address my colleagues.

'All aspects of the case are progressing well. The persona I've created – Penny Mullings – is engaging with Dunn daily via text messages and' – I take a steeling breath – 'we have a video call scheduled for tonight.'

Fellow agent Nasrin sends me a commiserating grimace across the table.

'I know,' I say to her. 'I'm not looking forward to it, but it's designed to progress the relationship with "Penny". The aim is to prod Dunn into making a sizeable donation to our chosen not-for-profit. He has a track record of flashing his wealth about, so we have reason to be confident.'

'Importantly,' Ursula says to the others, 'we're not only hitting Dunn in his hip pocket, but also his ego. When it emerges that he's donated to an arts' education program – and we plan to make his donation as visible as possible – he will have to grin and bear it.'

'Or suck it up, as we'd say in Australia,' I add with a smile.

'A charming expression, as always, Poppy,' says Ursula with a sideways glance in my direction.

'The other update,' I continue, 'is that Kate and the second fiancée's brother, Willem de Vries, are off to Verona this afternoon where they will approach Lucia Rossi and inform her that Dunn isn't who he says he is. They're racing the clock, however, as there is every indication Dunn plans to propose to Rossi tomorrow evening.'

George, also an agent, raises his hand. To keep staff meetings running to time, we're encouraged – rather, *expected* – not to interrupt another agent's update, but I call on him. 'Yes, George.'

'Why isn't the second fiancée going to Verona with your client? Why is it the brother?'

'Well, if we were to ask them, I reckon they'd all have different reasons. The second fiancée – Adriana de Vries – is all for retribution and she'll be here for the finale but, till then, her brother will act as her proxy. From what Kate tells me, she's still processing the news about Dunn.'

'And what about the brother?' asks Nasrin. 'Is he the vigilante type? He's not gonna go all John Wick on this bloke, is he?'

There are sniggers around the table. 'Er, not to my knowledge, no,' I reply with a smile. 'Marie Maillot has vouched for him, so we should be safe on that front.'

George raises his hand again.

'That's enough for now,' says Paloma. 'If you have follow-up questions for Poppy, talk to her afterwards. Thank you, everyone.'

Most of my colleagues disperse, but George stays back and so does Freya, my closest friend at the agency.

'You want the goss, don't you?' I ask them.

'Well, obvs,' George replies with a dramatic roll of his eyes.

'I do too, Poppy,' says Freya. 'I mean, don't you think it's a little...'

She trails off, leaving the rest of her thought unsaid, one of her endearing foibles, and George seamlessly finishes her thought with, '*Suspect?*'

'The entire *case* is suspect – which part are you referring to?' I ask, looking between them.

They exchange a glance, which tells me they've already discussed this.

'Well?' I press.

'Your client and the brother,' George states, hands on his hips.

How did I not see that coming? Maybe having to sully my Friday night by talking to Dunn has distracted me.

'Agreed,' I reply. 'I'm suss about that part too.'

George's eyes light up. 'I did wonder. So, are they... you know?' He waggles his brows.

'George, you're a grown man. Just ask if they're sleeping together instead of talking like a self-conscious teenager.'

'Are they?' Freya asks.

'Actually, I'm not sure.'

'Oh,' they sigh in disappointed unison.

'Because de Vries is *hot*, Poppy,' says George. 'If it were me – if I were in your client's position – I'd have climbed him like a tree by now.'

'Setting aside that rather graphic imagery, how do you

know anything about him? I've barely mentioned him in my briefings.'

He tips his head to one side. 'Poppy, how many times do I have to tell you? I have excellent hearing – there's nothing happening in this office that I'm not aware of. And I was curious.' He shrugs, as if that excuses him snooping around my case.

'Well, as you've so astutely guessed, I'm concerned that Kate is unwittingly transferring her feelings from Dunn to de Vries. Although...' My gaze unfocuses as I sift through my concerns, still unsure where to land.

'*Poppy*,' says Freya, and my attention returns to the conference room.

'Sorry.'

'Although *what*?' George prods.

'It could be that Willem de Vries is actually Kate's perfect match. Every time she mentions him, her cheeks flush, but underneath the outward display, there's this calm contentedness about her. It's a vast contrast to when we're discussing Jon Dunn.'

Freya grins, clapping her hands softly beneath her chin. She's a die-hard romantic and even in a case that's ostensibly 'a revenge case' (no matter how unpleasant it is to admit that), she'll want an HEA for our client. And if anyone deserves a happily ever after, it's Kate Whitaker.

'So, how are you going to help make that happen?' George asks – a timely reminder of my *actual* role at Ever After.

'That's a good question,' I reply. 'Hmm.'

'Well, you said they're going to Verona together...' says George. 'What if there was an issue with their accommodation and they had to – I don't know – share a hotel room?'

I give him a sceptical, oh-come-on look. 'The one-bed thing? That only works in romcoms, George.'

'That's not true,' he retorts. 'My friends, Luca and Alistair, got together because of a room mix-up. A group of us rented a chateau in the south of France and we thought it had enough bedrooms for each of us to have our own. It didn't and guess who volunteered to share? They've been together two years now.'

'Could Marie help?' Freya asks. 'With the hotel reservations?'

'Probably,' I reply, looking at them in turn. 'Do you really think this could work?'

'If they're not into it – or each other – they'll go somewhere else, make other arrangements,' says George. 'And if they are... they'll make it work – even if they pretend to be put out by the inconvenience.'

'Hmm.' Am I really considering playing matchmaker in the middle of this complicated case?

Freya, who seems to understand my hesitation, places a hand on my shoulder. 'I suppose you just need to decide, Poppy. Do you think it's too soon for Kate to be pursuing romance with someone else, or is this exactly what she needs to move on with her life?'

This is one of the most difficult aspects of matchmaking – having to make a call on behalf of the client, particularly a call they might disagree with.

'Look,' says George, 'if you do nothing, it could eventuate anyway. They could get together on their own.'

'Yes, but what you said just now, Frey... about Kate moving on with her life. Maybe I've been looking at this all wrong. Maybe Kate spending time with Willem de Vries is exactly what she needs – especially as he's such a vast contrast to Dunn.'

'Most people are,' says George, and I nod in agreement.

'So, where are you landing?' asks Freya. 'See how things go on their own, or give them a little nudge so they fall madly in love?'

I snigger. 'That's quite the binary view, Frey.'

She shrugs unapologetically.

'I suppose it can't hurt to meddle,' I say, making them both wince. Fair – because in our line of work, the word 'meddle' has particularly negative connotations. We prefer 'intervening'.

'Sorry, it can't hurt to create a situation in which my client might fall madly in love,' I say, and they both smile. 'As you said, George, if I've misread the situation – or if one of them isn't into the other – they'll simply make other arrangements.'

'Oh, they won't do that,' says Freya, and I let it slide, even though she clearly considers it a sure thing. We can *hope* for an outcome but expecting it can lead to disappointment.

'I'll give Marie a call,' I say, trusting that for Marie, this latest request will be a piece of cake. 'And thanks – both of you. It's been really helpful talking it through.'

'You're welcome,' they reply together.

'And, Poppy,' says Freya, 'good luck tonight. Freddie and I are having a night in, so if you need to debrief afterwards, give me a call.'

'Thanks, Frey,' I reply, my stomach clenching with nerves.

Now that we've got a course of action for progressing Kate towards an HEA, the focus is back on me and Penny.

Ugh, how did I ever agree to this?

* * *

When I emerge from the guest room after my call with Jon Dunn, wearing pyjamas to give the illusion of it being morning in Melbourne, Tristan looks up from the book he's reading and inverts it on the sofa.

'How was it?' he asks.

I squirm from top to toe, then shake out my hands.

'That good, eh?'

'I feel disgusting. He's so *awful*, Tris.'

'Well, you are comparing him to me,' he says, clearly trying to lighten the mood.

I give him a lipless smile.

'Come here, darling.' Tristan pats the sofa and I go to him, accepting the offered hug. Eventually, I gently ease away and face him, rocking back on my heels.

'You know, on the one hand, I can understand how he manages to charm these women, but on the other...' I shudder, revolted, and Tristan reaches for my hand.

'Do you think your reaction is because you're privy to who he really is?'

'Oh, absolutely. And that's the thing – if I were in Kate's situation, I'm not sure I'd see past his charm offensive – not at first anyway. He's just so... *calculating*.'

'Where did you leave it?' he asks.

'Well, that seed I planted – him having to front up with a donation to get me back to London – it seems to be germinating. Especially 'cause I laid it on extra thick: I can't stop thinking about him... I want to return to London as soon as possible... Maybe I'm better at role playing than I thought.'

'Mmm,' he murmurs; it's clear how much this bothers him. 'And there's one more thing I'm curious about,' he says.

'What's that?'

'You want him to donate to the Creative Futures Foundation, but won't that become obvious to him at some point – that it's an arts' program?'

'Ah, well Marie did some digging, and it turns out to be a subsidiary. If Dunn does agree to cut a cheque, it will be to the parent organisation, which deals in broader educational objectives – likely far more palatable to Dunn. And Saskia has agreed to don her solicitor's hat again to draw up the contract. She's confident we'll be able to cover the paper trail until it's time to reveal where the money's really gone.'

'Is that legal?' he asks, giving me the side-eye.

'It's Saskia, not Marie. If she's overseeing it then, yes, it will be legal. Now,' I say, getting up from the sofa, 'I'm going to shower.'

'Any chance that's an invitation?'

If anything can wash away the residue of talking to that ghastly man, it's a romp in the shower with my handsome hubby. I reach for his hand, and he grins.

Kate

It's like déjà vu being back in the airport lounge on a Friday night, waiting to fly to Europe. Only this time, I'm going straight to Verona and Willem is meeting me at the hotel.

Willem. The man has dominated my thoughts all week.

When I first wake up. As I'm getting ready for work. On my commute to the office. Between meetings. During lunch. At my desk when I should be working. On my commute home. And when I lay my head on my pillow at night... Willem, Willem, Willem.

I'm like a teenager with a crush on the cute boy at school –

moments away from scribbling his name on my folder in loopy lettering, then drawing a heart around it.

Though, Willem hasn't been the only thing on my mind. There's also what Poppy said to me on Sunday and Margot's warning from Monday night.

It can take time to heal... Meaning: don't rush into anything.

Be careful with your heart... Meaning: don't rush into anything.

Is that what I'm doing, monkey-barring from one man to the next before I've properly recovered from Jon's betrayal?

Before he and I started seeing each other, I was 'chronically single', as Margot liked to say. I'd gone *years* without being in a serious relationship. Have I now become the type of woman who struggles with being single?

As I sip my pint of beer, I scrutinise the question. *No*, I tell myself. If Willem weren't a part of the equation, I would happily move on from Jon, content to be on my own until I got up the nerve to 'get back out there' – another of Margot's favourite soundbites, even though she doesn't follow her own advice.

Willem's on my mind because it's *him*, not because I'm desperate to be with someone and he just happens to be around.

Right?

I let out a lazy sigh. Maybe I won't know for sure until I see him again.

I picture his blue eyes... How they're framed with lashes so thick, he could star in a mascara advert... How that shirt he wore to dinner in Amsterdam matched their shade exactly... How they crinkle slightly at the corners when he's trying not to let on he's amused, betraying him... How they linger on mine when he's mulling over what to say next...

My phone rings, cutting through my romantic musings, and I answer it without checking who's calling, expecting it to be Margot.

'Hiya,' I chirrup.

'Hello, Kate.'

I plummet back to reality with a thud.

'Jon,' I say, my mouth suddenly dry.

I take a swig of beer – as much for the Dutch courage as to quench my thirst. I cannot let on that this call is anything but a welcome surprise.

'I've missed you, darling. I so wish I could have seen you this week,' he says.

Has his voice always had that whiny quality? I wonder.

'It's a shame,' I reply.

He'll take that at face value, no doubt, even though I've internally imbued it with a different meaning. *It's a shame you're such a lying, conniving, spineless snake, Arseface.*

'Indeed.'

An idea pops into my mind, and I act on it before I can second-guess myself. 'What about this weekend?' I ask cheerfully. 'I'm as free as a bird tomorrow – *and* Sunday.'

My heart is in my throat as I wait for him to respond.

'Oh, darling, I *wish*, but I've got to be in Frankfurt first thing to pick up the Tokyo route.'

'*Oh, no,*' I whine, doing a brilliant job of sounding devastated (if I do say so myself). 'That's such a pity. I haven't seen you in an *age*.'

'I *know*, darling,' he says in the most patronising tone. If he tosses in a 'there, there' I won't be surprised. 'That's why the phone call,' he adds. 'I've missed your voice.'

'Aww, how lovely,' I say, sounding as if I mean it.

I glance at my half-drunk beer. Either it has magical properties, or I'm in a far better place than I thought I was when it comes to Jon. I'm actually *enjoying* this, stringing him along.

'Look, I best be getting on – flight preparation.'

'Oh, right. *Very* important.'

'I'll let you know when I'm back in London. Hopefully sooner rather than later.'

Trotting out the typical bog-standard vagueness, I see. Jon has rarely ever committed to a specific date more than a few days out, something I only realised recently when combing over our entire relationship.

'Of course,' I say reassuringly.

'Bye, darling. Love you.'

'Byeeee,' I sing-song.

I will happily lie to Jon about most things, but he will never get another 'I love you' from my lips. I'd sooner lick a public toilet seat.

21

KATE

My flight to Verona dragged, even though it was only two hours long – anticipation, I suppose. I'm now in a cab, zipping through the winding streets, both looking forward to seeing Willem and anxious about the purpose of this trip.

Poor Lucia has no idea we're about to deliver devastating news.

The cab turns onto a narrow street, then stops outside an arched doorway. While the cabbie retrieves my case from the boot, I get out, looking up at the hotel's façade. Like many of the buildings in Verona, it's beautiful. I pay in cash – with a generous tip – then wheel my case into the hotel.

As soon as I enter the lobby, I spy Willem at reception. He's leaning on the counter and seems to be having an intense conversation with the receptionist.

I sidle up right as he says, 'I don't understand how this happened. The reservation was for *two* rooms.'

That doesn't bode well, but surely it's fixable.

'Hi,' I say, drawing his attention.

He looks down at me as if he's surprised I've appeared by his side.

'Hi,' he says, clearly frustrated. 'There's an issue with the reservation.'

'I heard. What's the problem?'

The receptionist, who seems just as baffled as Willem, explains that the second room from the confirmation email has disappeared from the system. 'I'm very sorry, sir,' she says.

'And you can't just add the room back to the reservation?' I ask.

'No, I'm sorry. Unfortunately, all our rooms are booked for the weekend.' She shrugs sheepishly.

I look to Willem. 'What do you think?' I ask. 'Try another hotel?'

Please say we should just stay here. Together. In the one room they do have.

'I don't know,' he replies, glowering at the reception desk.

In all our interactions, this is the most uncertain I've seen him, and there's something endearing about someone as capable Willem being this rattled.

'Are you *sure* there are no other rooms available?' I ask the receptionist, even though I'd be happy with the one. 'Or what about a suite? Do you have any suites available?'

Her chocolate-brown eyes meet mine for a moment, then she steps in front of the desktop computer and starts typing quickly. She frowns at the screen, shaking her head and breathing noisily out of her nose. She jerks the mouse across the mousepad and types again. Eventually, she sighs and looks up.

'I am sorry – I even checked our sister hotel near Ponte Nuovo. But I can call around and find you a second room somewhere nearby.'

Willem scrubs his hand over his face, then turns to me. 'We really need to get to Lucia's gallery. What if we leave our luggage here, go see Lucia, then figure out the rooms later?' he asks.

It occurs to me that by then it might be too late to organise another room – perfect!

'Sounds good.'

We turn towards the receptionist, who hands over luggage tags with a smile. She seems pleased to be able to help us with *something*. We tag our cases and she takes them from us, securing them in a locked room behind the reception desk.

'Ready?' Willem asks.

'Yep,' I reply.

As we step out into the cool evening air, my heart rate increases – and it has nothing to do with the handsome Dutchman by my side. This is it. We're going to break the news to Lucia.

* * *

We arrive at the gallery to discover it *is* open, alleviating concerns about tracking Lucia down, but she seems to be hosting some sort of event. It's brimming with people drinking wine and chatting animatedly, with some spilling out onto the footpath.

'Not ideal,' I say to Willem. 'What do you think we should do?'

His eyes scan the small crowd, then land on me and he does that thing where he's obviously thinking things through, but his eyes are locked onto mine the entire time. It's incredibly sexy and far less unnerving than it was at first. But even so, I look away, refocusing on how I plan to break the news to Lucia.

'We could get dinner and come back later,' Willem says eventually.

'But we have no idea how long this will go on,' I say, looking back at him. 'What if by the time we return, she's locked up and gone somewhere else?'

'Good point,' he says, twin lines forming between his brows. 'And you definitely want to be the one to tell her?'

'Yes, it should come from me.'

'Okay, let's go in.'

He lets me go first, uttering an apology in Italian as we slip past the people blocking the doorway.

As we weave through the jovial party guests, I take in the long, narrow, beautifully appointed gallery. The pieces on the righthand wall appear to be by the same artist and when I peer at one more closely, Lucia's signature is scrawled across the bottom-right corner.

The artwork on the opposite wall must be by other artists – they're hung in small groups, each with a distinctive style. And along the middle of the room are narrow wooden tables showcasing pottery, wood carvings, and blown-glass sculptures.

A trill of boisterous laughter fills the space, and when I look up from an intricate glass paperweight, I spot Lucia at the back of the gallery, perched on the edge of a desk and laughing heartily at something an older, stylishly dressed woman just said.

Photos do not do her justice. She is absolutely stunning: a petite but curvy figure, jet-black hair worn pin-straight past her shoulders, a heart-shaped face with full lips and high cheekbones, and enormous dark-brown eyes, framed by expertly shaped, full brows.

I turn and make an 'eek' face at Willem. 'I'm nervous,' I say.

He stares at me intently, then gives my arm a squeeze. 'It will be okay,' he says reassuringly. It helps – a little.

'But how do we... you know... *approach* her?'

'We wait for their conversation to end,' he says, nodding towards Lucia, 'then introduce ourselves.' He's replied as if this is a normal, everyday situation. It isn't.

'Right, okay.'

I draw in a deep, fortifying breath, then expel it slowly. And before I can overthink it or hedge a moment longer, I beeline for Lucia.

'Hello, Lucia,' I say, interrupting. So much for waiting for a natural break in the conversation, but nerves took over and now it's done.

'Hello,' she says, eyeing me curiously.

'Sorry to interrupt,' I say to them both.

The other woman smiles at me tautly, then says something to Lucia in Italian. Lucia accepts a kiss on each cheek and when the other woman leaves, she looks at me with a smile. She must think I'm an admirer of her art or even a prospective client.

I look behind me and signal for Willem to step closer, then turn back to Lucia. 'I'm Kate Whitaker and this is Willem de Vries.'

'Hello,' she says again, reaching out to shake our hands in turn. Then her head tilts expectedly. This is the part where I'm supposed to tell her who we are and why we're here.

'Uh...'

It's a poor start and I mentally chastise myself. *Come on,*

Kate. Margot would just blurt it out, like ripping off a plaster, but I've practised what I want to say, so I start there.

'We'd like to speak to you privately about something important.' I glance to my left, where a narrow glass-paned door leads to a compact office. 'Perhaps we could go in there?'

Lucia seems confused – and why wouldn't she? We're random people who have shown up uninvited.

'It's about Jon Dunn,' Willem says.

'Oh,' she says, breaking into a wide smile, 'you know *Jonny*. Are you also art lovers, or have you just stopped by to say hello?'

God, this is going to be harder than I thought. And *Jonny*? Jon is anything but a 'Jonny'. But perhaps Lucia sees a vastly different side to him.

'Ah, well, we *are* art lovers,' I say, smiling up at Willem, who nods along, 'and you have a *beautiful* gallery. Your work is incredible.'

She beams at me, but I'm about to wipe that smile from her face.

'I'm afraid this isn't about art, however. We have something to tell you and it's probably best done in private.'

Her face falls instantly. 'Is everything all right? Is Jonny okay?'

It's not lost on me that Lucia's first thought is of Jon's well-being; whereas, when Willem broke the news to me, it took me much longer to consider that he might be unwell or injured. And considering how her face lit up at the mention of his name, Lucia may have a far closer connection with Jon than I ever had. Even closer than how Adriana described *her* relationship with Jon.

This really *is* much more difficult than I imagined.

'It's nothing like that. As far as we know, he's fine,' I say, and she sighs with relief. 'But we do have information about Jon, and it concerns you.'

'Okay,' she says, finally seeming to grasp the gravity of the situation. She pushes off the edge of the desk and goes into the office, beckoning for us to follow, which we do.

* * *

'*You're engaged to Jonny?*' she asks, every word imbued with incredulity. 'I don't understand,' she adds with a please-tell-me-you're-joking laugh.

'I am, yes,' I reply, steadily meeting her gaze. 'He proposed nearly four months ago – in London.'

'No – no, it isn't possible. He's in love with me.'

She states this as an unassailable fact, and having anticipated her reluctance to believe me, I take out my phone and unlock the screen. As planned, it opens on the photo of me and Jon from the night he proposed – the one I showed Adriana in Amsterdam.

I look away because I hate seeing myself with him, blissfully unaware. I could have deleted it from my phone when I first found out, along with the other photos of us. But now I'm glad I didn't.

Lucia takes the phone from me and stares at the screen, her brow furrowed and her jaw tight.

'But, Lucia, there's more...' I say, gently taking back my phone.

As I tell her about Adriana, myriad emotions cross her face and eventually, her features settle into an open-mouthed grimace.

I gesture towards Willem. 'Willem is Adriana's brother.

He's the one who discovered what Jon was doing and came to tell me – like we've come to tell you.'

She regards me closely, then looks up at Willem.

'We've brought additional proof if you nee—'

She holds up a hand, and he stops talking. The silence that follows is thick with tension as Lucia's gaze fixes on the wall between us, thoughts tumbling behind her eyes. I wonder if she's conducting a mental audit of their time together – like I did.

Her eyes snap back into focus and she looks at me. '*Bastardo*,' she says, her voice laden with vitriol.

Instinctually, I recoil, thinking she's referring to me. But when Willem steps in with, 'He *is* a bastard,' I realise my error.

Though if Lucia did direct some of her anger at me, I would understand. This is a tricky situation no matter which way it's spun, and it's forgivable if she wants to shoot the messenger.

It also occurs to me how little it has taken to convince her, especially compared to Adriana – or even me. Lucia must have had her suspicions, or perhaps she had niggling doubts but dismissed them – also like I did.

'That's why we wanted to tell you,' Willem continues, 'to prevent him from doing any more damage than he already has.'

'But you don't even know me,' she says. 'Why do you want to help me? *Either* of you.' Her eyes land back on me, and from the way she's asking, she's not lobbing an accusation; she's genuinely curious.

'Because Jon is a snake and we don't deserve his lies,' I reply evenly.

Her expression softens slightly. 'So, you were the first?' she asks, and I only now notice her mild Italian accent.

I recall from Marie's research that although Lucia was born and raised in England, she's lived in Italy for the past decade.

'Yes,' I reply. 'But it was fast – the courtship – so there's a lot of overlap between us. And I have no idea if Jon has done anything like this in the past – strung several women along at once – but as far as we can tell, there are only three of us. For now, anyway.'

She nods. 'And does he know you've caught him in the lie?'

'No. As far as Jon's concerned, Adriana and I are both in the dark.'

Her eyes narrow again and there's a flash of intrigue. 'You have a plan, don't you?'

'We do. And if you're willing, we'd like you to be part of it.'

'Will it make Jon pay for what he's done?'

'In more ways than one,' I reply.

She nods, then puffs out her cheeks and exhales slowly. 'I think I've always known,' she says, her mouth bunching to the side. 'Too good to be true – this handsome, worldly wine merchant enters my life, out of the blue... tells me how beautiful I am, how talented... how he wants to introduce me to his art-dealer friends... That's why I thought he'd sent you.' Her gaze lifts to the ceiling and she shakes her head at herself. '*So* gullible.'

'I felt exactly the same way when I found out – I still do, sometimes.'

'Adriana too,' says Willem.

'But Jon's lies are layered and textured and calculated,' I continue. 'For one, he's not a wine merchant. *Or* a pilot,' I say, pointing to myself, 'or a diamond dealer, like he told Adriana.'

'What is he then – besides a *bastard*?' she asks sarcastically.

There's an explosion of laughter from the gallery and we all look towards the door.

'Sorry,' she says, 'I should probably get back to my party.'

'Before you do,' I say, flicking a glance towards Willem, 'there's one more thing.'

'Don't tell me – he's really an alien. No, no, a time traveller.' She laughs at her own joke but soon realises we're not laughing along and stops. 'Just tell me,' she says with resignation.

'You're seeing him tomorrow night, right?' Willem asks.

'How do you know that?'

'Because Willem and a woman called Marie Maillot have been investigating Jon. That's how we've pieced this together, and there's every indication that he's going to propose tomorrow night. To *you*.'

I probably didn't need to clarify that last part, but I'm not exactly my most switched-on self at the moment. Though I'm not sure who would be in this situation.

There's a beat of silence before Lucia erupts. 'He's going to *propose*? Well, he can fuck off. I'm not marrying that... that... *stronzo*.'

I have no idea what *stronzo* means, but I can guess.

'Of course – no one would expect you to,' I say. 'But...' I hesitate, because what I'm about to ask is big – *enormous*.

'But?' she prods.

'But it's better if Jon doesn't get to propose in the first place.'

'I don't understand.'

'It's like I said earlier – he's still of the belief that Adriana and I are none the wiser. We've been in contact with Jon, but when he's asked to meet up in person, we've made excuses.'

'So, you're stringing *him* along?'

'Yes.'

'Okay, but why? Why not simply confront him?'

'Because of the plan,' I say. 'And this may sound completely bizarre, but Adriana and I are working with a matchmaker called Poppy. She's currently posing as Jon's *fourth* potential love interest, and she's working on getting him to donate a huge sum of money to a charity he would *never* donate to if he weren't trying to win her over. All going well, he signs the cheque, then the four of us confront him together.'

Lucia regards me thoughtfully. 'That's good. I like it. But I have *so* many questions.'

'We'll answer every question we can,' I say.

'Definitely,' Willem concurs.

'Well, we can start with how I avoid seeing Jon tomorrow night.'

22

KATE

You would think that between the three of us we could come up with *something*, but after several minutes of brainstorming, we've got nothing.

There was a ludicrous suggestion from Lucia that she and Willem stage a lovers' spat outside the restaurant where Jon intends to propose. Jon would catch them, then she'd tearfully confess 'the affair' and ask Jon for time to sort out her feelings.

Channelling my inner project manager, I vetoed it immediately – far too many factors that could go awry. There was also the sickening sensation of imagining Willem with Lucia – even as a ruse – which I did my best to ignore. Willem is not mine to be jealous over.

'You could stand him up,' I suggest. 'Just don't show.'

There's something satisfying about the thought of Jon sitting alone in a restaurant, diamond ring in his pocket, brimming with anticipation of adding yet another fiancée to his collection, then realising Lucia is a no-show.

'But as soon as he realises I'm not coming, he'll call me,' she says, extinguishing my fantasy. 'And if I ignore his calls, won't he come looking for me? I can't hide inside my flat with the lights off.'

She's right, especially as she's already told Jon she can't wait to see him. Standing him up might worry him enough to alert the authorities.

'Family emergency back in England?' I ask when nothing else comes to mind.

She considers this. 'That could work.'

'But you have to time it right – when you tell him,' says Willem. 'Otherwise, he might change his plans and ask to meet you in England.'

'Of course,' she murmurs. '*And* there's the danger of running into him here in Verona.'

'That could be a problem for us as well,' Willem says, glancing at me.

Wonderful – something else to worry about. I hadn't even considered that until now.

'Maybe we all need to leave Verona in the morning, before Jon gets here,' I say. 'Just to be sure.'

Lucia sighs. 'This is a lot to take in,' she says, staring past us at the wall again.

'I know – *truly*,' I reply, reaching out to briefly grasp her arm.

She meets my eyes and smiles sadly right as someone knocks on the office door. Through the window, a couple signals that they need to leave. Lucia holds up a finger, asking them to wait a moment.

'We should let you get back to your guests,' I say.

'First, let me give you a way to contact us,' says Willem sensibly. They tap phones and twin chimes confirm the exchange.

'Kate,' says Lucia, turning to me, 'this might seem a bit bonkers, but I really want to hug you.'

It *is* bonkers, but like with Adriana, I feel a sense of solidarity with Lucia. I break into smile, then reach for her and we hug. She promises to keep us informed and Willem and I say our goodbyes.

Outside, we set off into the cool evening without a clear destination in mind. Soon after, we end up by the river and by an unspoken agreement, we stop to take in the view. I rest my elbows on the stone wall and gaze towards Ponte Pietra. It's even more beautiful at night, its arches with their hodgepodge of stonework illuminated by the lights of Verona.

Across the way, Castel San Pietro sits proudly, silhouetted by the late-dusk sky, a dozen or so Cyprus trees standing sentry. Below, halfway down the hillside, the Roman theatre is bathed in purple light and strains of music float across the fast-flowing river.

'It's so beautiful here,' I say with a sigh.

I sense Willem moving closer, the warmth radiating from his large frame cutting through the evening chill, and I couldn't be more shocked when his hand rests on the small of my back and he leans in. '*You* are beautiful, Kate.'

Lips parted in surprise, my head whips in his direction. Our eyes lock and he steps back slightly, his hand falling away. He suddenly seems unsure, as if he might have misread my feelings.

But he hasn't.

I turn to face him and before he can second-guess himself further – and before I can talk myself out of it – I raise onto my tiptoes, close my eyes, and press my mouth to his.

His hands land lightly on my waist, then meet on my lower back, pulling me close. I slide my hands up his muscular chest, then around his neck, where they clasp. Our bodies melt into each other as his mouth moves hungrily against mine, our shallow breaths mingling as I sink into the kiss, tasting him, breathing him in.

One of his strong hands finds the nape of my neck, and his thumb gently caresses my jawline. The kiss intensifies, igniting every nerve ending and sending tingles down my spine to my toes. Warmth floods my body, igniting my insides.

How many times have I thought about kissing him, encircled in his arms, my body pressed to his? Countless times. And this kiss is everything I've imagined, only a thousand times more mind-blowing.

I couldn't say how long we kiss for – it feels like seconds *and* years – but eventually, we ease apart and open our eyes. I drop back onto my heels, keeping my hands clasped behind his neck.

'That was...' I say, breathless.

'Yes,' he says with a nod, then he breaks into a grin, which I return.

We stare at each other for a long time, and I wonder if this is as much of a pinch-me moment for Willem as it is for me. I've never been kissed like that, not once in my entire life.

'So...' he says after some time.

'So...' I parrot with a tilt of my head.

He looks away as if he's trying to work up the courage to say something, then it dawns on me what it might be.

'Are you thinking about our hotel-room issue?' I ask, and his eyes land back on mine.

His lips disappear between his teeth for a few seconds, then he releases them, his eyes narrowing. 'Yes. How would you feel about shar—'

'I'd feel brilliant,' I say, interrupting him.

Wowser, I like this Kate. Wanting a man as much as I want Willem must have unlocked something inside me that I never knew was there – a bold, sexy, confident goddess of a woman who is undoubtably about to have the best sex of her life.

Willem's brows lift, then he breaks into another smile. 'But we should have dinner first, don't you think? There are lots of choices around here,' he adds.

'Willem, that's what room service is for.'

I reach for his hand, lacing my fingers with his, then lead him in the direction of the hotel.

Forget about like – I *love* this Kate.

* * *

When I wake, I'm instantly aware of Willem in the bed next to me, even though it's a super king. I carefully roll onto my side, not wanting to disturb him. His back is to me, broad and muscular, and I long to reach out and run my fingertips along its ridges, but that might wake him.

Instead, I roll onto my back and stare at the ornate ceiling – likely centuries old – and cast my mind back to last night.

I've never been kissed like I was by the river, so it shouldn't surprise me that Willem is without question the best lover I've ever had.

We arrived at the hotel practically at a trot and Willem went straight to reception to get our cases and the room key. We rode the lift in silence, the air between us fizzing with desire. And inside the room, the second Willem latched the door, we came together, tearing impatiently at clothes, kissing passionately, clinging to each other...

And like I'd imagined many times before, our first time was up against the wall, my legs wrapped around Willem's waist, and him holding me up – fast and hard and passionate. I felt like I'd been winded when he carefully lowered me onto the floor afterwards.

The next time, we moved to the bed and took our time.

It was only when I was lying in Willem's arms and his stomach growled loudly that we realised how late it was and that we still hadn't eaten. Fortunately, the Italians eat late, so we ordered room service and devoured enormous plates of pasta while enjoying a delicious bottle of Valpolicella.

It was the perfect night.

But back in the present, reality looms and I ask myself that intrusive, troubling question: now what?

Because until recently, I prided myself on being level-headed, on my ability to apply logic to any situation and come up with a feasible solution designed to meet as many objectives as possible.

Now I'm a woman who has hard, against-the-wall sex and has fallen – also hard – for someone she probably shouldn't have.

I glance over at Willem, mesmerised by the rise and fall of his torso.

We only met a few weeks ago – and under the most extraordinary circumstances – but in many ways, it feels like I've known him much longer than that. I'm certainly closer to Willem than I ever was to Jon.

But is this really the right time to embark on something new? Both a matchmaker and Margot, who understands me better than anyone, have warned me to guard my heart – warnings that I've boldly ignored. *Highly* uncharacteristic of Kate the Rule Follower.

And is that what this is, the start of a new relationship? Maybe for Willem, this was strictly a one-night thing and when this absurd situation is resolved, I'll never see him again.

Gah! There I go catastrophising again. Nothing about Willem indicates that he's a fuckboy who likes to bed women, then mess them about.

Like Jon.

Suddenly, my phone starts chiming with notifications – it must be 7 a.m., which is when my quiet hours end. I snatch it off the bedside cabinet, trying desperately to silence it before it wakes Willem.

I succeed, but my heart's racing almost as much as it was last night. Now wide awake with no hope of falling back asleep, I check my emails – mostly spam plus a lovely, newsy email from Mum in which she gossips about people I've never met – and then navigate to my messages.

There's a whole string from Margot spaced out over the evening, the last one arriving right before midnight Italian time:

Let me know how it goes with the Arseface's girlfriend.

Stupid autocorrect. Had to type Arseface four times. *eye roll emoji*

How's the hotel? Did you get adjoining rooms? *winking face emoji*

Did you find her? What's she like?

Hello? Update please! And how's Thor?

I consider how to reply for some time. If she's awake – not

likely, but possible if she was out all night – and my reply is too juicy, she'll phone me immediately. Finally, I settle on this:

Sorry! Went well with Lucia. She was shocked at first (natch) but she's agreed to the plan. She's waiting until Jon's plane lands in Verona then making an excuse not to see him. She reminds me of you a bit (feisty). You'd like her. Saw a bit of Verona afterwards, then back to the hotel.

She'll hate that I haven't mentioned Willem, but that's not a conversation I want to have with him lying next to me.

I've also heard from Poppy, which means that even on a Friday night, she was looking out for me – that is, *working*:

I hope you're able to find Lucia in time and that she's receptive to what you have to say. Keep me posted on how it all goes and I'm here if you need to talk – about anything.

There are those words again – 'about anything' – which clearly mean 'Willem'. I type out a reply, filling her in on the conversation with Lucia and how we've scuppered Jon's plans. I blatantly omit mention of Willem, which I'm sure Poppy will read into, but that's also a conversation for another time.

The last message – no surprise – is from Jon:

Missing you already. Have a lovely weekend, beautiful. Hoping to be back in London next week or the week after. Catch you then. *kissing face emoji*

I stare at the little yellow face after Jon's message, its pursed lips blowing a heart-shaped kiss. There was a time when it would have filled me with warmth, a feeling of being loved. Now it's repulsive.

'Good morning,' says a gruff voice, startling me.

'Good morning,' I reply, quickly inverting the phone on the bedside cabinet. I roll over to face Willem, plastering a smile on my face.

It's like vertigo, swinging this wildly between disgust at Jon to lust for Willem. Lust with a generous measure of like.

Willem returns my smile, then leans across the gap between our pillows to land a chaste kiss on my mouth.

Well, that's not very one-night-stand-ish, I think, a familiar flutter invading my chest.

'How did you sleep?' he asks.

I blink at him, then break into a wider smile. 'Actually, I slept really well.'

He laughs. 'You sound surprised.'

'I am. You know, late night, strange bed...'

What's left unsaid is that I was sharing that strange bed with someone new, something that until now has always meant a fitful night's sleep.

'And you?' I ask, reciprocating.

'I also slept well.'

'Good.'

'Yes.'

This is hardly a scintillating conversation, and I wonder if it's because Willem feels uncomfortable. *I'm* starting to.

'So...' he says, his eyes piercing mine.

'So...' I say, delighted by the seismic shift in the mood.

Willem's hand reaches for my face and he trails the backs of his fingers down my cheek and along my jawline. It's gentle, his touch, belying that he's a hulk of a man – or a Thor of a man, as Margot would say – and it makes me quiver.

This time when Willem closes the gap between us, his kiss is anything but chaste.

* * *

'I was thinking...'

We're at a café near the hotel having a light breakfast of coffee (which may be the best I've ever had) and croissants (also delicious), and Willem is watching me closely.

'Are you planning on finishing that thought or should I try and guess?'

Get you, Kate Whitaker! That's a Margot-worthy quip right there. Orgasms must have magical powers. Not only have all my early-morning doubts been banished, I'm also my most comfortable, confident self – the Kate from last night.

Or that could be how *Willem* affects me. He even reached for my hand as we left the hotel – *very* un-fuckboy-like.

He grins. 'It's about changing your flight...' He's referring to our decision to vacate Verona to avoid accidentally running into Jon. 'What if you came to Amsterdam with me instead of going to London?'

My eyes widen in surprise. Definitely not one-night-stand-ish!

'You don't have to—'

'No, I want to,' I reply enthusiastically.

We stare at each other for a few seconds, then he reaches across the table for my hand.

'Kate, I—'

My phone chimes loudly with a message notification – I must have overcorrected after I unsilenced it. 'Sorry,' I say, turning off the screen. I look back at him, expecting him to pick up where he left off, but he doesn't.

'Don't you want to check that?' he asks. 'It could be Lucia.'

'Oh, of course,' I say, feeling a little foolish. I open the phone screen and navigate to my messages. Only it isn't Lucia – it's Jon.

I groan involuntarily.

'What is it?' asks Willem.

I look up from my phone, grimacing. 'It's Jon. I forgot to reply to his message this morning and sometimes he gets a bit... stroppy.'

'Stroppy?' he asks, a shadow of confusion crossing his face.

'Annoyed, pissed off.'

'*He* gets pissed off with *you*?' he asks incredulously.

'Uh, yes. Sometimes.'

Willem inhales through his nose, his nostrils flaring.

I turn my head away, giving him an amused side-eye. 'You don't like him – I get it. I'm not Jon's biggest fan either, but soon this will all be over and we never have to mention him again.'

'Any chance I can get five minutes alone with him?'

'Based on how your knuckles have turned white, I'd say no.'

His mouth twitches and with a self-deprecating eye roll, his scowl gives way to a smile.

'Now, after I reply to the lying prick,' I say, holding up my phone, 'we're changing our flights. *And* I'm coming to Amsterdam with you.'

His smile stretches into a grin. 'I like it when you take charge,' he says, his voice dripping with inuendo.

Remembering exactly how I 'took charge' last night, my cheeks colour and Willem bursts out laughing.

23

POPPY

I wake with a start – namely because Saffron's bum is in my face and her swishing tail is flicking back and forth over my mouth. I swat it away, then push her over to Tristan's side of the bed and fish a cat hair out of my mouth. If I didn't love her so much, I'd ship her off to Siberia.

My mouth stretches into a silent yawn and I stretch my legs out, twisting my hips from side to side. I'm awake far too early for a Saturday morning but there's no way I'll get back to sleep now. No doubt part of Saffron's evil plan to usurp me as 'lady of the house'. Since the day we brought her home, she's been in love with Tristan.

I prop myself up on my pillows and check my phone. Mum messaged overnight. She and Dad are excited about their upcoming trip to London and she's now sending daily count-downs of how many sleeps it is until they arrive.

I'm excited too, but I *really* hope I'm done with the Whitaker case before they arrive. They're already baffled by the machinations of my profession. If 'Penny' is still in operation, especially if she's having video chats with Jon Dunn, there will be some serious explaining to do.

I also heard from Kate overnight – a brief message saying that she and Willem found Lucia and successfully foiled Dunn's intended proposal.

She didn't mention Willem specifically, which *could* be telling. Is she deliberately not mentioning the room mix-up because they shared a room, or did they figure out something else, so she didn't think it was worth mentioning?

Other than asking her outright, which would reveal my hand in the mix-up, I have no way of knowing. Unless...

After replying to Kate, I fire off a message to Marie. She keeps all kinds of odd hours and is constantly travelling for work, so I'll either hear from her in the next few minutes or not until the end of the day.

It's the former. A minute after sending the message, she replies:

Confirming they shared a room. Seen leaving hotel this morning, hand in hand.

Hand in hand! I have no idea how Marie procured *that* information, but it's what we call in the matchmaking biz 'proof of romantic entanglement'.

'Yes,' I whisper, punching the air.

'That's either good news, or you've started without me,' says Tristan dryly.

I glance over and he's watching me through slitted eyes, one hand lazily petting Saffron, who's purring loudly.

'Good morning, babe. I haven't started without you – we can do that later,' I say, casually moving sex with my hot husband down on the schedule. 'It's my client – she and the potential love interest spent the night together in Verona.'

'The client who's engaged to your boyfriend?' he teases, the corners of his mouth lifting slightly.

'Hilarious,' I retort. 'And yes.'

Tristan sniggers, then his eyes narrow again. 'Hold on, I thought this case was about retribution.'

'It still is. But now there's a potential HEA.'

'Since when?'

'Since my client spent the night with the love interest,' I state matter-of-factly.

'Makes perfect sense,' he quips, his head shaking slightly.

'It doesn't, not really,' I acknowledge, 'especially as, until recently, I didn't think Kate was ready to get involved with someone new – not this soon after finding out about Dunn.'

'What changed your mind?'

'Freya and George. They helped me see the situation differently,' I admit. 'Nearly six years in and I'm still evolving as a matchmaker. And *that* could mean an HEA for someone who came to me seeking revenge. *Revenge*, Tris. Talk about a turnaround.'

We share a smile that speaks to a deep understanding of how invested I am in my career, how much I love what I do.

Neither of us *has* to work any more, not with Tristan's inheritance and how shrewdly he's invested it. Financially, we're set for life, but it has never occurred to either of us to simply stop working. Tristan loves his job as much as I love mine.

'And how do you know they spent the night together?' he asks.

'Marie,' I reply with a waggle of my brows.

Tristan's eyes widen. 'So, you had Marie spy on your client?'

'Yep.'

'I see, and is this something you've done before?'

'Spying?' I ask, stalling. Because the only other time I've spied on a client, it was Tristan – long before we recognised we were into each other – and *I* was the spy.

'Mm-hmm,' he replies.

'Maybe.'

It must click why I'm being cagey, and he sits up suddenly and gawps at me. 'Was it *me*?'

'Mmm, I don't recall,' I lie.

'Poppy Elizabeth Dean!'

Uh-oh, he's busting out my full name. Time to come clean.

'Okay, yes, it was you.'

'When?'

'During your lunch with Alexandra,' I reply, referring to one of his potential matches.

He frowns in concentration. 'The lunch at City Social?'

'That's the one.'

He's wearing a far-off look, as if he's trying to remember that day.

'This was *way* before I fell for you, don't forget,' I hasten to add. 'Or at least before I admitted it to myself.'

He refocuses on me, his mouth twitching.

'Anyway, I wanted to make sure that it went as planned, so Freya and I spied on you.'

'You dragged *Freya* into it?'

'Yes, and she agreed on the proviso that I buy lunch. Only that place was so exxy! I said we had to stick to starters and Freya ordered the scallop. As in singular. And it was twenty-two pounds – for a lone scallop!'

'You appear to be skirting around the issue, Ms Dean,' he says with a smirk. 'Can we revisit the part where you spied on me?'

I sigh. 'No. It's water under the bridge now. How about we shoo Saffy off the bed and get to the sex part instead?'

Still smirking, he tilts his head at me knowingly. But then he puts Saffron on the floor, and turns and gathers me in his arm.

I'm off the hook! And if he ever brings it up again, I will stress that it was all in service of the case. Like my surveillance of Kate and Willem.

Hand in hand! Huzzah!

* * *

Kate

'It's a shame you don't get to spend more time in Verona,' says Margot after I fill her in on the change of plans.

It *is* a shame, but as far as consolation prizes go, spending the rest of the weekend in Amsterdam with Willem makes up for it. Now I just need to tell Margot without getting reprimanded for turning one night of rebound sex into a cosy weekend at his.

I listen out and the shower is running, so I can speak freely.

'Actually, I'm heading to Amsterdam,' I say with (what I hope is) the breeziest of breezy tones ever to be voiced in the history of humanity.

She doesn't buy it – not surprising, considering. I've always been the opposite of breezy.

'So, you finally slept with Thor.'

My eyes fly to the bathroom door – still shut, like it was a moment ago. But Willem won't stay in there forever, so I need this part of the conversation to be over as soon as possible.

'So how was it?' she asks before I have a chance to respond. 'Was it hot and sexy or dreamy and romantic?'

'Both,' I reply. Then I giggle – *actually* giggle.

'Oh my god, Kate! Tell me everything!'

I knew this was coming, of course. Since I lost my virginity, Margot has insisted on detailed accounts of my sexual encounters. Except when it came to Jon, that is. When I first started seeing him and Margot asked how he was in bed, she concluded that I was too young to settle for vanilla sex. We had a row over that, but in hindsight she was right.

'I will,' I say, dropping my voice. 'But not right this minute.'

'Okay, you're off the hook – for now, but I'm holding you to that.'

'I promise,' I say, even though I've barely grasped this situation myself.

'Wait, I've just had a brilliant idea,' says Margot.

Uh-oh. Margot's 'brilliant ideas' are either absurd or destined to get me into trouble – sometimes both.

'What if I popped over to Amsterdam for the remainder of the weekend?' she asks.

I laugh. 'Right, sure. The three of us can order pizza, then play Uno. I'm sure Willem would love that.'

'I'm not joking.'

'Margot, *no*,' I say, panicking. How can she be serious?

'Not to cock-block you, you muppet. Just the opposite. I'll take Adriana out for the night – give you two some privacy.'

'That's...' I want to say 'bonkers', but is it? Sure, Willem and I can go out for dinner, but we'll want to return to his place at some point in the evening to... well, have sex. A lot of sex. Actually, I'd be happy to skip dinner and just have sex. All. The. Sex.

Who am I right now?

'That's perfect, Margot, thank you,' she says sarcastically.

'That's perfect, Margot, thank you,' I parrot sheepishly. 'Hang on – what if Adriana already has plans?' It's a reasonable assumption; it's Saturday and she seems to have an active social life.

'She doesn't,' Margot replies, sounding certain.

'And you know this how?'

'Uh... we've been messaging.'

There have been so many twists and turns in this conversation, I may develop whiplash. Margot should come with a seatbelt.

'You've been messaging with my fiancé's fiancée?'

'Well, yes. She's my silver lining.'

'Your silver lining?' I ask, confused.

'Mm-hmm. Jon is a massive shit of a human being, *but* if he hadn't been such a massive shit of a human being, we wouldn't have met Willem and Adriana. Now you get to have rebound sex with a hot guy – *your* silver lining – and I've... well, I've made a new friend.'

'I *love* how you've spun this to be about you,' I say sarcastically.

'Situational narcissism – practically my only flaw,' she says immodestly. She has others, of course – like everyone – but I let it go.

'Well, if you want to get yourself to Amsterdam *and* pay for accommodation *and* take Adriana out for the evening, then I won't stop you.'

She laughs heartily. 'As if you could.'

Resigned and somewhat frustrated, I lift my eyes to the

ceiling. 'But can you hold off a bit?' I ask with a sigh. 'Willem hasn't talked to Adriana yet. I don't want *you* breaking the news that we're showing up unexpectedly.'

'Course not.'

'Does that mean you *will* hold off?'

'Yes. Now, I've got to go – lots of plans to make. See you in Amsterdam, cuz,' she says, ringing off.

After the call, an odd thought pops into my mind.

Is it still called cock-blocking if I don't have a cock? What's the female equivalent? Box blocking?

'Eww, *no*, Kate,' I say out loud to myself.

'What's that?'

Willem is standing in the doorway to the bathroom, a towel wrapped tightly around his waist, his penis prominently outlined. The timing is uncanny, considering the whole cock-blocking tangent, and I stifle a laugh. 'Er, nothing... That was Margot on the phone,' I say, shifting the focus off me.

'And how is she?' he asks, coming into the room and rifling through his case.

'She's coming to Amsterdam,' I say – ripping off the plaster Margot style. He stops what he's doing and looks up, one brow arched. 'All right, you need to stop that,' I chide playfully.

'Stop what?' he asks, clearly baffled.

'You're standing there in a towel and you're all...' I cup my hands in front of my chest, then over my biceps – makeshift sign language to denote 'muscly' – which makes him snigger. 'And now I discover you can raise one eyebrow? That's far too much power for one man to possess.'

'You mean this?' He arches that brow again, then shrugs. 'I can only do it on the right side. It's not that impressive.'

'Pretty sure that's in the eye of the beholder,' I assert.

'Okay. And what else would you like to behold?' he asks, his voice low and rumbly.

My breath catches as heat blooms between my legs. We're supposed to be making travel plans before we check out, but all I can think about is round four. I haven't even packed my case yet, and I don't care. This is all very un-Kate-like behaviour, like a fresh, unbuttoned version of myself.

He's still watching me, waiting for a response.

'Oh, sod it,' I say, slipping the straps of my dress over my shoulders and letting it fall to the floor. Willem grins at me, then untucks the towel and whips it off with a flourish.

I must say, we are getting our money's worth out of this hotel room.

* * *

We're in the lobby waiting to pay our room-service bill when I receive a message from Lucia:

Thinking of going to London for some family time. Would you be interested in meeting up later? I feel like we've got a lot more to talk about.

I suck in a breath through my teeth. I didn't expect that Lucia would want to see me again so soon.

'Is everything okay?' Willem asks.

I hold up my phone so he can read her message. 'Oh,' he says, looking up to meet my eyes. 'Would you rather return to London?'

We haven't changed our flights yet. We got a little side-tracked, barely making the expected checkout time, so we'll do it on the way to the airport. But I don't want to go back to

London right away. I already have my heart set on Amsterdam – other parts of me are set on it too.

'Would it be completely mad to ask if she wants to come to Amsterdam?' I ask.

'Not completely, but won't that affect *our* plans?'

'And what are our plans exactly?'

In a fit of bad timing, it's our turn in the queue. Willem asks the receptionist for the bill, but I'm quicker in handing over my credit card than he is – only fair because he paid for the room. He doesn't argue like Jon would have. Then again, Willem isn't a macho arsehole who has to pay for everything to feel like a man.

We don't resume our conversation until we're in the backseat of a cab, zipping once again through the narrow streets of Verona. I'd gawp out the window like I have before, but I *really* want Willem to answer my question.

'Right, so, picking up where we left off: what *are* our plans for the rest of the weekend?' I ask.

Before responding, he captures my hand in his, making my pulse quicken. I never knew how erotic handholding could be until I met Willem.

Looking across the backseat, he says, 'I thought we could go for dinner and...'

...go home and shag each other senseless.

'...talk.'

'Oh,' I say, taken by surprise.

He breaks into a grin. 'You don't want to talk?'

'No, I do. I just...' My cheeks heat up and I look away. It's one thing to unleash my inner sex goddess within the confines of a hotel room; it's another to be caught out practically begging for sex.

Willem leans across, his mouth close to my ear. 'And after

dinner... after talking... I want to take you home and pick up where we just left off.'

Tingles. Everywhere.

I quiver with anticipation – *and* relief – because it seems this *isn't* one-sided. Willem wants me as much as I want him. Physically, anyway. I'm not sure what he wants to talk about, but I'm fully prepared for the let's-just-be-friends-with-benefits talk.

All right, that's an abject lie.

I do not want to be friends with Willem. Well, not *only* friends. God, this is a lot. Maybe Poppy and Margot were right. Maybe it *is* too soon to get involved with someone else.

'How does that sound?' he asks when I don't respond.

I send him a smile. 'It sounds perfect,' I reply, and he beams at me.

But almost instantly, his smile falls away and he's suddenly serious. 'So, what do we do about Lucia?'

'Honestly,' I say, giving in to the momentum of this situation, 'it might be good for all of us to be together – Jon's... "menagerie"? Is that the right word?'

He lifts one shoulder in a half-shrug.

'Doesn't really matter what we call it,' I continue. 'But Lucia's right – we *do* have a lot to talk about. Even with Adriana, I've only scratched the surface.'

'Hmm,' he says, his expression pensive.

'What did she say, by the way? When you told her I'm coming to Amsterdam with you.'

'I haven't had the chance to tell her yet. I was going to message her after we changed our flights.'

'Right.' Somehow, this information makes a dent in how cheery I felt only moments ago. But rather than dwelling on that, my pragmatism kicks in.

'Okay, how about I say yes to Lucia and tell Margot she shouldn't come? The three of us spend some time together this afternoon, talking things through, then later, you and I go to dinner. How does that sound?'

He nods, giving me a weak smile. 'Okay, I'll message Ady. And, Kate, I'm really sorry.'

'Sorry?' I ask, surprised. 'For what?'

'Wanting you all to myself when you've got so much going on.'

There's a lot to unpack in that apology, but it will have to wait. Because Willem's right; there's too much going on right now.

24

KATE

A two-hour flight goes fast when you and your travel companion are swapping embarrassing stories from your childhood to avoid the elephant in the room – well, aeroplane. Namely that our timing is terrible and it's probably ill-advised to be embarking on whatever this is. And 'ill-advised' is the best-case scenario.

Still, it's been entertaining hearing about his childhood antics – *and* Adriana's – especially the story he's telling right now from when he was thirteen.

'Our parents aren't prudes – they're typically Dutch, very progressive,' he says, 'but my mother...' He shakes his head, his eyes comically wide. 'I would have been in *big* trouble if she'd found *Playboy* in my room.'

'But that was Daan. *He* brought it over. It wasn't your fault.'

'I doubt she would have cared about that distinction, so I hid it under my bed, then we went to make some food – sandwiches or something – and I forgot about it.'

I give him an I-don't-believe-you look.

'I promise. I forgot all about it.'

'Hmm, okay. So, what, your mum found it?'

'Oh no. *Much* worse than that.'

'What's worse than that?' I ask with a laugh.

'Well, that night, my parents went out and I stayed with Ady to look after her.'

'You were babysitting.'

'Right. And she was playing in her bedroom, and I was watching TV or something... Anyway, when my parents came home, they found Ady in her room, cutting out pictures of the "pretty ladies" from the magazine and making a collage.'

'Oh my god!' I exclaim loudly, irking the woman across the aisle. She glares at me, and I apologise. She tuts and resumes her crossword with a shake of her head.

'So, what did they do? Your parents?' I ask in a hushed tone.

'My mother calmly calls me into Ady's room to admire this "artwork" – and I am standing there, my mouth open, feeling...' He seems to search for the right word.

'Mortified? Horrified? Wanting the ground to open up and swallow you whole?'

'Yes,' he replies with a chuckle. 'Exactly like that.'

'Then what happened?'

'Then we leave Ady to finish her collage.'

'No. *Really?*'

'Really, and then my mother tells me that it's normal to be curious about these things.'

'Oh, interesting.'

'Yes, and I think, "Okay. I'm not in trouble. My mother is fine with this."'

'I sense a "but" coming.'

'You sense correctly. *Then* she says that if I ever bring this type of thing into the house again – before I am an adult – she will send that collage to my grandparents and tell them what I did.'

'Oh, wowser, that's genius,' I say with an appreciative grin.

'It was convincing, and I never let something like that happen again.'

'But *Daan*... It was *his* fault and you were the one who was punished.'

'Oh, no. His father found out he'd taken it and when he couldn't give it back, because Ady had destroyed it, Daan had, er... we say *huisarrest*. Except for school, he had to stay home for two weeks.'

'Ah, he was grounded, yes.'

'Right – *grounded*.'

'And I'm assuming it never got sent to your grandparents?'

'No, but when I was renovating, I found it in a box of my old schoolwork.'

'What? Your mum kept it?'

'Apparently, and when I showed Ady, we laughed *so* hard – for at least five minutes.'

The idea of stoic, measured Willem laughing that freely is endearing.

'Well, that *is* a good story – top-notch parenting by your mum.'

He smiles. 'I think you will like her. I'm sure she will like you.'

His use of future tense yanks me back to the present – for Willem too, I can tell. He's quiet for a moment, then he reaches for my hand. I let him take it, even though hand-holding means *far* more than I'm prepared to examine right now.

'Kate, I want to ask you...' He pauses, his gaze fixed on the seatback in front of him, then he turns towards me. '*How* did you end up with Dunn?'

'Oh...' I look away, then puff out my cheeks. Ordinarily, I'm good at formulating succinct answers, but this isn't a Monday-morning standup. This is my topsy-turvy love life and I'm not sure I even *want* to answer.

But there's a minute possibility that this thing between me and Willem could turn into something more, so I want to be truthful. I owe that to both of us.

'Well,' I say, glancing at him, 'in my twenties – and way further into my thirties than I care to admit – I fell for blokes who were emotionally unavailable, and I would mould myself into what I thought they wanted.' Uncomfortable, I look away, focusing on the emergency evacuation card in the seat pocket. 'And just over four years ago, after a rather ugly breakup, I finally understood what I'd been doing and I self-imposed a moratorium on men, which went on for a long time – *years*. And to be completely truthful, I felt lonely sometimes.'

I inhale deeply, then steady my breath.

'Anyway, around six months ago, I was talking with a colleague – she'd just invited me to her wedding – and she told me that she and her husband-to-be had met through a matchmaker. I was intrigued and she offered to refer me, which after a couple of weeks of contemplation, I agreed to. But of course' – I point to myself with both forefingers – 'prag-matist that I am, *I* stupidly thought, "What's better than *one* matchmaker? Two!" and I signed on with a second agency, the one that matched me with Jon. The rest you know.'

He runs his thumb along the back of my hand, then gives it a squeeze.

'Thank you for telling me,' he says, and I look over again.

We share a smile, then lapse into silence, and I turn and stare out the window as we descend into Amsterdam.

I'm overcome with nerves when the cab turns down Willem's road. Understandable, considering Adriana's lukewarm response when Willem told her I was coming to Amsterdam – *and* that Lucia would be joining us.

Even though Adriana and I seem to get along well enough, I've never expected us to become lifelong friends. But we're both invested in Jon getting his comeuppance and I'd like to think we're on the same side.

It could be that we're simply processing this differently. From what I can tell, Adriana is either holing up at home, miserable, or going out on the town with her girlfriends, drowning her sorrows.

Whereas I've skipped two full stages of grief – bargaining and depression – and have gone straight from anger to acceptance. I have no doubt it's because of Willem, but is he simply a diversionary tactic or are my feelings for him – as muddy as they are – real?

And maybe Adriana's reaction has nothing to do with me at all. Well, I'm about to find out.

The cab pulls up outside Willem's house and while I pay, he gets our cases from the boot. Then it's just us, standing outside his front door.

'Is everything all right? You look a little...'

'Freaked out?' I ask, breaking into a nervous grin.

'Yes.'

He stares at me while I go back and forth on being honest or brushing my feelings under the carpet. But before I can decide, the front door flies open and Adriana fills the doorway. Is this her idea of a welcome or is she acting as a human barricade? She says something to Willem in Dutch, then her eyes land on me.

'Hi, Kate,' she says, her expression unreadable.

'Hi.'

She steps back and signals for us to pass, which is difficult because she's in the way and it's a narrow space.

'Ady, out of the way,' says Willem gruffly, but she stays put. He sidesteps her, our cases in hand, and I follow. Adriana closes the door behind us with a little more force than is probably required.

Yep, she's definitely out of sorts and I *really* hope it's not because of me.

Willem walks over to the wide doorway that leads to the bedrooms and sets our cases down. Adriana watches him closely, her hands on her hips.

'*So*, you two are toge—'

She's interrupted by the sound of a toilet flushing.

Did Lucia beat us here? I wonder. We'd hoped to arrive first to make the introductions. But with Adriana obviously pissed off, polite introductions are the least of my worries.

'Who else is here?' Willem asks Adriana.

'The ghost of the old lady who died here,' she replies sarcastically, and he huffs with annoyance.

'Hi, cuz.'

I thought I'd had my fair share of surprises over the past few weeks, but the fates clearly have something else in mind and here's yet another one.

'Margot, what the hell are you doing here?'

She wipes her still-damp hands down the front of her trousers.

'What?' she asks defensively.

'I told you not to come. Lucia's arriving soon and we have—'

'I know, I know,' she says, 'but I'd already bought my ticket and besides, Ady was expecting me.'

I look over at Adriana, who's now nibbling on her thumbnail. A moment ago, she was about to give me a bollocking; now she looks like she's expecting one from me.

Then it dawns on me, and my head swivels towards Margot.

'Is this what I think it is?' I ask.

'I'm not sure. What do you think it is?' she replies evenly.

'Don't be coy, Margot. Are you and Ady seeing each other?' I glance back at Ady, who hurriedly looks away, then return my gaze to Margot.

Margot drops her head back and sighs, then looks at me again. 'Yes.'

'Since *when*?'

'Since the weekend you showed up to tell me about Jon,' Adriana replies quietly, drawing my gaze. Right, so they must have got together after the girls' night out while Willem and I were at dinner. 'We like each other – and it's fun,' she adds with a casual shrug.

I stare at Adriana, dumbstruck. There's so much to unpack here, and most of it is contradictory.

Adriana's pissed off about me and Willem, yet she's been shagging my cousin. Margot warned me not to fall in love, but she and Ady seem to be embarking on a relationship.

What the actual fuck?

I drop my face into my hands and groan, and Margot comes over and pats me on the back.

'Are you okay?' she asks.

I lift my head and glare at her incredulously.

'Er, no, Margot. No, I'm not okay. I am so far from okay, I'd need a *passport* to get there. How is any of this even happening? *Any* of it!'

I break away from her, crossing to the tall windows and staring out into the lush garden. 'Less than a month ago, I was just living my life – happily living my life – just normal. All very normal,' I say, my voice high and pitchy. 'I went to work and I spent time with my friends and with you' – I flap my hand over my shoulder towards Margot – 'and I was engaged to a nice man – a man who I *thought* was nice – who I saw every few weeks and it was good. Life was good.'

I spin around and they're all gawping at me, but I'm not finished, so I ignore their wide eyes and open mouths and start pacing the width of the room.

'But then *you* show up,' I say, my hand shooting in Willem's direction, 'and you tell me the most *unbelievable* news. Like, full-on, *bonkers* news. And if that weren't enough,' I say, rounding on him, '*then* you ask me to come here and present myself to your sister as living, breathing proof that our sodding, bloody arsehole of a fiancé was living a double life!'

Willem's mouth snaps shut and he looks away, appearing sheepish.

'But even that wasn't enough... No, suddenly, I'm one of *three* and I'm flying here, there and every-bloody-where, plotting and scheming as if this is *Charlie's Angels* and I'm Cameron bloody Diaz! And *today,* I discover that my cousin and my fiancé's other fiancée are in the midst of a love affair, something neither of them thought to tell me even though we're in communication all the sodding time!

'And, yes, Adriana, your brother and I have slept together. Was that misguided? Probably. Was the timing ideal? It was not. But did I enjoy every minute of it? I absolutely, bloody well did, yes. So, if you want to be pissed off at me, particularly in light of this latest development, you hypocrite, then go ahead.'

'Kate—'

'I'm not finished!' I shout at Margot, who presses her lips together. 'And you want to know the worst thing? *None* of this is me,' I say, my arms thrown wide. '*None* of it – not the complications nor the messiness, not the running about and becoming embroiled in a revenge plot – a revenge plot of all things! It's not even me to be standing here, screeching like a banshee. I'm typically calm and collected and... and... not, well, like this. And it is *especially* not me to jump into bed with someone, simply because I fancy the hell out of them, knowing it would only complicate an already complicated situation and would be a stupid, *stupid* mistake!'

As the words leave my mouth, I realise I've gone too far, something confirmed by the hurt on Willem's face.

'Fuck!' I gasp. 'Willem, I—'

He holds up his hand and I fall silent.

'Lucia will be here soon. I'll leave you all to talk.'

And he does. He leaves and the silence that fills the room is so epic, I can hear my heartbeat hammering in my ears.

What have I done?

* * *

'Don't worry, he doesn't usually stay angry very long. He'll calm down,' says Adriana reassuringly. Only it's not reassuring because I thought Willem was hurt, not angry. She sets a mug of coffee in front of me, made on her brother's fancy machine.

'Thank you,' I say softly, the fight having left my body the moment Willem left this house.

Why did I go off like that? How humiliating. *And* I've upset Willem.

'Ady,' says Margot, scrutinising me from the other side of the dining table, 'I think she's going to need something stronger than that.'

She's not wrong – a stiff whisky wouldn't go amiss, but I'm not exactly in the position to make demands.

'Okay. How about rum?'

'*Surely* you've got something else?' asks Margot with a laugh, not one to mince words. 'I haven't had that crap since uni days and if I catch even a whiff of it, we'll be re-living Vomagedon 2006 before you can say, "Margot, don't you dare throw up on that rug!"'

This makes me and Adriana laugh, and our eyes meet briefly before she looks away. I don't blame her. When I was here last time, we found common ground; we were on the same side. But that was when we were entangled in a simple love triangle. Now that it's become a love *hexagon* – and far more complex than either of us could have foreseen – we seem to be back at square one. She's wary of me and I'm at a loss for how to fix everything.

'I'll see what else we've got,' Adriana says, crossing to the tall cabinet where they keep the liquor.

Margot leaps up and reaches past her. 'This,' she says, taking out a bottle of Redbreast.

'Margot, no,' I say, recognising the bottle immediately. Jon drank it – it's very expensive and he ordered it nearly every time we went out. Of course, some places didn't carry it and he'd always make a big to-do.

'Not that one,' says Adriana softly. She takes the bottle and places it back on the shelf.

'Because of Jon?' I ask.

She spins around quickly. 'How did you— Oh, right. Never mind.'

'Must be one of the details he kept the same,' I say.

'Yes.' She sighs heavily. 'Kate, I'm sorry I reacted that way – about you and Will. And you're right, I *was* being hypocritical. But I...'

I stand, facing her. 'No, you don't need to apologise. I can understand why you're upset.'

'It's just... first Jon and now my brother.'

'I get it, and you have every right to be pissed off at me.'

'That's the thing... I'm not – not at you, anyway,' she says. 'It's Jon. *All* of this is his fault, that... that...'

'Fucking wankard,' Margot supplies, which makes us both laugh again.

'I *love* it,' says Adriana. 'Fucking wankard – it feels good in my mouth. Fucking wankard,' she says again, hitting the consonants with precision.

'What about this?' Margot holds up a bottle of vodka.

'Perfect,' I declare.

'*Ja*,' Adriana agrees, striding to the fridge and opening the door. 'And we have orange juice and limes...'

She and Margot get to work and I observe the easy way they interact, how Margot beams up at Adriana and how Adriana's eyes soften when they meet Margot's. I haven't seen this side of Margot since... well, I can't remember when. And even though they couldn't be more different, they seem to work. Margot looks *happy*.

A few minutes later, we're each holding a vodka-orange garnished with a wedge of lime.

'*Prost*,' says Adriana, lifting her glass.

'*Prost*,' Margot echoes.

'Oh, we can do better than that,' I say. 'To the fucking wankard who brought us together.'

There's a beat of silence and for a moment, I worry that I've gone too far – again. Then Adriana bursts into laughter, and Margot and I join in.

'Kate,' she says, looking me in the eye, 'no matter what happens – no matter how this situation is resolved – I hope we can be friends.'

'Huzzah!' Margot exclaims.

I smile at Adriana, grateful for the olive branch, but a niggling thought takes hold.

That's one of the siblings on side, but what about the other?

25

KATE

Lucia is due in ten minutes and Adriana and I are deep into a tit-for-tat exchange of Jon's lies – the big, the small, and the (very, very) ugly.

'So, what did Jon tell *you* about his parents?' I ask.

'They're estranged and he never sees them.'

'Hmm – convenient,' I retort tartly. 'He told me his father is deceased and that his mum is in aged care. Only whenever I suggested we go and visit her, he made up some excuse.'

'And which is it?' she asks.

'Willem didn't tell you?'

'I wouldn't let him. I didn't want to hear it – too depressing.'

'And now?' I ask.

'Now... maybe it's better to know,' she says, resigned.

'Well then, his father *is* deceased, of course – hence the enormous inheritance – but his mother lives on a beautiful estate in Scotland with three dogs and live-in staff. It's likely she has no idea what Jon is up to.'

'If my son ever pulled anything like this,' says Margot, 'I'd drag him through the streets by his ear and give him a right bollocking in the town square.'

'How very *Victorian* of you,' I quip, and she chuckles.

'Kate,' says Adriana, and I look over. 'What's she like?'

It takes me a second to grasp who she's asking about, because my first thought is of Jon's mother.

'You mean Lucia?'

She nods.

'Different – to *us*, I mean. Opposite to you in looks – petite, dark hair – and polar opposite to me in personality.'

'So, he doesn't have a type,' Margot observes.

'Not as far as I can tell,' I reply.

'Just gullible women,' says Adriana, her lips flattening into a peevish line. I don't disagree and, once again, I feel a stab of regret for being so willing to swallow his lies.

'But other than that,' Adriana adds, 'Jon must like variety.'

'It appears that way,' I reply. 'Even the persona Poppy's playing is quite distinctive, a deliberate tactic that seems to have worked.'

'Do you think this will all be over soon?' Adriana asks wearily.

'It should be. Poppy says she's making progress.'

Adriana clasps her hands behind her neck, the way Willem does when he's frustrated, then expels a long groan of a sigh. 'I just want this to be over. I want to confront Jon, revel in seeing the terror on his face, then move on.'

'I hear you,' says Margot.

Adriana drops her hands and looks at Margot, the left corner of her mouth lifting. 'Yes, this *has* been hard on you,' she says, her lips twitching.

Margot swats the air. 'You know what I mean. I just feel for you – *both* of you. It's a horrible situation and neither of you deserve to be in this position.'

'Thanks, Margs,' I say.

I'm actually glad she's here, despite my initial shock at her showing up when I asked her not to – *and* at whatever's going on between her and Adriana.

The doorbell sounds, startling all of us, and Adriana leaps up to answer the door. There's a polite exchange in the entry-way, then Lucia's larger-than-life presence fills the vast room, with Adriana coming up behind her.

Lucia drops a leather duffle bag on the floor and before I have a chance to greet her and introduce her properly, she looks directly at Margot. 'Don't tell me you're number four?'

Margot presses her hand to her chest. 'Me? God, no. I wouldn't touch that prick with a ten-foot pole. I'm the cheer squad.'

Lucia sniggers, then crosses the room, her hand outstretched. 'Lucia Rossi. Number three.'

'Margot Whitaker – number one's cousin,' she replies, jerking her head in my direction.

'*Ahh*, I see,' says Lucia with a guarded smile. Her gaze drops to the half-drunk drinks on the table. 'So, what are we having?' she asks no one in particular.

Adriana seems to snap out of her trance. 'Vodka with orange juice. Have a seat. I'll make you one.'

The rest of us sit around the table, Lucia next to me, while Adriana sloshes some vodka into a glass freehand, then tops up the glass with orange juice. As an afterthought, she adds two ice cubes, splashing liquid onto the benchtop.

She's nervous, I think. Completely understandable, consid-ering I've felt the same way at least a dozen times over the past few weeks.

'Here.' She sets the drink in front of Lucia, then takes a seat opposite her.

'Thank you – and for letting me come,' says Lucia.

'Sure,' Adriana replies, as if she'd invited Lucia here herself.

'But I have to say,' Lucia continues, 'it's weird, meeting you. Same as when I met Kate last night... Sorry, I don't mean that as an insult,' she adds quickly.

'It's okay, it's the same for me,' says Adriana. 'Kate too, right?' she directs at me.

'Surreal doesn't even begin to describe it – even now and I've known the longest.'

Lucia laughs. 'So, you're saying it doesn't get easier with time?'

'I bloody well hope it does!' I say emphatically, which makes the others chuckle.

'Right,' says Lucia, looking between us, 'who wants to listen while I tell Jon I'm not in Verona?'

'Oh, that's right,' I say, checking the time. 'His plane will have landed by now.'

'Uh-huh,' replies Lucia with a mischievous grin.

She stands and retrieves her phone from her duffle, then returns to her chair, sitting cross-legged. She sets her phone on the table, then dials Jon and puts the call on speakerphone.

'Hello, darling,' he answers, and I shiver with disgust. How did I ever love that man?

'*Mio amore!*' Lucia exclaims. Then she waggles her brows at us.

* * *

Lucia is masterful on the call with Jon, lying to him with an ease that makes me wonder if she's ever done any acting. She certainly sounds more natural than I must have when I last spoke with him.

After he begs her to return to Verona for the third time, she says, 'I wish I could, but my grandmother…' Her voice breaks convincingly. 'This may be our last time together. You understand, don't you?'

He acquiesces reluctantly and Lucia ends the call. She reaches for her drink, then sits back against her chair with a satisfied sigh.

'That was amazing,' says Margot, awestruck.

'It really was,' I agree. 'And I hope this doesn't come across the wrong way, but you're a very good liar.'

She shrugs. 'I studied theatre before I changed to fine arts. My father says I get my dramatic side from my *nonna*.' She smiles. 'She was a tiny woman – even tinier than me – but what a *force*. And *everything* was OTT with her. When we'd visit her in Italy, I'd go with her to the butcher, to buy fresh produce… and at every shop, it seemed like she and the shop-keeper were arguing. But she was just getting the best meat, the best tomatoes – *and* the best price.'

'She sounds like an incredible woman,' I say.

'Oh, she is.'

Adriana, who has been quiet until now, speaks up. 'You seem… *okay*,' she says to Lucia, eyeing her curiously.

'You mean about Jonny?'

Adriana nods.

'Well, I'm massively pissed off with the bastard. As long as I stay mad, I'll be fine. I can cry when all this is over.'

It's a sobering thought and we're quiet for a moment, even Margot. Then Lucia raises her glass.

'To us, Jonny's prey. May we make his life a complete and utter misery. *Salute.*'

'*Salute,*' we chorus.

Lucia takes a generous sip and almost spits it out. She covers her mouth as she splutters and coughs. 'That's really strong,' she manages in between coughs.

I pat her on the back as Adriana jumps out of her chair, returning to the table with a glass of water.

'Sorry, that's my fault,' she says, looking at Lucia apologetically. 'I was nervous about meeting you and I...'

Lucia raises a hand, attempting a smile through the spluttering. 'It's okay.'

Eventually her coughing subsides and she takes a long drink of water. Adriana sits heavily in her chair, shaking her head at herself. 'I really am sorry.'

Lucia reaches across the table. Adriana hesitates for a second, then lets Lucia take her hand.

'I was nervous too,' says Lucia.

'You were?' we all say at once. Adriana, Margot, and I exchange amused glances.

'Luv, you could have been a *star* if you'd stuck with the theatre,' says Margot. 'You swanned in here like Meryl Streep in *The Devil Wears Prada.*'

Lucia laughs. 'I don't know about that – it was bravado more than anything. Must be how I'm coping – being pissed off and pretending everything's okay.'

'"Pissed Off and Pretending" sounds like the title of a self-help book,' Margot jokes, sending sniggers around the table.

'So...' says Lucia, sitting up taller. 'Shall we place bets on who Jonny contacts first?'

'Oh,' I say, 'you're right. He's bound to contact at least one of us.'

'Or both,' says Margot. 'Up his chances of getting a shag this weekend.'

'Margot!' I chide.

'What?' She seems genuinely baffled by why that might be inappropriate.

'Perhaps consider your audience,' I reply, casting my eyes between Lucia, who's smiling sardonically, and Adriana, who has gone pale.

'Sorry,' Margot says contritely.

My phone chimes, followed almost instantly by Adriana's. We pick them up at the same time and Lucia leans close to read over my shoulder:

Hello darling. My work commitments have changed last minute and I'd love to take you out tonight. Shall I hop on a plane?

'*Stronzo!*' Lucia declares. 'What does yours say?' she asks Adriana.

Adriana reads out the exact same message Jon sent to me. He must have copied and pasted it, the *stronzo*.

'I like how he doesn't even ask if you're free,' says Margot. 'He just expects you to drop everything and run into his arms. Arsehole.'

She's not wrong. And hearing from Jon, especially under these heightened circumstances, only emphasises the vast chasm between him – snake, turd, arsehole – and Willem.

I wonder where he is. I wonder *how* he is. God, I feel like a proper shit having said those things.

'Hey,' Adriana says, dragging me from my bout of self-reproach. 'What if we both reply yes?'

Lucia starts laughing. 'Oh, that would be *brilliant*. Talk about painting himself into a corner.'

'It *would* be brilliant,' I say, 'but only until he chooses which one of us to let down. Then he'll expect to see the other one.'

'Oh, right,' says Lucia.

'Of course,' mutters Adriana, spinning her phone in her hands.

'Wait a minute,' I say. 'If we both turn him down, he'll reach out to Poppy next.'

'Oh yeah,' says Margot. 'If he can't see one of you, he'll move on to his Australian girlfriend.'

'We'd need to warn her though,' says Adriana.

'This is the matchmaker?' Lucia interjects.

'That's right,' I reply.

'But does she work on weekends?'

'From what I can tell, she works any time she's needed.'

Lucia blinks at me, clearly impressed. 'Wow.'

'I know, right? I'll call her now.'

Like Lucia did before, I set my phone on the table and dial Poppy's number, then put it on speakerphone. She answers after the third ring.

'Hi, Kate,' she says cheerfully.

'Hi, Poppy. I'm here with Adriana, Lucia, and my cousin, Margot.'

'Ooh, the whole gang,' she says with laughter in her voice. 'How's it going? Is Dunn aware that his proposal isn't happening?'

'Yep!' Lucia proclaims. 'I told him my grandmother is sick, even though she's fitter than a fiddle, and I had to rush back to the UK unexpectedly. Oh, this is Lucia, by the way.'

'Hi, Lucia. You sound *liberated*.'

'I feel it,' she replies with unfettered laughter.

It occurs to me that in the short time since she arrived,

Lucia's bright spirit has made a considerable dent in the day's gloomy mood. Maybe she and I will become friends as well.

'Poppy,' I say, getting to the purpose of the call. 'Adriana and I have already heard from Jon – he's asked to see us tonight.'

'Both of you?' she asks, surprised. 'Oh, of course – he's hedging his bets. So, you've both said no?'

'Not yet, but we will,' I reply.

'Then he'll probably ping Penny next,' she says, catching on straight away.

'That's what we were thinking.'

She audibly sighs.

'Sorry, Poppy. No doubt this will derail your evening.'

'Ahh, it's no worries,' she says, even though it's clearly an imposition.

'Poppy, this is Margot. You know, *you* could put him off as well,' she suggests.

'I *could*... but if he can't propose and neither of his fiancées are available, it might make him ripe for taking the next step.'

'Agreeing to the donation?' I ask, looking at the others excitedly.

'Yep. And if I can get him to do that, then "Penny" could be in London by next Friday.'

'Are you saying that we could be confronting Jon in less than a week?'

'Is that Adriana?' Poppy asks – I should have made this a video call.

'Yes, it's Adriana.'

'It's sounds like you're ready to wrap this up,' says Poppy, commiserating.

'I am – we all are,' she replies.

Poppy laughs. 'To be honest, that would suit me as well.

My parents are arriving from Australia soon and I'd like to have all this done and dusted before they get here.'

Adriana smiles at me across the table; she seems relieved.

'Okay,' says Poppy, 'how about you both tell him no – maybe space your messages out twenty or thirty minutes, so you don't raise his suspicions – and I'll wait to hear from him. In the meantime, I'll check in with my boss and make sure we've got the contract sorted – for the donation.'

'Sounds good, Poppy,' I say, also relieved to see the light at the end of this tunnel.

'Just be ready,' she advises. 'Once the final pieces start falling into place, this could all unfold very quickly. Jon Dunn is an impatient man, and he wants what he wants without delay.'

'Okay, Poppy. And thank you.'

The others thank Poppy, and we say our goodbyes.

'Right,' I say, looking at Adriana. 'You want to go first?'

'It would be my pleasure,' she says with a satisfied smile, and she starts typing on her phone.

I've got at least twenty minutes to kill, so as Lucia and Margot start chatting about Verona, a city high on Margot's bucket list, I busy myself with clearing the glasses from the table, including Lucia's undrinkable cocktail.

From the sink, I eye my case, which is sitting mere feet from Willem's bedroom door. Only, it's unlikely either of us will see the inside of that room. Not after I made a total hash of it, shouting that I've essentially been using Willem for sex, as if that's all this is. Total and utter bollocks, of course, but *he* doesn't know that. And I can't make it right if he isn't here... *Gah!*

'You bloody idiot,' I tell myself glumly as I wipe the benchtop.

'I've done it, Kate,' Adriana calls out, dragging me from my miserable thoughts.

She gets up and brings her phone over to show me.

I'd love to but my students have their performance tonight, remember?

'Nice touch, highlighting the performance angle,' I tell her.

'Thanks,' she says, accepting the praise with a smile.

'Wait, *do* your students have a performance tonight?'

'*No*, I made it up.'

'Ahh, gaslighting the gas lighter... Also a nice touch.'

'And it makes his reply even funnier. Look.' She scrolls down to his instant reply:

Of course. Silly of me to forget. Though you know how I feel about school performances *winking face*

'He's such a first-class prick,' I say. 'Though we *definitely* chose the right cause for him to donate to.'

'Mm-hmm. So, what's your excuse going to be?' she asks.

'How about a migraine?' Margot suggests.

'He'd just tell Kate to take a headache tablet,' Lucia replies. 'That's what he said to me when I actually *did* have a migraine. Have you ever sat through a five-act opera with a pounding head?'

Her mention of the opera reminds me of Willem, but I need to focus on Jon right now, not how royally I've cocked things up with Willem.

'What if you've got something contagious?' Adriana suggests.

'Yes, like the flu!' Margot agrees excitedly.

'You seem oddly pleased about infecting me with a fake illness,' I say.

'I'm *pleased* that Jon's getting what's coming to him,' she replies. 'I wish I could be a fly on the wall when you all confront him. Unless... ooh, do you think I could—'

'*No*, Margot. And this time, I mean it.'

She shrugs. 'It was worth asking.'

I don't agree, but I let it go.

26

POPPY

'Babe, don't hate me,' I say, entering our bedroom after my call with Kate.

'I'd be hard-pressed to come up with any reason to hate you, but what's going on? Is it your case?'

'It is, and I need to stay home tonight.'

His mother is hosting a swanky event for one of the charities she's on the board of. It's for the beautification of an affluent, already beautiful area of London that needs charitable funds about as much as Jeff Bezos.

Tristan's eyes light up with glee. 'You mean we don't have to make small talk with horrible people, then sit through a sub-par meal and boring speeches?'

'Well, *I* don't but you could go by yourself.'

'Oh, no, no, no. You being there is the only thing that would make it bearable. If you're not going, then neither am I.'

'Okay. So, will you come up with a plausible excuse?' I ask.

'Why not just tell the truth – that you have to work?'

'Oh, yes, I'm sure Helen would *love* that. She already thinks my job is a load of hooey. She's hardly gonna believe there's such thing as a matchmaking emergency. She'll think we're making it up.'

'Hmm, how about I say *I* have to work?'

I cross to him where he's stretched out on the bed, an inverted book on his chest, and bend down for a kiss. 'I trust you to figure it out, babe. Now, I have to go get ready to talk to that horrible man.'

'Oh,' he says, sitting up, 'I hadn't realised *that's* why we're staying in.'

'Yeah, sorry. Hands-down the worst thing I've ever had to do in the name of a case. But I reckon it'll be over soon.'

'All right.' He gives me a weak smile and I leave, going into our guest room, which doubles as my office.

The first thing I need to do is ping Saskia about the contract for Dunn's charitable donation. It's not ideal, having to interrupt my boss on a Saturday night, especially as she insists that we 'switch off' over the weekend, but sometimes that's not possible.

She answers my call almost right away, the distinct sounds of family-night festivities in the background. I apologise, but as always, she tells me it's no trouble before getting down to business.

'Is this about the Whitaker case?' she asks. It's a fair assumption, even though I have other active cases.

'Yep. I could be hooking him as soon as tonight.'

'Oh, good work, Poppy. And you've phoned about the contract?'

'Yes.'

'It's almost good to go. I've got a former colleague looking it over this weekend, so it'll be ready to send as early as Monday, if needed.'

'Perfect, thank you.'

'Of course.'

We chitchat for a minute or two about her family, then wrap up the call. All I need to do now is wait to hear from Dunn. In the meantime, I make another call – this one to Shaz.

'What's up?'

'Do you always answer the phone like that?'

'Hah! Only when my bestie calls. So, what *is* up?'

'I've got a hypothetical for you,' I begin. 'For that case with the multiple fiancées.'

'Go.'

'You've got a narcissist with tendencies towards grandiosity who sees you as a gullible, naïve innocent that he can manipulate into falling for him. *And* you need him to agree to something outrageous – in this instance, donating a huge sum of money to the charity you work for in Melbourne, so your bosses will let you return to London where you'll resume the courtship. How do you play it?'

'Fuck me, this is a juicy case.'

'Juicy, yes, but I also want it to be over – *ASAP*. So, what do you reckon?'

'Lean into the narcissism. Only *he* can solve your problem. And if you can swing it, cry.'

'Cry? But how do I do that?'

I do cry sometimes – I'm not shut off from my emotions or anything – but I can't cry on queue. I'm not a trained actor – far from it!

'I'll send you something. It's an exercise I use with my patients to access deep emotions.'

'Okay, sure,' I reply, unconvinced.

I ask her to say hi to Lauren for me, then end the call. Less than a minute later, an email hits my inbox and I read though the attachment. Shaz is right – this exercise could be my magic bullet.

Now I just need Dunn to contact Penny. It's possible that he won't, but with the other three turning him down and his Saturday-night plans turning to shit, I'm confident he will.

* * *

Tristan taps softly on the door as he opens it and peeks in.

'Are you finished with— Oh no, you've been crying,' he says, concerned. He crosses to me and bobs down, one hand cupping my cheek.

'*Fake* crying. I had to really sell the whole I-miss-you-and-I-can't-come-back-to-London-unless-you-write-a-huge-cheque thing.'

'Oh.' He sits back on his heels. 'And?'

'And he said to send over the necessary paperwork as soon as possible, then book a flight.'

Tristan gives me a concerned side-eye. 'How does he expect someone who works for a not-for-profit to afford a last-minute flight across the world?'

'You make a salient point, Mr Fellows. But he's so out of touch, it didn't even come up. Anyway, *Penny* will be back in London this Friday and she told him to book a suite at the Langham.'

'Nicely done, darling,' he says, giving me a quick kiss. 'And now that we're staying in, what do you say to one of your fancy-pants antipasto platters and a bottle of Chianti?'

'And the new romcom with Florence Pugh?' I ask with a wide grin. I *love* a good romcom, but Tristan would rather a thriller or a gritty crime drama any day.

His mouth twitches. 'Since you've had a less-than-ideal evening so far, all right.'

'Woohoo,' I shout, waking Saffron, who glares at me from the bed. Then I go into the kitchen to start assembling a platter for dinner.

* * *

Kate

It's after 7 p.m. and Willem still hasn't returned.

Lucia and Margot have gone to get ready to go out with Adriana, who's in her studio getting dressed, and I'm sitting here like a numpty waiting for him.

The others invited me to join them, but I won't be able to enjoy myself unless things are right with Willem. Not even Poppy's news that she convinced Jon to donate £150,000 to our chosen charity has made a dent in my I've-behaved-like-an-arse-and-maybe-ruined-things-forever blues.

Eventually, Adriana comes back into the house, gorgeous in a sparkly mini-dress and four-inch heels. 'You look smashing,' I tell her.

'Thanks!' She points one toe to show off her shoes. 'I could never wear these with Jon – they make me taller than him and he didn't like it.'

'That sounds about right,' I say with a wry laugh. 'Why is it that all his flaws suddenly seem so obvious, especially his vanity? Is it like that for you as well?'

'God, yes. It's what's keeping me sane. Any time I miss him, I remember the red flags – so many!'

'Precisely! Yet we didn't notice them at the time. I asked Poppy about that and she answered with "love is blind".'

'Hmm. She's probably right. It was easy to ignore his faults when he was being charming.'

'Exactly.'

'So... I should go meet Margot and Lucia,' she says, looking hesitant.

'Oh!' I say, realising she probably doesn't want to leave me here alone. 'I should go too – sorry.' I give her a tight-lipped smile, then go over to my case and extend the handle.

'Kate, I don't mind if you wait here. But I'm not sure Willem—'

'No, no, it's fine. I wouldn't want to upset him further – or get you into trouble with your big brother,' I joke, only it's not funny and we both know that.

I start rolling my case across the wooden floor, the sound echoing ominously throughout the large room. And right as I swing my handbag onto my shoulder, a key sounds in the lock. My eyes fly to meet Adriana's.

'Perfect timing,' she says with an ironic smile. She comes over and leans down to give me a hug, which I return one-handed. 'See you in London,' she says, stepping back.

With a pang, I note that she doesn't say 'see you tomorrow', so it's unlikely she thinks I'll be here in the morning.

I don't think I'll be here either.

I look over and Willem is standing there, watching us. My heart starts racing. Why does he have to be so bloody handsome – even with that troubled look on his face?

Adriana stops to give him a cheek kiss. 'I'm staying with Margot tonight. See you in the morning.'

He grunts his reply, then she goes, and the sound of the door closing reverberates around the room like a death knell – the death knell of our fledgling relationship, if Willem's scowl is anything to go by.

'I didn't expect you to be here,' he says gruffly.

'I gathered that,' I say with an embarrassed smile. 'I was just leaving.'

He nods and this is the part where I am supposed to go, but my feet are rooted to the spot. It doesn't help that he's standing between me and the door. His gaze latches onto mine, but it's unbearable and I look away, hitching my handbag strap further up my shoulder.

'Okay, I'll get out of your hair.' I stride towards the door, deviating around him, only as I pass, he captures my free wrist with his hand.

'Kate...' he whispers, and for a millisecond, I think he's going to ask me to stay so we can talk things through. 'Safe travels,' he says instead.

Suddenly, there's a lump in my throat the size of Trafalgar Square and tears prick my eyes.

How? How did I give my heart freely to a prick like Jon, but when a good man like Willem comes along, I cock it up?

I don't trust my voice, so I nod sharply, then leave, and this time when the front door closes, it feels final.

I look up and down the road where cars are parked bumper to bumper on both sides and the footpath is littered with bikes. It's unlike me to not have an exit strategy – I should have ordered an Uber or called a cab – but a lot of my behaviour of late is unlike me.

Worried that Willem might be watching me out his front window, I walk down the road away from the canal. Margot gave me the name and address of her hotel, but the thought of checking in, then sitting there by myself all night, stewing, is unbearable.

No, if I'm going anywhere, it's home. I get to the corner and fish out my phone to order an Uber to the airport.

* * *

Sunday arrives wet, grey, and miserable – typical of London spring weather to lull us into a false sense of 'it's getting warmer!' then have us digging out winter woollies at least one more time.

The weather's also a fitting accompaniment for my grim, miserable mood. Only yesterday morning, I woke up next to Willem in Italy – blissful, hopeful, thoroughly ravished – and now I'm back in London. *Alone.*

I bundle myself into my fluffy robe and Uggs and go to the kitchen to make myself a coffee. Even before the water boils, I know this will be a poor cousin to the coffees I enjoyed in Italy – or the coffee Willem made me in Amsterdam. I may be spoiled for drinking instant coffee ever again.

That's not the only thing I'm spoiled for.

Now that I've discovered there are decent men in this world – kind, honest men, men who can make my toes curl simply by looking at me a certain way – I will never be able to accept 'good enough' again. The Kate of today would *never* fall for someone like Jon. I suppose that's one good thing to come from all this. I've upped my standards.

But I've also cocked things up with the decent, clever, sexy man across the Channel, so it's hard to chalk this up as a 'win'.

I eye my phone, which is sitting on the benchtop face-down. I haven't yet summoned the nerve to check my messages.

No doubt, Jon will have sent his obligatory I-miss-you message without bothering to enquire about my ailing health, despite me telling him I have the flu.

But worse, I won't have heard from Willem.

I heave out a self-pitying sigh. I really didn't think this

through, being back in London without Margot and with nothing to keep my mind off things. Though I seem to have made a habit of not thinking things through.

The kettle boils and I pour hot water into my mug, absent-mindedly stirring while I consider how to spend my day. There's always work I can catch up on but Mina frowns upon working over the weekend unless absolutely necessary. I doubt replying to bog-standard emails or getting a jumpstart on my monthly reports will count as 'absolutely necessary'. Working would only earn me a friendly earbashing tomorrow about work–life balance.

What about Poppy? I think. She *has* become a confidante of sorts and she doesn't judge me – even when I'm behaving like a complete idiot. She also has terrific insight; maybe she'll have advice for me about how to stop sabotaging my own happiness.

I suppose I could ask her to lunch – she can only say no. I pick up my phone to message her and it vibrates in my hand. It's Margot:

Heading down to Rotterdam with Adriana and Lucia for the day. Flying back to London tonight. Love you. And stop moping. It will all work out.

Of *course* she knows I'm moping – more so now that she's shared her plans for the day. If I'd just stayed in Amsterdam, *I* could be on a day trip to explore a new city with my bestie and my new pseudo-friends.

'Gah! Just message Poppy and ask if she's free, you silly muppet.'

I do and she is. Finally, a bright spark in this otherwise bleak day.

We make plans to meet at The Black Penny in Covent Garden at 12 p.m. and I head into Central London early to take myself to the National Gallery. Hard to stay miserable when basking in the greatness of Degas, Monet, Cézanne, and Van Gogh.

27

KATE

Despite the rain and wind, which has turned my umbrella inside out twice on the walk from the National Gallery, I'm feeling more like myself when I arrive at The Black Penny. Poppy waves from a table at the back, and I skirt past the waiter with an apologetic, 'My friend's already here.'

'Hi – sorry, am I late?' I ask with a grimace.

'Nah,' she says, 'I'm just habitually early.'

She rises, leaning across the table for a cheek kiss. It's a kindly gesture, considering this is ostensibly a work lunch, and it instantly sets me at ease.

'Have you been here before?' she asks as I sit opposite her. 'The menu looks amazing.'

'A few times with Margot. They're famous for their brunch menu.'

'And their cocktails?' she asks with raised brows.

I laugh freely, and it's like a weight lifting from my chest. 'Okay, yes, the cocktails *might* just edge out the food. If you like a Bloody Mary, you're in the right place.'

'Hmm.' She starts perusing the menu, and I do the same,

deciding on the same dish I had last time – and the time before that. Sometimes it pays to stick to what's familiar – less chance of disappointment.

The waiter takes our order, then leaves with the menus, and Poppy gives me a smile.

'So, we're here to talk about Willem de Vries.'

It's a statement, not a question, and her forthrightness catches me off-guard. I'd planned to make small talk before raising the topic of Willem, but why faff about when he's the reason I asked her to lunch?

'Ahh, yes,' I reply with an uncomfortable smile. 'It's gone to shit, Poppy, and it's all my fault.'

'Oh no, what's happened?'

We're interrupted by our drinks arriving – a Bloody Mary for me and a Bellini for Poppy – and I raise mine in a quick toast. 'Cheers.' We clink glasses, but I set mine down without taking a sip. I need to get this out.

'Okay, so at first, I thought I just fancied him. I mean, I'd have to be *dead* not to have noticed how handsome he is. Anyway, I wrote my emotions off as lust, pure and simple, so every time I was around him and there were tummy flutters or my heart started racing, I would tell my libido to check itself. There were far more important things on my plate with the whole Jon situation.'

Poppy regards me intently, nodding along and sipping her drink.

'But that first time we were in Verona together... I didn't tell you this, but our accommodation wasn't as expected. Willem thought it was a two-bedroom flat, but it was open-plan and the only thing separating our beds was this giant shelving unit.'

Poppy sniggers – she must see where I'm going with this.

'So, there I am' – I mime holding covers up to my chin, eyes like saucers – 'wide awake for most of the night, hyper aware that he was lying *right there*, a half-naked, glorious specimen of man.'

Poppy grins.

'And *every* time I heard the rustle of sheets, my eyes would pop open. It was torture, Poppy, torture! I mean, not only was the timing less than ideal, but he was off-limits – or so I told myself. What good could come from complicating the situation with Jon and Adriana and Lucia by throwing myself at my fiancé's fiancée's fit brother?'

'And when did you figure out it was more than attraction?'

'Lust?' I ask, talking over her. 'Oh, "attraction" sounds much better. Less like I'm a randy sad sack whose fiancé cheated on her.'

'Eh, same difference,' she says.

'You're being kind,' I reply, and she shrugs good-naturedly. 'Anyway, to answer your question, it was the following day. We were killing time before Lucia's gallery opened and Willem was playing tour guide. And Verona's *beautiful*. I would have thought that even if I'd been on my own, but Willem really brought it to life for me, taking me to some of the lesser-known parts of the city, as if he was sharing its long-held secrets. Then, when we got to the gallery and Lucia had stuck that sign on the door, saying she was in Mykonos, we didn't pack up and leave right away. Instead, we had this incredible lunch and we talked – really *talked* – about all sorts of things. And that's when I realised I liked *him*, the person behind the film-star looks. And *that's* when I knew I was in trouble. It's only intensified since.'

'And you've tried to talk yourself out of it – out of feeling the way you do.'

'Yes, how did you know?'

'It's my job to know,' she says with a modest shrug.

'Ahh.'

'And after this realisation, the one you had that day in Verona, was there any indication he reciprocated?'

I flush, my flaming cheeks betraying me yet again, and I reach for my drink and take a gulp, hardly noticing how good it tastes.

'I take it that's a yes, then,' she says.

I nod. 'We slept together. In Verona. On Friday night,' I blurt.

'You don't seem particularly happy about it,' she says, a bewildered expression on her face.

The waiter arrives and we're quiet as he places our dishes in front of us. Now too worked up to eat, I pick up my fork and start moving food around my plate, stalling. Finally, I look up.

'It's because I'm supposed to be in Amsterdam with him right now, but he's upset and possibly angry and it's likely he never wants to see me again. I've completely fucked things up and I have no idea how to fix it.'

'Geez, Kate, I'm really sorry to hear that. What happened?'

While continuing to push my food around my plate, only taking the occasional tiny bite, I tell Poppy about yesterday afternoon.

'And you haven't heard from him?' she asks, setting her knife and fork next to each other on her now-empty plate.

I look down at my own and give up, my appetite having abandoned me completely.

'No,' I say gloomily. I suck my lips between my teeth and exhale noisily though my nose.

'Hey...'

I look up.

'There's every chance this is fixable.'

'I doubt it. You didn't see how he looked at me before I left his house.'

'No, but that doesn't mean it's over before it even began. People mess up – *we* mess up. We say stupid, hurtful things that we don't mean and, yes, they can do damage, but never underestimate the power of a heartfelt apology.'

'But I shouted to a roomful of people that I used him for sex.'

'Yeah, but how many of them actually believed it? *Margot* would know better, and from what you've told me about Adriana, I doubt she would have come around if she thought you were only after her brother for sex. It's likely even *Willem* knows you didn't mean it.'

'Really? That means there's hope, right?'

'In my experience, there's almost always hope when two people care about each other and want to be together – even if one of them makes a massive misstep along the way.'

'Okay,' I mutter. I should probably be rejoicing about the hope part, but Poppy's characterisation of my behaviour as a 'massive misstep' stings. Rather than dwelling on that, however, I ask my other burning question.

'Poppy, let's suppose I can make things right with Willem,' I say. 'Is it stupid of me to embark on a relationship so soon after Jon? You said something along those lines, and I can't seem to get it out of my head.'

'I did say that, yes, but even I get things wrong sometimes,' she says with a self-deprecating smile.

'So, I should try and fix things? Apologise to Willem?' I ask. I'm not exactly seeking Poppy's *permission* – more like her endorsement.

'An apology's the bare minimum, yes. Of course, it will be up to him whether he wants to pursue a relationship.'

'Right,' I say, nerves wrenching my stomach, because what if he doesn't?

'But I will say this: when I was reviewing your case file a few weeks ago, in preparation for our meeting, something struck me about your response to the first question – why you wanted to engage the Ever After Agency. You said – and I'm paraphrasing here – "because I'm ready to find my special someone, a man who shares my values and loves me for who I truly am, a man who will become my best friend." Again, I'm paraphrasing, but it was something along those lines.'

'I remember,' I say softly. 'And I'm almost certain I told Perfect Pairings the same thing. How they matched me with Jon...' I say with a disbelieving shake of my head.

'Well, trust me, we're going to ensure they get theirs. But that aside, you *did* fall for Dunn's charms.'

'I know. I legitimately have no idea what I was thinking – even now, weeks after finding out about him.'

'I might have an idea,' she says, looking at me intently. 'You see, sometimes we don't reveal our truest self until we meet the right person. We're instinctually protective, we keep that side of us hidden, cocooned. And when we meet our "someone", it emerges. You weren't yourself with Dunn because he wasn't your someone. As an aside, I doubt he's anyone's. But that would explain why, when you think about how you were with Dunn, you don't recognise yourself.'

'God, Poppy, I've never thought of it like that before. It makes so much sense. Thank you.'

'Again, it's part of the job. But you know what this means, right?'

'That there's every chance Willem's my someone,' I reply reverently.

'There is every chance,' she echoes. 'So, how are you going to win him back?'

* * *

Poppy

'Good morning, Poppy,' says Ursula as I arrive at the office. I can count on zero fingers the number of times Ursula has beaten me to the office. She always arrives precisely at 9 a.m. and not a moment earlier.

'Good morning.'

She beams at me, and I keep my eyes trained on her as I drop my handbag on my desk.

'What's going on?' I ask.

'I had the *best* lunch yesterday,' she says cryptically.

'Oh, so did I as a matter of fact. I went to The Black—'

'Poppy, I've done it!' she interjects.

'Great. Done what exactly?' I ask, stumped.

'I've confronted Clarissa.'

It takes me a moment to remember that 'Clarissa' is Clarissa Blackheart, who runs Perfect Pairings and was once Ursula's friend and business partner.

'Ooh, that's some serious goss,' I say, fascinated.

'I'm positively *bursting* with it, Poppy.' This must be why she was first into the office this morning – she needed to tell someone.

'Okay, I'm all ears. Let me just...' I drag another chair over to my desk and she sits facing me.

'Shall I set the scene?' she asks.

'I'd expect nothing less.'

In great detail, she tells me how she lured Clarissa Black-heart to lunch at the Ivy under the guise of burying the hatchet.

'So, there we are making pleasant chitchat and right as she took another sip of her Lillete Blanc, I said, "I'm onto your reckless matchmaking practices, Clarissa, and I have proof."'

'Oh, I *love* that. And how did she respond?'

'By spluttering and coughing and covering half the table-cloth with wine.'

My jaw drops. 'Ooh, I would love to have seen that!'

'It was quite spectacular. She was horrified, particularly because the waiter was there in an instant, offering to exchange the tablecloth! Can you imagine? Such a spectacle,' she says, starting to laugh. 'Obviously, she declined and when he stepped away, she leaned close, her face contorted and her halitosis wafting through the air, and that's when the claws came out.'

'What did she say?'

'Well, it was more of a hiss,' says Ursula, and it's clear she's getting a kick out of this, 'but she said I was obviously delu-sional, and she had no idea what I could possibly be talking about.'

'What a piss-weak comeback,' I say. Oops – forgot who I was talking to. 'Sorry, that was crass.'

'It is, but I agree – it *was* a piss-weak comeback, as you say. Anyway, I gave her my death stare,' she says, demonstrating, 'then reached into my handbag and took out the invoices for three identical engagement rings – all charged to Jon Dunn, of course – and handed them over.'

'Did she get it right away, or did you have to make the connection for her?'

'Oh, she might have figured it out eventually, but rather than wait for her dull synapses to fire, I took great pleasure in pointing to Dunn's name and saying, "You matched *this* man with one of the Ever After Agency's clients, and he is not who he says he is. He's a fraud and if you had one ounce of professionalism in that bony little body of yours, you wouldn't have *dared* match him with *anyone*!"'

'Wow. Remind me never to piss you off.'

'Poppy, if you keep saying "piss" you will piss me off,' she says with a slight quirk of her left brow.

'Sorry. So, what happened after that? Did she leave? Did *you* leave?'

'On the contrary, I continued to hand her proof – pages and pages of indisputable evidence that Perfect Pairings was *aware* of Dunn's proclivities but disregarded them in favour of his enormous fee.'

'Wow, that's even worse! And where did you get *that* informa— *Oh*, Marie.'

'Mm-hmm. And as Clarissa sat there red-faced, looking as if she might *explode*, I outlined my terms for keeping mum.'

'Which were?' I asked, rivetted. I knew she'd planned to confront Clarissa Blackheart, but I hadn't known there would be *terms*.

'First, that she issue Kate Whitaker a full refund for their so-called services.'

'Well, that's good – Kate will be pleased – and what else?'

'That Perfect Pairings conduct a thorough audit of their database and weed out any other undesirables. They have three months. You know, if this were any other industry, we'd report them to the governing body. As it is, we need to self-regulate!'

'Agreed, and awesome job, Ursula.'

'Why, thank you,' she replies, bowing her head. 'Now, your turn,' she says, a glint in her eye. 'Tell me where you're at with the rest of the case.'

28

KATE

Today's the day. I'm meeting Adriana, Lucia, and Poppy at the Langham this afternoon to confront Jon.

Surprisingly, this past week has flown by, which I attribute to two things: I threw myself into work – even more so than usual – and I actively ignored the gaping hole in my inbox where messages from Willem would be if I hadn't cocked things up.

I know I need to apologise – of *course* I do – but the moment I said goodbye to Poppy on Sunday, I had a stark realisation: I need to apologise in person. If I want things to work out with Willem, I'll need to look him in the eye so he can see how truly sorry I am. *And* how much I feel for him. I'm not sure if it's love – not yet, anyway – but whatever it is, it's worth fighting for.

But before I can apologise to Willem with all the care and sincerity he deserves, I must say my piece to Jon and put him and his lies behind me, once and for all.

As I wait for the kettle to boil, I check my messages.

Adriana and Lucia posted to our group chat overnight,

saying they missed me at dinner. They both arrived in London yesterday and had invited me to join them, but I already had plans with Margot at mine. Besides, I wasn't really in the mood for a girls' night out – *nor* for another bout of comparing notes on Jon.

Margot was her typical cheerful self over dinner – her signature spag bol – giving me her version of a pep talk. But she suddenly turned serious while we did the dishes.

'I really wish I could be there,' she said.

'Only because you're drawn to the spectacle of it all,' I replied with a laugh. 'You just want to watch the onslaught.'

Her eyes bored into mine, concern etched on her face. 'It's not that. If I could I'd go in your place and challenge the bastard to a duel – or whatever the modern equivalent is – I would.'

'That's sweet, Margs,' I said, reaching for her hand and giving it a squeeze. 'But I'll be with the others. We're there to support each other as much as to put Jon in the hotseat.'

'Okay,' she replied solemnly. 'But if you change your mind, I'm there in a heartbeat. You're the closest I'll ever have to a sister – *and* I'm older than you. It's my sisterly instinct wanting to protect you – with or without the use of gardening shears.'

We shared a smile at that. Then she gave me a tight hug, told me she loves me, and made me promise to send a selfie once I'm coiffed and dressed today – for posterity.

Though I suspect 'posterity' means she reserves the right to whip it out any time she assesses that I'm doubting myself. I can just imagine it: 'Look at how fucking gorgeous and fierce and brave you are, Kate! *Look!*'

Margot is a lot sometimes, but I love her just as fiercely as she loves me.

She left right after that, heading to Adriana's hotel, and I tried not to be jealous that she wasn't spending the night alone.

The kettle dings, yanking me to the present, and I make a coffee. If I weren't so nervous, I'd eat something, but I can't bear the thought of food. Maybe after Jon gets what's coming to him.

Right as I'm stirring in the milk, my phone chimes. It's probably something pithy from Margot – most likely a meme of some kick-arse woman doing something kick-arse.

But it isn't Margot.

It's Willem and my stomach plummets. Forget eating breakfast, I doubt I can even finish my coffee.

I swallow – hard – and summon all my courage to tap on the message.

I hope it goes well today. Thinking of you.

I expel a short sharp breath of relief. Surely he can't hate me if he's sending messages like that. But the relief is short-lived, and I'm wracked with guilt – *I* should have been the one reaching out with an olive branch, not Willem. Regardless, it means more to me than he can possibly know, and I type out a reply:

Thank you. Just want it to be over.

My thumbs hover over the screen. I want to ask about seeing him, but what if that's pushing my luck? What if he's only being friendly – or worse, *polite*? And didn't I tell myself I needed to get past today before I could properly make things right with Willem?

No, I should wait. I want to have a clear head and an unfettered heart before I see Willem again – or even ask to see him.

I set my phone down and go shower.

* * *

As the cab stops in front of the Langham, everything I want to say to Jon, along with everything Poppy has coached me on, flies out of my head. It doesn't matter that I've been mentally rehearsing for days now. I'm a ball of nerves.

Though a gorgeous ball of nerves, I'll admit, having spent a couple of hours at the salon to have my hair and makeup done. I'm also dressed to kill in a tailored suit, lacy camisole, and black heels. But no sense in looking like a million pounds if my mind is blank and I can't utter a coherent sentence.

I should have expected that showing up here, where much of our courtship took place, would knock me sideways. Hopefully, seeing the others will stem the rising tide of panic.

I pay the cabbie and step out into the sunshine, and the doorman, dressed in opulent finery, marches up the steps ahead of me to open the door.

'Good afternoon, madam. Welcome to the Langham,' he says, his warm smile shaving a sliver off my nerves.

'Thank you.'

Once inside, I cast my eyes about for the others. Poppy's meeting us in the lobby to take us up to the suite Jon booked. As instructed, she checked in earlier as Penny to 'freshen up after her flight' while Jon is at Mayberry's for a manicure and straight-razor shave.

I was worried about him showing up earlier than expected, but Poppy assured me the agency has eyes on him and will know precisely when he's on his way up to the suite.

No doubt that odd French woman is lurking nearby disguised as a topiary.

I catch sight of Poppy and she waves me over.

'You look fantastic,' she says, eyeing me from top to toe.

'Thanks,' I say before sucking in a gulping breath. *Breathe, Kate, breathe.*

'Hiya, we're here.'

I turn at the sound of Lucia's voice and she and Adriana are striding across the lobby, their footsteps echoing. They also look gorgeous – Adriana in a floral silk maxi-dress and Lucia in a fitted linen shift in siren red. Like me, they're both wearing heels, and I wonder if it's for the same reason – to be as tall and formidable as possible when we face Jon.

We greet each other nervously – I'm glad I'm not the only one who's anxious – then Poppy, who's the calm in the eye of this storm, says, 'Let's go up.'

The ride in the lift and the walk along the carpeted hallway is silent as we collectively fizz with anticipation – and a large serving of trepidation. Poppy leads us into the suite and as expected, it's spacious and luxurious.

This is really happening. Breathe, Kate, breathe, I remind myself.

'I thought I could stand here when he comes in,' says Poppy, indicating a spot right in the line of sight from the door. 'And you three could be over there.' She points to a sofa. Silently, we cross to it and sit with me in the middle.

'I haven't been this nervous since taking my final exams to be a teacher,' says Adriana.

'For me, it's since my first exhibit,' says Lucia.

'I'm glad it's not just me,' I offer in solidarity.

'God, no,' says Lucia with a laugh, and Adriana agrees.

'Ah, ladies,' says Poppy. We all look up. 'He'll be here soon.'

'Ady and I were talking,' Lucia says to me, 'and we'll follow your lead.'

'All right,' I agree.

We haven't discussed this previously, but it makes sense. I was the first fiancée, after all.

We make forgettable small talk as the minutes tick over and my nerves ratchet up. Inevitably, the beep of the keycard sounds, silencing us immediately, and the door swings open. Poppy dons a neutral expression, her eyes fixed on Jon as he sweeps into the room, his overbearing cologne instantly permeating the air.

If I didn't know Jon – and I wasn't repulsed by the sight of him – I might say he looks good. He's dressed in a lightweight suit, one that will have cost several thousand pounds on Saville Row, and a white dress shirt unbuttoned at the neck.

'Darling!' he declares, crossing to Poppy. She steps aside, dodging the incoming embrace, and his features morph into confusion.

Eyes laser-focused on Jon, I grope for Adriana and Lucia's hands either side of me, clasping them tightly. And as though we rehearsed it, we stand in unison then drop hands.

'Hello, *Jon*,' I say, drenching his name in rancour.

He turns abruptly, his shock so extreme as his eyes dart between us, it would be comical if I didn't want to cut his bollocks off – metaphorically speaking, that is.

'Wha— I don't— I can't—' he stammers. His eyes bug out and his mouth gapes then closes without making any sound. He's like a well-groomed goldfish.

His gaze swings back to Poppy. 'Penny?' he asks, clearly confounded.

This is when I should start speaking, but my mind has gone blank and my mouth bone-dry.

'I'm not Penny Mullings,' Poppy says coolly. 'She doesn't exist.'

He recoils in shock, then breaks into incredulous laughter. When he looks at us to share the joke, his ridiculous smile falls away the instant he sees we're not laughing with him.

'Sit. Down,' I say firmly, finally finding my voice.

'Sorry?'

'I said, *sit*. Over there will do,' I say, pointing at a low wing-back chair.

He hesitates, obviously perplexed, then ever so slowly edges towards the chair, watching me warily, as if I'm a lioness who might gobble him up if he makes a sudden move.

He sits, sinking into the chair. I couldn't have planned it any better, him now peering up at us like a little boy. Adriana moves first, skirting around the coffee table and standing over him, her arms folded and glowering. I follow and so does Lucia, who slots in beside me.

'Obviously, we three have met,' I say to him. 'And you can imagine our surprise, discovering that the other two existed, that you were involved in love affairs with three different women in three different countries.'

He goes to speak, but I silence him with, 'No, I'm still speaking.'

I glare at him, unblinking, as a flash of shock crosses his face. He presses his lips together and looks away.

'But we know all about you *now*, Jon Theodore Dunn,' I say, imbuing each of his names with condemnation. 'We know that you're not a pilot, nor a diamond dealer, nor a wine merchant. And you're *not* a geologist,' I say sarcastically, flicking my eyes towards Poppy where she's leaning against an ornate desk, staring coldly at Jon.

Jon glances over his shoulder then turns back to me. It's

clear he's starting to piece things together, and his gaze falls to his hands, which are fisted in his lap.

'We know that as the beneficiary of a substantial trust, you're obscenely wealthy, that you have *no* profession, contributing nothing meaningful to society, and that you live in this hotel fulltime – and *not* because your home is being renovated. We also know your mother lives on a vast estate in Scotland, rather than in a care facility, and that she's completely oblivious to what her son has been doing.'

This last statement – an educated guess – is confirmed by the split-second of horror in Jon's eyes before he regains his composure – well, as best he can. He looks absurd in that low chair.

His eyes harden and he puffs out his chest. 'I *haven't*—'

'You haven't *what*?' I ask, cutting him off again. God, Margot would be so proud of me right now.

I bend down, my face close to his, like a nursery teacher chiding an errant child. 'You haven't lied to all of us, including "Penny"? You haven't pretended to be someone you're not, to be some*place* you're not, time and time again?' I stare right into his eyes, then straighten, looking down my nose at him. 'Because you *have*. And we have proof.'

'You even bought us the same engagement rings,' Adriana spits at him.

'Yes, and why was that, Jon?' asks Lucia, notably abandoning the name 'Jonny'. 'Lack of imagination or something more sinister? Some sort of sick branding, perhaps? Behold my fiancées, blinded by love and each wearing the same sodding ring!'

'I have no idea what you're talking about,' he says dismissively. 'I didn't even give you a ring.'

'Hah!' she barks. 'But you'd *planned* to. Ristorante Il Desco? Hotel Gabbia d'Oro? Do they ring a bell?' she asks smugly.

Jon's mouth starts working again, then he clamps it shut. He must be wondering how we can possibly know all this – hah!

'And how was this supposed to work, Jon?' asks Adriana, glaring down at him while he blatantly avoids eye contact. 'Were you *really* planning on becoming a polygamist?'

'*I* bet you never planned on marrying any of us,' Lucia interjects. 'If you hadn't been caught, you'd have strung us along indefinitely. You weird, sick bastard.'

'*Ja!*' Adriana chimes in.

Lips pressed together, Jon stares hard at the carpet in front of him. We've *definitely* got him on the ropes now. And it really doesn't matter what his intentions were or how he thought he'd get away with being engaged to three women – possibly even four. He's clearly delusional – or as Lucia says, a 'weird, sick bastard'.

'Right,' I say, getting to the part I was coached on, 'this is what's going to happen. There's going to be a close watch on you, Jon Dunn. You've already been blacklisted at every matchmaking agency and on every dating app in the UK – *and* Europe *and* North America. And if your tiny little brain thinks that's of no consequence, guess again. Because if you so much as *think* about attempting to dupe another woman with a false persona, every shred of evidence we've accrued against you will be sent to your mother. And with her as the named trustee of your inheritance...' I trail off with a shrug, leaving the rest of the threat implied.

I'm not entirely sure how the Ever After Agency plans to follow through on this threat, but Poppy assures me it's legitimate.

Jon heaves out a frustrated, guttural sigh, then places his hands on the arms of the chair and stands. 'Are you *finished*?' he asks viciously.

I look to the others, who murmur their agreement, then back at Jon. '*Almost*,' I say. I smile at him serenely, which seems to confuse him even more. 'Poppy?'

'Poppy?' Jon murmurs. He looks over at her. 'Oh, of course, *you're* Poppy.'

'I am. And before you leave, you should know that the Creative Futures Foundation is *extremely* grateful for your generous donation.'

'Creative Fut— Oh my god.' He claps his hand over his mouth, then drops it like it weighs a tonne. 'Oh my god, I signed that donation over.'

'Yes, you did,' she replies with a broad smile.

'Only because you asked me to – no, *begged* me to.'

'*Penny* begged you to.'

'Well, that won't stand. That donation was procured under false pretences. Wait,' he says, his eyes narrowing with realisation. 'The not-for-profit *I* donated to was called Urban Growth something, not Creative Futures... whatever it was you said.' He flaps his hand about as if he's shooing flies.

'Urban Growth Collective is the parent organisation,' Poppy says evenly. She points at him, mirth in her eyes. 'But *you* generously donated specifically to the Creative Futures Foundation, which supports arts' education for underprivileged youths.'

'Oh, no. We'll see about that. You tricked me. You've committed *fraud*.'

Lucia is the first to break, her laughter filling the room, then Adriana and I exchange a glance and join in.

'Oh, Jon,' says Lucia, waving her hands in front of her face. 'That's the funniest thing you've ever said.'

Now we're proper laughing – all three of us – and the release is incredible. Meanwhile, Jon is standing there, hands on his hips, glaring at us.

'I'm not sure what you find so amusing,' he bellows. Our laughter reduces to sniggers, but none of us stop laughing outright. 'I think you'll find that what this woman has done,' he says, pointing at Poppy, 'is illegal. And if you had anything to do with it, you'll go down with her.'

'Mr Dunn,' says Poppy, grabbing his attention. His glowering eyes slide in her direction. 'You're not in the position to issue threats and I'm sure once you consult your solicitor, you will learn two things. First, that contract you signed is watertight. Top-notch solicitors have seen to that. Second, this wasn't a one-off donation. You agreed to donate £150,000 *annually* for the next ten years – all going towards the Jon Theodore Dunn Arts' Education Bursary.'

Jon turns beet-red, rounding on us.

'I don't know where you found this... this... *harpy*, but you will rue the day, I can promise you. Especially *you*!' He stabs his finger at Adriana. 'Arts' education? Is this some sort of joke?'

'No more than you proposing to me when you were already engaged to Kate,' she replies pointedly.

Jon vigorously shakes his head, his face now purple. 'This is... *outrageous*, that's what! You'll be hearing from my solicitor. Gah!!!' he shouts as he storms out.

I'm sure he wishes he could have slammed the door, but this is a hotel and hotel doors don't work that way.

'Harpy,' says Poppy with a laugh. 'Well, I've been called worse.'

And we all break into raucous laughter.

29

KATE

It's like a fragrant spring breeze has blown through the suite, sweeping away the remnants of Jon's presence.

It's done.

'That was brilliant,' says Lucia, pacing in front of the windows, shaking out her hands. 'Just *brilliant*.' She turns to us with a grin.

'*Ja, briljant*,' Adriana agrees. She throws back her head, closes her eyes, and presses her hands to her chest, expelling several sighs in a row, the last one turning into laughter. '*Niet te geloven*,' she says to herself, sighing again.

Even without knowing exactly what she's said, her meaning is clear. I plop back onto the sofa, depleted but elated.

'Uh, ladies,' says Poppy, 'a reminder that this suite is paid for until Sunday if you'd like to stay.'

Adriana and Lucia exchange an excited look. 'What do you think?' Adriana asks.

'It's the least Jon could do,' says Lucia. 'What if we order one of everything on the room service menu and have a girls' night in?'

'*Or* we have cocktails and dinner downstairs and charge it to the suite,' says Adriana with a waggle of her brows.

'Well, we do have two nights here…' says Lucia with a sly grin. 'I say we do both. And you should invite Margot. But first, let's ask them to send up a bottle of Champagne.'

'Yes!' exclaims Adriana. 'Oh,' she says, looking my way. 'Sorry, Kate. What would *you* like to do?'

'Quite frankly, this hotel doesn't hold the best memories for me. I'd rather go home, but you two stay and enjoy it. You deserve it,' I reply with a warm smile.

But Adriana responds with a frown. 'Will you at least have Champagne with us before you go? You too, Poppy.'

Poppy and I agree and Lucia calls room service and places the order. While we wait, I sidle over to Poppy.

'I wasn't aware Jon's donation was going to be annual,' I say. 'That's a lot of money.'

'It is and it isn't for someone that wealthy. Hopefully, what will sting the most is the annual reminder that he was tricked.'

'Oh, good point.'

'And the contract *is* above board. If Dunn has a bone to pick, it's with the person who manages his legal affairs, not the agency.'

'You really came through, Poppy. I feel like I've been exorcised.'

She laughs.

'Seriously, though, thank you.'

'Eh, all part of the service,' she says with a modest tilt of her head.

I doubt that *anything* she's had to do for this case is typically 'part of the service'. I wish I could do more than give her my thanks.

We're interrupted by a young woman delivering the Champagne, cracking it expertly with a whisper and pouring into four flutes. When she leaves, we raise our glasses.

'To Kate, who totally kicked Jon's arse,' says Lucia. 'You're our *eroina,* our *amica. Grazie mille.'*

I flush, chuffed but also embarrassed by her words. 'To Kate,' say Poppy and Adriana.

I tap the rim of my glass to theirs and we all take a sip. It's delicious but I know that as soon as it hits my empty stomach, it'll go straight to my head. Maybe that's not such a bad thing.

Adriana and Lucia break into excited chatter about how they're going to spend the weekend at Jon's expense, and my gaze wanders to the window. Now that I've closed the door on this chapter, I can give my full attention to making things right with Willem. *He did message me this morning*, I think, and a glimmer of hope bubbles up inside me.

But if it *is* too late, if the damage is done and Willem doesn't want me, at the very least I'm free and clear of Jon. My romantic slate is clean and I'm ready for a fresh start.

'Penny for your thoughts?' Poppy asks quietly. 'And no pun intended.'

I turn to her with a closed-mouth smile. 'Willem,' I whisper, and she nods in understanding.

Then the realisation lands like a shockwave: why am I still here when I should be on my way to Amsterdam?

'Er, sorry,' I say, setting my glass on the nearest table, 'but I need to go.'

Lucia and Adriana look over, both clearly baffled, then exchange a glance. Ignoring their obvious disappointment, I race over and drop kisses on their cheeks and say goodbye to Poppy, promising I'll be in touch.

I leave the suite, rushing down the hallway and stabbing at the button to call the lift. It takes an aeon to arrive and once I'm inside, another one to descend to the lobby. The doors finally open, and I sidestep a waiting elderly couple, apologising over my shoulder for my brusqueness. When I turn back around, I run smack into a human wall.

The deep, guttural timbre of the 'oof' sparks recognition within me a split second before I glance up and gasp at the sight of Willem's handsome face.

'*Hallo*, Kate,' he says, an amused twinkle in his beautiful blue eyes. 'Fancy running into you like this.'

'What are you doing here?' I ask, breathless.

'You keep asking me that,' he says, and for a moment, I'm lost. But then I recall the time he showed up at Elev8te unexpectedly. 'Should I go?' he asks, turning as if he's about to leave.

'No!' I say, grabbing his arm. I'm instantly aware of how loud that was, and when I glance about, several people are watching. I wave my apology, and most look away.

'Sorry,' I say to him.

'It's okay.' His eyes scan the lobby, then land back on me. 'Kate, can we talk?'

'Absolutely,' I tell him. 'But not here. This is where Jo— Just not here,' I say again, and he seems to understand.

'I saw a café around the corner,' he suggests, reminding me how observant he is.

'Sure, okay.'

Once outside on Portland Place, he indicates which direction we're going and we fall into step. I long for him to take my hand, but he doesn't. There's every chance he's only in London to support Adriana and is about to give me a polite, but heart-breaking, goodbye.

We arrive at the café and he opens the door for me, signalling for me to go ahead, as always. I scout for a table and choose one towards the back, away from curious eyes and ears. If this *is* goodbye, I'd like as few witnesses as possible.

A waiter bustles over and we both order coffee, but when he leaves, the silence between us grows to gargantuan proportions. If it had a physical form, it would fill this entire café.

'I was about to fly to Amsterdam—' I say, right as Willem says, 'I've never been any good at this.'

At least, I *think* that's what he said. 'Sorry?' I ask to clarify.

He clasps his hands behind his neck, expelling a loud breath, then dropping them back in his lap.

Oh, so this is *goodbye.*

The Champagne curdles in my stomach and my breath catches, shallow and fraught. This is far more nerve-wracking than confronting Jon. Perhaps because it's my future at stake, not my past.

'Willem,' I say, just as he starts speaking again. We both laugh nervously.

'Go ahead,' he says with a gentle smile. I attempt to read what's in his eyes, but they're now clouded with a maelstrom of emotions.

Breathe, Kate, breathe.

I can't recall any other day when I've had to coach myself to breathe as often as today. I inhale deeply, steeling myself.

'Before, when I ran into you – *literally*,' I add, stalling with a feeble joke, 'I was on my way to see you.' His lips part in surprise, which I take as a small sign of encouragement. 'Willem, I owe you an apology.'

He regards me intently and I swallow – *hard*.

'Last Saturday at your house... that rant... *Most* of what I said was the truth. This whole mess has me turned inside out and there have been so many times over the past few weeks when I've hardly recognised myself. I'm *not* the adventurous type who takes off to another country at a moment's notice or plays the leading role in a revenge plot. That's not me.

'Only, maybe it *is*, which I realise is confusing – it's confusing to me – but not recognising myself, seeing myself through others' eyes, like Lucia's and Adriana's... *yours*... it's been *liberating*. When I faced Jon earlier, it was like something had been unleashed in me. I felt powerful and in control – and not in the way I usually do, where I'm governed by schedules and procedures, following rules to the letter – but like I was setting the terms for my own life. Because before all this, before you buzzed my flat, my life was tidy and predictable and, in many ways, *small*.

'But I don't want small any more. I want new experiences and possibilities and to view the world through fresh eyes. I want to feel alive inside, to slough off the Kate who willingly believed the lies of a narcissist, simply because they gave the illusion of novelty when, in reality, those occasional disruptions to my status quo merely mimicked excitement.

'And *that* Kate, the one who's no longer satisfied with small and safe, she started to emerge when I met you. And, yes, I'm wildly attracted to you but that's not the reason, that's not what *affected* me, what gave me a glimpse of a different way of... well, *being*.

'So, when I said what I did about falling into bed with you and dismissing our time together as purely physical... that part *wasn't* the truth. Because you are so much more – as a person and to me. And I'm sorry. I'm sorry I said those things and I'm sorry I didn't stop you from leaving and I'm sorry I didn't apologise the second you came back. I'm sorry for all of it.'

I've rambled on long enough and I sit back against the chair, slowly blowing out a breath, my eyes fixed on his. His expression has softened since the start of my meandering monologue, which both terrifies me – he could be trying to let me down gently – and fuels that glimmer of hope.

Please let it not be too late.

Willem licks his lips, then reaches across the tiny table to take my hand. The glimmer takes hold, swelling inside me as his thumb runs along the back of my hand. I study him closely, holding my breath, and he's about to speak when our coffees arrive.

When the waiter leaves, I meet Willem's eyes again. *Breathe, Kate, breathe.*

'Bad timing, yes?' Willem asks with a rueful smile, and my stomach plumets. Because it was bad timing, us meeting – I was engaged to someone else, for starters – but surely that doesn't matter now?

I try to pull my hand away, but he holds on tightly.

'Kate,' he says, smiling, 'I was talking about the coffee.'

'Oh!' I exclaim, relief flooding through me. 'Sorry,' I add with a shake of my head.

'No more apologies. Well, except from me.'

'You don't owe me—'

'I do and I'm terrible at them, which is why I've been such a coward. I shouldn't have let this much time go by... And I shouldn't have walked out – that was wrong of me, but I convinced myself that you meant what you said.'

'I didn't.'

'I know.'

'Really?'

'Yes.'

'Well, good. Because our time in Verona last weekend... that was... *everything*. And not just because of the sex,' I hasten to add. 'I mean, the sex was amazing, don't get me wrong. You're the best lover I've ever had but—'

His mouth quirks.

'I'm going to shut up now.'

'Don't. I like it,' he says with a grin.

'Only because I'm complimenting your sexual prowess,' I retort.

He shrugs, earnest again. 'So, you forgive me for being an idiot?'

'I wouldn't say you were an *idiot*,' I reply.

'Well, that's what Ady called me when she told me off.'

'Adriana told you off?' I ask, taken aback. Even after the shock wore off, she didn't seem enthused about the idea of me and Willem together.

'Mm-hmm,' he replies. 'She told me you were just venting – and that I was being an idiot.'

I bark out a laugh. 'Your sister is rather... *forthright*.'

'She is, especially when she knows she's right.' We exchange a smile. 'Kate, you're not the only one who's been living half a life.'

The way he's expressed it – living half a life – resonates so strongly, it thrums through me. Because isn't that what prompted me to engage a matchmaker in the first place: recognising that there was more to life than my work and visits home and the odd mini break with Margot?

If only I hadn't convinced myself that *Jon* was the gateway to a fuller life.

Although, if I hadn't, I wouldn't have met Willem.

'What's happening in there?' he asks, pointing to my forehead.

'Is it that obvious?'

'When you're deep in thought? Yes.'

His eyes bore into mine, as if he's seeing right into the heart of me, and I don't mind one bit.

'I liked the way you put that, about living half a life. And then I was chastising myself about Jon. And then it occurred to me that if it weren't for him, I wouldn't have met you.'

'The only good thing to come from all of this,' he says.

'Not the *only* good thing,' I reply, and his head tilts in interest. 'I also met Adriana and Lucia, and I get the sense we'll be friends – *good* friends.'

He smiles.

'And I've been to Verona now. I've discovered a whole new city to fall in love with. Oh—'

Fall in love with...

I inhale sharply and look down at the tabletop.

'Kate?' His voice is soft, hesitant, *vulnerable*. I look up. 'Do you think... could we maybe start fresh? Without all the...' He seems to struggle to find the right word.

'Noise?' I offer.

'Noise, yes. Just you and me.'

Just you and me...

Tears prick my eyes and, unable to speak for the lump in my throat, I simply nod.

Then he leans across the table, one hand cupping my cheek, and kisses me.

Everything else falls away – the doubts and overthinking, the self-reproach and regret – and it's just me and Willem, hopeful and eager about embarking on a new adventure.

Together.

EPILOGUE
SEVERAL WEEKS LATER

Poppy

'They're in the car!' I look up from my phone and grin at Tristan. He grins back, but then I have a troubling thought. 'We should have met them at the airport. Should we have met them at the airport?' I ask, suddenly doubting myself.

Tristan captures me in his arms and lands a soft kiss on my mouth. 'Darling, your mum insisted that we not do that. It was a miracle she agreed to us sending a town car. Now, what's really got you so out of sorts?'

I peer up into his whisky-brown eyes.

'I want to tell them. I know it's early but—'

'I do too,' he says, cutting me off.

'You do?' I ask, my eyes wide.

'Darling, this is the most *brilliant* news we've ever had to share. *I've* barely been able to contain myself – I've nearly told Ravi half a dozen times.'

'You have?'

'Yes,' he says with a laugh. '*And* you're nearly seven weeks along.'

'True. And Dr Prior was pleased with how it's going.'

'Exactly. So, let's tell your mum and dad that they're going to be grandparents.'

I grin at him again, excitement infiltrating every part of my body, every nerve ending, every hair follicle, every *cell*.

We're going to be parents!

And with Baby Sharma arriving in a couple of months and Shaz and Lauren another step closer to becoming mums, it won't be long until our friendship family will grow by three.

'Meow.'

Saffron appears at our feet, her tail curling around Tristan's legs. He bobs down to scoop her up.

'What do you think, Saffy?' he asks. 'Ready to be a big sister?'

She mewls disdainfully, struggling in Tristan's embrace. He lets her go, and she drops to the floor and saunters away.

'So, that's a no,' I say.

'She'll come around.'

'Sure she will,' I reply sarcastically.

'We'll just have to make sure our new home has enough bedrooms for Saffy to have her own,' he says, and I narrow my eyes at him. Is he being serious? He looks back at me, guileless. He is being serious.

'You indulge her.'

'I do. Because I love her. But don't worry, I love you more.'

'Nice save, Fellows.'

'Well, I mean it. I love you, Poppy.' He rests his hand on my belly. 'And you,' he says to our unborn child.

That earns him a kiss and were it not for my parents

arriving soon, I'd be dragging him into the bedroom – or over to the sofa – for a whole lot more.

Kate

'I'm as full as a tick,' I say, sitting back in my chair with a satisfied smile.

Willem and I are at Wolf Atelier, a restaurant near the Westerdok in Amsterdam with panoramic views of the bustling water traffic and further off, Amsterdam Noord.

It's been an incredible meal, a degustation of imaginative taste combinations and plating so creative, each dish was a work of art. And the curated wine list paired perfectly with the food, but I'm also tipsy as well as full.

'So, you enjoyed the meal?' he asks.

'Slight understatement,' I say with a wink. 'Thank you for bringing me here.'

'A pleasure. I didn't want you thinking that Dutch food is only *stroopwafels* and *bitterballen*,' he says.

'Oh, don't knock those. They've both earned their place on my list of favourite foods.'

'Always with the lists,' he teases.

'I like lists,' I retort. 'Especially to-do lists. There's an incredible sense of accomplishment in crossing off each item, no matter how small a task it is.'

'I've noticed,' he says, picking up my hand and pressing his lips to the back of it. My heart does a flip, something that happens frequently when I'm with Willem. 'So,' he says, 'anything left on that to-do list before you leave tomorrow?'

His question is a jolt back to reality. Because tomorrow I

head back to London, having spent my two weeks' leave in Amsterdam with Willem. Two glorious, thrilling, and romantic weeks, during which we've explored the city *and* each other – heart, mind, and body.

I'll miss Willem.

I'll miss him next to me as we linger in bed long after the sun has come up, reading or talking... I'll miss the gentle touch of his large, strong hands and how his eyes light up when he laughs at his own jokes... I'll miss his tender kisses and our lengthy conversations about life and what our futures hold – individually and together... I'll miss how he looks into my eyes as he makes love to me...

But I won't be missing him for long. Because I'm accepting Mina's proposal.

The new Kate – fledgling that she is – is *thrilled* at the prospect of spearheading Elev8te's expansion into Europe. The old Kate still lingers, peering into the future with optimistic caution, and I imagine she'll always be there, tethering me to reality while allowing enough space for the newer side of me to soar.

And there with me, which makes me happiest of all, will be Willem. My very own Norse god, my champion and friend, my love.

Oh, and Margot of course. Now that she and Adriana are officially an item, she's promised to visit twice a month, if not more – and 'promise' is her word, not mine. I would have gone with 'threatened'.

I look across the table where Willem is patiently waiting for me to sift through my thoughts. 'No,' I say, my head swivelling from side to side. 'I just want to spend as much time as possible with you.'

He smiles and I beam back at him.

* * *

MORE FROM SANDY BARKER

Another book from Sandy Barker, *Someone Like You*, is available to order now here:

    https://mybook.to/SomeoneBackAd

Would you like to read an EXCLUSIVE epilogue to find out where all the couples of The Ever After Agency series are now? And would you like to access a whole bundle of FREE exclusive content from Sandy? Sign up to Sandy Barker's newsletter to start reading! (SPOILER WARNING if you haven't finished the series yet!)

ACKNOWLEDGEMENTS

This is the last book in the Ever After Agency series – for now anyway (never say never, right?) – and my first thank you is to the readers who fell in love with the series, especially with fellow Aussie, Poppy, and her cast of supporting characters. Poppy has been my proxy throughout the series, giving insight into the love stories that the protagonists didn't have, and it was an absolute joy writing her into every book, so thank you for embracing her.

A massive thank you to my wonderful editor, Emily Yau, who loved this story from the moment I pitched it more than two years ago. We were both excited to get to this story and it was her brilliant idea to include the 'honeypot' subplot, something that really elevated it. Emily, thank you as well for your insight and guidance during the editing process.

Thank you also to the rest of the Boldwood Books team, especially the editorial and marketing teams. I have loved working on this series with you and I can't wait for our next book together. Readers, watch this space!

And I cannot wrap up this series without thanking Nicolette Chin, the talented voice artist who did such a fantastic job bringing Poppy, Elle, Greta, Gaby, and Kate to life, along with the rest of the characters in the series. The audio books would not be the same without your incredible work – especially the accents! – so thank you.

Another huge thank you to my incredibly clever and

supportive agent, Lina Langlee. This is our thirteenth book together, which blows my mind when I think about it for more than half a second. Thank you for being my partner and co-steward of my writing career. We have so much to look forward to in the coming years.

I've dedicated this book to my author friends, who are a special kind of friend and very dear to me. Because author friends get it – *all* of it.

They get when you're in the flow and don't respond to messages for days on end. They get when you're devastated by a one-star review and why it has the power to overshadow a hundred five-star reviews. They get it when you are frustrated, baffled by the publishing industry, and deep in the editing cave, crying, 'I can't remember the difference between an em dash and an en dash!' They stand up and cheer, celebrating every one of your milestones (even the little ones), and shout/sing/yodel your praises from the rooftops. They offer a safe place to be all facets of an author. They offer guidance and counsel and commiserations.

And most importantly, they are your true friends – even if you've never met them in person.

So, thank you to mine – especially the Renegades, who I got to see in person in 2024 (while I was writing this book), Nina, Fi, and Andie, and to my fellow Boldwood romcom gals, Portia, Olivia, Leonie, Laura, and Camilla. I am in awe of your talent and so grateful for your friendship.

A quick but important thank you to my brother-in-law, Mark Penrose, and dear friends, Jenna Lo Bianco and Lyndall Farley, for letting me check in with you about French, Italian, and Dutch, respectively.

I also wanted to mention that this is the first book in a long time I've written *and* edited while on sabbatical with my partner, Ben (I wrote two books during our 2018 sabbatical). We spent the better part of 2024 (and some of 2025) travelling, living, and working around the world, including a month in Amsterdam, the setting of this story. It's been brilliant – thank you for another incredible year, babe. And thank you to the family and friends we've seen along the way, especially Vic, Mark, and Alex. I always leave a little piece of my heart in England when we part ways. Huge thanks to my mum, who reads every chapter as I write them, spurring me on by asking for more, and my dad and stepmum and the rest of my family, who proudly make space on their shelves for each new book I write. Your support means the world to me.

That's all for now, as I need to crack on with my next book. Till next time, happy reading...

Sandy xxx

ABOUT THE AUTHOR

Sandy Barker is a bestselling romance author. She's lived in the UK, the US and Australia. She has travelled extensively across six continents, with many of her travel adventures finding homes in her books.

Sign up to Sandy Barker's newsletter to start reading where all the couples of The Ever After Agency series are now? (SPOILER WARNING if you haven't finished the series yet!)

Visit Sandy's website: www.sandybarker.com

Follow Sandy on social media here:

facebook.com/sandybarkerauthor
instagram.com/sandybarkerauthor
bookbub.com/profile/sandy-barker

ALSO BY SANDY BARKER

The Ever After Agency Series

Match Me If You Can

Shout Out to My Ex

The One That I Want

Someone Like You

I Knew You Were Trouble

Boldwood
EVER AFTER

x♡x♡

JOIN BOLDWOOD'S
**ROMANCE
COMMUNITY**
FOR SWEET AND
SPICY BOOK RECS
WITH ALL YOUR
FAVOURITE
TROPES!

SIGN UP TO OUR
NEWSLETTER

HTTPS://BIT.LY/BOLDWOODEVERAFTER

Boldwood

Boldwood Books is an award-winning fiction publishing company seeking out the best stories from around the world.

Find out more at www.boldwoodbooks.com

Join our reader community for brilliant books, competitions and offers!

Follow us
@BoldwoodBooks
@TheBoldBookClub

Sign up to our weekly
deals newsletter

https://bit.ly/BoldwoodBNewsletter

Printed in Great Britain
by Amazon